DARK WHISPERS

DARK WHISPERS

CLAUDETTE NICOLE

CUTTING EDGE

ISBN-13: 978-1-970848-20-5

Published by
Cutting Edge Books
PO Box 8212
Calabasas, CA 91372
www.cuttingedgebooks.com

GLOSSARY

barbican
: A defensive structure outside a castle moat that guarded the drawbridge.

bartizan
: An overhanging, protruding turret on a tower or bastion.

bastion
: A tower projecting from the main walls of a castle.

cire-perdue
: A method used in casting bronze with wax molds which are lost (destroyed) in the process.

curvilinear design
: A aid:pstyle of architecture of harmonic, flowing curved lines, present in details such as windows, as well as overall design.

diaper pattern
: Designs of constantly repeated and joined patterns, usually symmetrical and balanced.

embrasure
: A slit or vertical opening in a turret through which defending archers fired.

entablature
: The architectural parts that rest horizontally on a column, consisting of the cornice, frieze, and architrave.

geometric foils
: The arc or rounded space between cusps in wall or window ornamentation.

gisarme
: Long lance with a double-edge, hooked blade.

halberd	A combination long spear and battle-ax blade.
keep	The central or main section of a castle.
Kentish tracery	Window design taking the undulating ogee curve pattern and breaking it into more crystalline design with reversed cusps.
merlon	The upright sides of an embrasure; the stones between two embrasures (vertical openings).
ogee curve	A double-curve joined in a peak, a form basic to Persian design and adopted widely in Gothic arch.
polearms	Any of a family of long weapons with varying blades: lances, pikes, gisarmes, halberds, etc.
spandrels	The curved, triangular spaces between adjoining arches.
string-courses	A horizontal band of stone along the face of a building, usually molded and ornamented.
triforium	Wall of a transept or nave built in the aid:pstyle of three blind, arched windows with ornate designs around the entire unit.
uncials	Rounded letters, unequal in size and thickness, set down by hand.

CHAPTER ONE

*It is a grand and glorious house, full of laughter and light,
and shrouded in darkness.*

*It is filled with music, and silent as a tomb. I am there
now, yet in another time and another place. I race through
its halls in terror yet I move with soft and careful steps.*

And as I scream, I make no sound.

The senses are confirmations, sight, touch, smell, all of them
guideposts for consciousness. I woke aware of the feel of the
bed quilt against my bare arms, the faintly musty odor of the
little room, the smell of age. I sat up, noted that I wasn't bathed in
perspiration and grateful for that. It hadn't been specific enough.
Small favors, I murmured silently. But I felt the touch of the chill
beneath the thick quilt, the sudden fear, at once all too real and
all too familiar.

I lay back down, very awake now, my mind dwelling on
dreams and contradictions, reality and unreality, and once again
I knew one thing, the line not so defined as most of us would
like to believe. Perhaps wanting it so clear was of itself revealing.
What were they? The question was never far away. The sexual
fantasies of Freud, the loosened libido indulging in withheld
wishes? I'd discarded that long ago and no psychiatrists, in person or in print, had made me change that. The psychoanalysts
clung to their murky inwardly-turned interpretations as fiercely

as the fortunetellers clung to their stars and tarot cards. The contradictions were too neatly turned away. For me, at least. The contradictions were keys, important perhaps beyond all else, I felt. Throughout the ages, dreams were held to be a form of wisdom, prophetic and visionary in nature, the stuff of saints and soothsayers, prophets and witches. Perhaps they were indeed just that, wisdom inside contradictions, the stuff of many things if we could unravel their contradictions.

I felt the little, wry sound escape my lips. I was a kind of contradiction myself, living as much in other times as in today, half in one age and half in another. I had a great-uncle, a shaggy bear of a man who hid his wisdom under a garrulous exterior. I always looked forward to his visits and the long talks we would have. He made confiding an easy thing. He had a sense of others, of what caused pain and self-doubt.

"Everyone thoroughly absorbed in their work, I mean really into it, lives a slightly schizophrenic existence, a life of separate halves," he once told me. I had questioned that then, rebelled at it, tucked it away in a dim corner of the mind. It was still there but I questioned it less now.

I shut off thoughts, reached for my robe, wrapped my nakedness in it. I wanted to stand, walk about, movement to dissipate a vague feeling of disorientation. I turned the nightlamp on and the room became a place of long shadows, the low, slanting ceiling ending against the top of the window frame. Outside, the night was total, not a light anywhere. I could have been in some underground, Stygian world. One of my suitcases lay on the table, the top up and the passport open atop a neat stack of sweaters. The picture in it stared back at me reassuringly, under it in neat letters the name: Patricia Conway.

It wasn't a bad photo as passport photos go. I saw a face with softly rounded cheeks, deep, brown eyes, a straight nose, and brown hair pulled back that cascaded down when I let it. It was a face that had been called a Renaissance face, something out of a Raphael drawing, a Frans Hals canvas, or a de Hooch interior. The remark had been a compliment, I felt, and I thought quite appropriate in its own way for someone who lived as much in the Middle Ages as I did.

I turned from the window, went back to sit on the bed. Even in the robe, I was chilly and I knew the chill was not just the unheated little room. Fear had left apprehension in its place, another contradiction. I'd come here eager, excited. looking forward to everything about my visit, and now I felt the small stirrings of uneasiness growing stronger and stronger, tiny, silent tickings of the psyche. Disregard them, I commanded myself. Give them names, faces, substance, and they'll disappear. Give them a *raison d'etre* and they'll cease to exist.

Secretly, I knew better, but I tried, starting a little catalogue. The delay in my flight at New York came first. I was not a good air traveler, anyway, and I hated delays at the beginning of any trip. Private omens are so unshakable. Hours had stacked up on each other and I'd grown more tense. We were a morning late when we finally left. On the way, we lost more time battling extremely strong headwinds. The pilot announced that fact over the plane's intercom in matter-of-fact tones. Perhaps it was of practical value to businessmen rescheduling appointments, but to me it was just added discomfort. That bad beginning was one thing of form and substance I could dutifully assign apprehension.

Landing at Shannon Airport, the little Morris Minor rental car I'd ordered had been given to someone else because of the long delay. I had to wait for another and when I'd finally driven from the airport it was dark, and nervous energy misled me into thinking I could keep going. The roads were unfamiliar, the feel of them unsettling. No lighted oasis for fuel and food appeared at regular intervals as on American highways. I'd taken the Ennis road north, made half a dozen wrong turns, and was only a little beyond Gort when I realized I couldn't go much further. I spied the little roadside sign soon after, *The Coach and Four Inn*, followed it at once, the name conjuring up instant visions. While I expected no noblemen and handsome coaches outside, I did look forward to a crackling fire, a warm hearthside atmosphere. I found a dark, cramped little place, a small pub to one side of the entranceway with figures hunched along the bar like so many crows on a rail. The room I was shown was this one, the sink and basin pointed out to me as part of its charms.

That was one more practical reason to explain away inner tensions and then, of course, the dream, amorphous, yet real enough. So the reasons were all there for assigning, for exercises in logic. I gave them names and of course it meant nothing. I gave them reasons for existing and yet the uneasy, inner ticking continued. Fearfulness continued to share me with eager, excited anticipation, one more contradiction. It was only fitting, though, for was I not in a land of contradiction, this little island where soft beauty and unyielding harshness were handmaidens, this green place called Ireland?

This was a land that forever looked to tomorrow while forever clinging to yesterday, a land of passion and penance, absolution and unforgiving enmity, a people simple and utterly complex. Sheridan called Ireland a place of "happy war songs and sad love songs." Its poets, painters, and writers have always known its contradictions. In a thousand ways they have sung of its bittersweet ironies, its darkness and its light, its black depressions and its laughing, dancing days.

The contradictions I brought were quite at home here. After all, the blood of Ireland flowed in my veins on my father's side a few generations removed. But there is an understanding of the heart that clings far longer than the understanding of the mind.

I spun around, shed the robe, and crawled under the quilt shivering, watching the lamp cast shadows along the slanted ceiling and grew angry with myself. I was no schoolgirl away for the first time. I was used to journeying alone and I'd been independent for enough years. I'd carved a career for myself, a considerable reputation. I'd achieved a definite measure of gratification and security as an individual. Yet suddenly I was terribly alone, terribly vulnerable. Inner warnings, I grimaced, veiled offerings. They shared their enigmatic wisdom with dreams.

I found myself wondering if my decision to come here bad been a right one. Decision. I always rebelled at the word. It was a masquerading word, implying an intellectual purity it seldom possessed. Decisions were really made of needs, desires, hopes, emotions, things of the heart. We added reason, logic, evaluation later, to justify our decisions, intellectual afterthoughts.

I let the things that had brought me here swim into focus— moments, people, places—as if I watched a film being turned backwards. The green lawn of the campus came into view, the neo-Gothic architecture of the university buildings, Tuesday afternoon, and my last lecture of the semester. My specialty was MAA-3, Medieval Art and Architecture Three, and the last day of looking into bright young faces that tried to appear interested in what I was teaching them. The effort always amused me, and saddened.

"Gothic architecture, constructional advances, what we call Gothic style, came into being from the intellectual collision of the adventurous Norman mind with Eastern craft and symbology," I would inform them and see that only the words were reaching through. Most of the young faces maintained a patient tolerance. "The study of Gothic architecture is not simply the study of design and new concepts and techniques. It is the study of philosophical and religious thought as it affected the works of man."

Information was being absorbed, I saw, but little beyond that. I used to become frustrated, wonder if it was my fault as a teacher that I couldn't impart the full measure of what I wanted to say. Then one evening, Timothy Conway, bless his big, shaggy soul and his avuncular interest in me, helped me over that hurdle. "You want the impossible," he'd said over his whiskey. "You want them to feel about medieval architecture as you do and you can't do that. It's not one of the universal subjects, it's an esoteric one and you've got the feel for it. Be happy if you can find a few who really share that with you."

He was right, of course, and recognizing that helped. A rare few took the course because they were really interested in the subject. Most took it for extra credits and because I was something of a minor campus celebrity, the only woman expert in my field, internationally recognized, and still under thirty. I'd even found a stock answer to the question most often asked: *Why did you choose your field?* They asked it as though I'd picked my discipline because it offered a quick road to notoriety.

"Why do you pick a man?" I'd answer. "Because you're attracted to him." It always sufficed as an answer and only in the dark nights, alone, did I wonder why we are attracted to a particular person, profession, piece of art? Why do we like what we like? What pulls us where we go?

In time, I came to realize that the question was seldom malicious. Surprise and the unfamiliar make people cast about for reasons. I added to the general picture by often signing articles and essays as Pat Conway and enjoyed the astonishment when I turned out to be a woman, a young and attractive woman as well, my own little shock treatment to rid the world of its prejudices and rigidities.

And so Tuesday afternoon had been a time of closing down, the finish of my term and of teaching, for a while, at least. I'd applied for a sabbatical, canceling myself out of the next term's curriculum, and the faculty had been cooperative, albeit disappointed. I hadn't realized how glad I was to get away from teaching until that moment when the last of the class filed from the room. I let a deep sigh escape me, gathered my notes, and walked out onto the campus. Going through the tall, wrought-iron gates, I felt almost disloyal at my lack of regrets.

Tuesday evening became a variation on a theme, also a time of closing down, and with less emotional turmoil than I'd expected. Sometimes we surprise ourselves. But then, something that you've known secretly, kept locked deep inside you, is never really a total surprise. Tuesday evening was Carter, as it had been almost every Tuesday evening for over a year. Saturdays were usually Carter, also, and often Sundays. Carter Stowall, tall with dark brown, wavy hair, slender and lean-bodied. Carter, charming, witty, urbane Carter, knowledgeable in bed and out of bed. At first, he'd seemed the fulfillment of every promise I'd ever made to myself. It took me almost six months to realize that Carter was magnificently superficial. The realization was a slow, gathering thing, almost painless because of that and by then he had become a habit, a pleasurable narcotic.

One learns to look away, to tell oneself that there is nothing missing, no silent hurting. To acknowledge hurting would be an admission that paradise was flawed. But even our needs can delude us only so long, even wanting can make one look away only so often. When the opportunity came, when I decided to take it and leave the university, it was only natural that Carter be taken out of my life, too. It was that time, a time for endings. He was genuinely surprised when I told him that night had been our last one together. He'd sat up in bed, looked at me as I donned a robe.

"Why afterwards, love?" he'd asked with almost idle curiosity.

"Affirmation. Another kind of knowing, beyond the mind," I had answered.

And so Carter had ended in a shrug, quite appropriate, I thought as I closed the door on him. Strangely, or not so strangely at all, I had had the sudden urge to call him back. It wasn't that I was uncertain or that I really cared that much. It was the thought that the searching had to begin all over again.

Had to? I asked myself and concluded that the phrase was indeed a correct one. The pairing instinct is deep in the human psyche, I'm convinced, the need for one, single, solitary, matching soul to complement our existence, to give ourselves to, and to receive in return. We need buttressing, like a Gothic arch.

Tuesday night faded away, the film continuing to reel backwards to that day a few weeks earlier when the letter had come that triggered everything else. It was in my bag now, and I reached over, pulled it out. I'd been captured at once by the offer itself and by the way in which it was presented, an unusual touch of charm. It had been written on parchment of some kind by what was obviously a quill pen. It was composed in a medieval, courtly style and manner entirely in keeping with the nature of it, everything charmingly perfect about it except its understandable reference to me as "Sir." The sender had obviously seen some of my articles that I'd signed as Pat Conway. I read it now, in the dimness of the little room.

My Esteemed Sire:

Youre knowledge having come to our attention, and having been highly praysed, we address this request for youre consideration and hope for a favourable reply.

As the fourth master of Castle Cashelderg, we finde that no proper record or accounting of the architecture, construction, carvings and artistry of this greate castle has ever been recorded. This shoulde be corrected, not only for our pleasures but for posterity. To this ende, we ask that you set yourself to this undertaking, stone by stone, halle by halle.

As we lyve in a temporal world, we offer the sum of 1,500 pounds for youre services. We awaite youre reply with all gude will.

Sir Brian O'Donnell
Lord of Cashelderg

The signature was ornate, highly distinctive, a kind of penmanship long since discarded in the world. I'd basked in the charm of the letter and its meaning, just for a short time, accepting quickly. It was like offering a conductor an orchestra, a botanist a new world of flowers to investigate. It was the kind of opportunity one dreams of and never gets. Within ten days, I received a draft on the Bank of Dublin and looked forward to meeting Sir Brian O'Donnell. He was obviously a man with a droll sense of humor and a flair for doing things with charm. I folded the letter now, put it back in my purse, switched the lamp off, and the room was plunged into blackness. I closed my eyes, lay very still, and let sleep creep up on me again. Rereading the letter had brought back all my eager excitement. It should have been enough to sweep away the gnawing uneasiness, the small, fearful stirrings that had taken root. It should have been, but it wasn't. Damn dreams, I murmured silently. Damn inner warnings. And damn heritage. That was the worst of all, but I refused to think about that, not now, not tonight. It would only add to the gnawing apprehension. I embraced sleep as a drowning swimmer embraces a life preserver.

CHAPTER TWO

The sun of the morning is a bright ally, a dispeller of inner as well as outer darkness, giving all things no-nonsense shape and form. I woke with the little room bathed in brightness, allowing no thoughts of shadowed dreams and contradictions, apprehensions and uneasiness. I washed and dressed quickly, putting on a gray skirt and a soft pink blouse, a light, white cardigan over my shoulders. I went downstairs to the smell of bacon and eggs—rashers and eggs here, I corrected myself.

The inn looked less dingy and a table was set. I breakfasted, eager to be on my way nonetheless. I'd had trouble confirming flights and had written that I'd arrive midweek but I wanted time to drive leisurely and enjoy the countryside. I paid the night's lodging, put my bags into the rear seat of the little Morris Minor, and drove from the inn. "The best to you," the innkeeper called after me and I felt warm and welcome for the first time. With a road map on the seat beside me, I took the scenic route along the coast, road signs bearing the names that I used to hear roll from Uncle Timothy's lips when he'd get to reminiscing after enough good whiskey. They were names with a lilt and a lift. They carried music in them and a hint of nonsense rhymes, sweet laughter and sounds made for the tongue. Ballyconeel, Killadown, Mallaranny, and Carrowmore, Clonacool, Tobercurry and Drumfin, Lissadell and Enniskillen. Timothy had taught me enough of the Gaelic to be able to understand some of them, the meaning behind the lilt of them: *Dunlee,* gray hill, *Loughmor,* great lake, *Shanderry,* old oak. It was fun to see how many I could put together and understand as I drove through and around and past them.

I halted for lunch at a little village in Mayo, had biscuits and wonderful salmon with soda bread and jam afterward. The map told me I'd been enjoying myself too much. I had a long distance to go, all the way to the tip of Donegal and it was already into the afternoon. I climbed back into the little car and turned away from the scenic coastal roads to drive through fields and towns equally scenic, village after village, some hardly more than a handful of thatched roof dwellings. I drove past lovely whitewashed stone "long farms" and squat little cottages, great stone houses that commanded long sloping hills and a *coteen* of wattles and thatch, ninth-century round towers that saw the Norse invaders, and pre-Christian *tumuli*, earthen burial grounds. But mostly I liked going through the little villages, each one pulling at me to slow and savor its charms.

Each, I was sure, had its own gifts and specialties, its own traditional, particular wares and services. I thought back to the wonderfully charming old list I'd once come upon, set down with obvious care and love by a Thomas Fuller in 1672. It was not only a directory of his native England but it evoked sights, sounds, places, and times, the very essence of an age and a kind of life. Fascinated with it, I'd copied it down and now it sprang to mind again just as Thomas Fuller had set it on paper:

> Staffordshire for *nails,*
> Wiltshire for *wool,*
> Somerset for *cheese, Mastiffs and lead,*
> Hampshire is *honey, red deer, hogs and wax,*
> Cornwall, *garlic, pilchards, slate, tin and diamonds,*
> Lincolnshire, *wild-fowl, pikes, feathers and pippins,*

Sussex, *wheatears, carps and iron,*
Kent, *flaxe, trout, Saint foine and Morello cherries,*
Northhampton, *pigeons and saltpetre,*
Nottinghamshire, *liquorice,*
Warwickshire, *ash, coal and sheep,*
Yorkshire, *horses, lime and alum*
and
Cambridgeshire for *hares, willows, saffron and eels.*

It was some time before I learned that *Saint Foine* was a forage plant akin to hay, that *wheatears* were a small, tasty bird about the size of a thrush, *pilchards* a small fish slightly fatter than a herring, and Morello cherries were black cherries.

But the list stayed with me and now, as I drove, I made up my own list for those villages and towns I passed through, not as real and accurate as Thomas Fuller's but enough fun to compile. By the late afternoon I crossed into Donegal, turned again to the coastal roads that would, according to my map, lead me to Horn Head and the Castle Cashelderg, the red earthern fort. I wondered if Sir Brian O'Donnell would be as courtly as his letter had been, certain that he'd be so with a twinkle in his eye.

The sea road took me down, almost to the water itself, with a succession of great rock cliffs to my right, interspersed with narrow defiles. I hurried now, conscious of the lengthening shadows, slowing when the little car skidded sideways on a corner. The sea lay at my left, blue and calm, only a strand of sand separating road and water. The cliff-like rock on the other side had grown steeper, more forbidding, the defiles cutting into it more infrequent and narrower. A cluster of red oaks appeared suddenly, an oasis of beauty against the slate gray of the rock. The sky was turning a delicate rose in the fading light of the day. I checked the map, saw I hadn't too far to go, and pressed the gas pedal, wanting to reach Castle Cashelderg before dark.

I'd gone another mile or so when I glanced out at the sea. My foot automatically moved to the brake pedal and, with disbelief, I saw it begin. I watched with hypnotic fascination, slowing the car to a crawl, uncertain I was actually seeing what I saw before me. It all happened so swiftly that it was as though I were watching an elapsed-time film that compresses hours into minutes, minutes into seconds. The delicate rose sky suddenly became indigo, streaks of deep red running through it, then turned into a deep purple. Great black clouds, appearing as if from nowhere, rolled in from the sea and the deep purple sky turned almost black. Fiery tongues of red rimmed the great clouds, then yellow flashes so brief they were almost gone before the eye could catch them. The calm, delicate sky had, in minutes, turned into a shifting turmoil of anger, deep purple to black to red-rimmed gray. It was as though the world had been turned upside down and I peered into a fiery pit. I saw the sea mounting upon itself, then rise up like a great angry beast shaking foam-flecked whiteness from its mouth.

The wind came then, erupting, sweeping down from the red-black clouds as a hawk upon a hare. I felt the little car move under me, shudder, the wheel start to turn and I clutched at it. In minutes, beauty had become rage. I heard the sound, then, faint at first but faint only for a few brief moments and then rising, gathering itself, a screaming that shook the very air. It grew louder, became a deafening, nerve-shattering screaming that came from all about me. I felt the wind moving the car from side to side, gunned the engine as I tried to keep the wheels on the road. The world had gone gray-black now and the rain swept down, slamming into the car, beating against it with the fury of nails being driven by a giant, unseen hammer.

The windshield let me see only glimpses of the onslaught outside but nothing could shut out the terrible, wild screaming. I thought of only one thing, *the dread women of Moher.* How often, as a little girl, I'd listened to my uncle tell tales of their screaming, shrieking cries as they swooped on the wings of a storm to devour the great schools of Atlantic salmon and anything else in their path. The dread women of Moher, part human, part bird, harpies who dwelled in the great cliffs of Moher to range far and wide when loosed by the elements. They were legend, folk tales, yet there were those who had seen them, those who testified to that with their dying breaths, others whose testimony was in the terror of their stilled faces.

Stories, I'd smiled then, even as I was caught up in the telling of them, stories, the fabric of legend and superstition. But now I felt only stark fear and a reality beyond reality. The wild, maniacal shrieking, the furious, battering rain, the wind that clawed at the car, all real, undeniable. Then, through the rainswept windshield, I saw dark shapes hurtling through the blackness, sweeping, screaming shapes I could see only as shadowed movement. Real, too, or my imagination seizing hold? I had to wonder when the wheel was almost wrenched from my hands, the wind catching the little car, sending it skidding sideways. I spun the wheel against the skid, felt the car go into a circle, the road slippery as ice now. I gunned the engine, spun out of the skid, heard the mud under the wheels offering no traction at all.

The screaming was pounding in my ears and I felt my head throbbing as if it could burst. The car shook, spun again. I tried to turn against the skid but I couldn't think, couldn't coordinate, the frantic, piercing screaming absolutely unnerving. The hurtling shadows continued to sweep in front of me, black shapes against rainswept blackness. I tried to hold the steering wheel steady but the wind pulled it from my grip. I felt the car skidding sideways, spinning. I glimpsed rock, the headlights falling on the sheer wall of stone, then turning from it as the car spun sideways. I heard the sound of metal scraping along rock, felt the car shudder. I yanked at the wheel and my hands, coated with perspiration, slipped from it. All I could hear, feel, sense, all my normal reactions were shattered by the terrible shrieking that filled my head. The dread women of Moher, legend or not, were fulfilling their role as omens of destruction and death. The car was whipped around as if a giant hand had seized it. The headlights flashed a water-filled glimpse of a narrow road cutting through the rock.

Desperation is the life-blood of survival. I clung to the wheel as the narrow road created a funnel for the wind. I felt the car being literally sucked into the funnel, lifted, carried forward, slamming against the side of the rock. I was flung sideways, felt the breath-catching pain in my neck and shoulder, and then my head hit the doorpost. I saw deep purple flashes, then yellow and red spots. I was somehow aware of the car moving forward, scraping along the rock at the side of the funnelled road. My head cracked against the doorpost again as the car jammed to a halt. The terrible screaming grew faint, a haze dropped over my eyes. My body seemed to dissolve and, for a moment, hang suspended in a nowhere place, and then there was only silence, nothing, unconsciousness.

The first return came slowly, tiny suspicions of being alive filtering through to me, a sense of something other than a void. Pain first, and I was actually grateful to it, evidence of life that it was. After the pain, the slow pulling open of my eyes, formlessness, a haze floating in front of me, then focusing, straining. The interior of the car took shape, defining itself. The seat had slid forward and I was close against the steering column. I pushed back and heard myself gasp in pain that ran down my neck and into my shoulder. But the seat had moved and I had more room. Slowly, fighting off the waves of pain that it caused, I turned my head, managed to see through the window. The rain still came down but without the wild fury. I leaned against the door, tried pushing, but it didn't move. Dimly, I saw leaves, branches, something wedged against the door. I steeled myself against the pain of my neck and shoulder again, reached over to the other door, and pulled on the handle. It opened about two inches and rested against a wall of rock. I pulled it closed again and lay back, hearing the rasping sound of my own breath. The small efforts had used up my little strength and I felt myself drifting away, falling back into unconsciousness. My head fell forward to rest against the steering wheel as the void wrapped itself around me again.

The second waking came more rapidly than the first, things defining themselves more quickly, conclusions remaining to help orient myself. I was in the car and wedged into a crevice, a tree against one door, the rocks holding the other shut. I sat for a moment collecting thoughts. I put a hand against my temple, my head throbbing, felt the warm stickiness at once end drew my fingers back, stared down at the redness on them. I moved, drew another gasp of pain from my neck and shoulder. All else was stillness, absolute quiet, and the blackness of the night. Slowly, I realized that the rain had stopped.

I found the handle for the window, tugged on it, and the window rolled down. Cold, damp air leaped into the car. I tried to turn, lift myself, gasped out at the pain in my shoulders and neck. Fighting it down, I tried to crawl through the open window, saw quickly that it had been a ridiculous thought, the space far too small. The tree was wedged against the car door, I saw clearly now, impossible for me to move. I leaned my head out the window and fought away the spearing pain of it again, began to call out for help. The night was Stygian and between cries I listened, heard no sound at all. I kept calling, at periodic intervals, until I felt my strength suddenly draining from me and realized that I was shivering. The interior of the car was filled with cold and dampness now. I rolled up the window and found I'd barely enough strength to do so. Shuddering with the cold, I felt myself slipping into unconsciousness again, a soothing siren song without words or music, a silent lullaby. I fought against it, dimly aware of the chilling cold as I inhabited a halfway world. I remembered hearing about people who froze to death because they fell asleep in the cold and I tried to stay awake by guessing how long it'd take for someone to find me. The effort was doomed to failure as strength slid away from me. The gray, half-light, the dim awareness of existence, drifted out of my grip. Strangely, the last, conscious flicker was the awareness of being cold, then place, time, existence evaporated and once again there was nothing.

It could have been minutes, hours, even days. The unconscious erases all trace of time. I only knew I felt a shaking, regained a dim consciousness at first. I thought it was my body shivering, then heard sound, a stab of light into my face making me blink. I opened my eyes, focused, slowly realized the car was being shaken. The light came again and I turned toward the window, saw the beam of brightness move away, a dark, shadowed shape behind it. Realization still trickled through with dreamlike slowness. Someone was there, someone had come. I turned, gasped in pain, focused again, and saw the tree blocking the door being pulled back, the beam of light making erratic motions in the air. The branches and leaves made scraping sounds against the metal of the car and then the door was pulled open, hands reaching in. I moved toward them, cried out again as my neck muscles sent sharp jabs of pain through me. I half crawled from the car, felt my knees give way, my legs suddenly not there. I sagged down, was caught, lifted, an arm around my waist. Suddenly I was as if in the center of a whirlpool, everything spinning around me. I could feel the blood racing through my head, a terrible dizziness. Once more I felt disembodied, ethereal, though this time without the dim half-world. This time only the terrible spinning that wouldn't stop and, once again, the obliterating blackness that descended.

CHAPTER THREE

Feeling before knowing. Warmth, delicious, cradling, comforting. My eyes opened and I lay very still, not wanting to move at all. I stared up at a whitewashed ceiling with dark wood beams crossing it. Shadows flickered against it, firelight, I realized. I smelled a liniment odor, not unpleasant, wintergreen, half-turned my head, and winced, realized the liniment odor was coming from my neck and shoulders. I grew courageous, moved a little more. The pain was not nearly so intense now. I turned further, saw the room take shape: slip-covered chairs, dark wood walls, a stone fireplace with thick logs burning in it, a drop-leaf table against one wall.

I lay still a few minutes more, felt the wool of the blanket against my skin, realized that I was wearing only my skirt. I pulled myself up on one elbow, reached a hand up to feel along my temple, found the neat patch of adhesive there. I turned my head to look around the room, a careful movement, felt the pain along my neck muscles had lessened to where it was now only a dull ache. I saw my bags along one wall, let my glance travel across the room to an open doorway leading into an adjoining room. I sat back against the couch, moved my head up and down and sideways, stretching muscles.

"Well, now, that's better," I heard the voice say, a quiet voice with a soft lilt to it. The figure moved into the room from the doorway. I saw a thin, rangy form that seemed all arms and legs. He wore an open-necked shirt with a dark red cardigan over it, slacks with a small hounds-tooth pattern. He stepped closer and I saw shaggy brown hair, a nose slightly large, a wide mouth, and clear blue eyes, a face that held a kind of affable, disarrayed attractiveness in it.

"How do you feel?" he asked.

"Not too bad," I answered. "Glad to be alive." I tucked the blanket around me, sat up straighter. "I was afraid I'd freeze during the night."

"Maybe. Double pneumonia, more likely," he said reflectively. "It wouldn't have been good, in any case. It wasn't a spot that's visible from the main road."

"How did you find me?"

"This place is set back quite a bit. The only road from it passes the spot where you were wedged into the rocks. I decided to walk out a bit after the storm," he said.

"Thank God," I breathed. He came closer, put a hand on my forehead, pulled my eyelids up, first one then the other.

"No fever, no sign of shock. You're a lucky girl," he said.

"Thanks to you," I answered, gratefulness surging through me.

"Liam Flaherty," he returned, almost solemnly.

"I owe you, Liam Flaherty," I said.

"Not at all, Patricia," he answered. He grinned, a warm, disarming little grin. "Your bag spilled open, the passport with it." He paused, moved to sit on the arm of the stuffed chair. "You went off the road in the storm, I take it."

"I was flung off, the car practically lifted into the air. I couldn't see anything. I had no control of the car," I recounted, the moment flashing before me with frightening vividness. "It was so sudden, everything just erupting all at once."

"It happens sometimes that way here. I imagine it has something to do with the formation of the coastline, wind patterns and sea currents, that sort of thing," Liam Flaherty said in his softly lilting voice. I felt a shudder race through me, my bare shoulders quiver.

"You heard the screaming, then," I said. "It was horrible. It went right through me."

"I heard the wind," he answered quietly and I caught the unsaid in his words. He had heard the sound of the wind and no more than that.

"You didn't hear the shrieking, almost human, like a thousand women screaming and wailing?" I prodded.

"No, not that," he said quietly. I fell silent, wondering, frowning. Had only I heard the dread women of Moher? Had only I heard their screaming? Were their wild shrieks only for my ears, an omen, a warning meant for me alone? I heard Liam Flaherty's voice cut in, quiet, reassuring.

"Down by the shore road you hear the wind differently," he said. "It whistles down from the cliffs and through the crevices in the rocks, a terrible sound, I'm told."

I smiled. He was offering explanations but there had been more than the wild screaming. There'd been the hurtling, shadowy shapes, and I lapsed into silence again. Once more his voice broke into my thoughts, almost as if he could read them.

"And I've heard that the sea birds, the cormorants, gulls, and petrels take wing and set up a fearful screaming," he said.

The sea birds, I repeated to myself. Not harpies, not apparitions, the dread women of Moher, really the flocks of cormorants. I was grateful for his words, so reasonable, so plausible, and so unable to satisfy. I lay back against the couch, winced as my shoulder stabbed pain.

"That'll fade after a spell," he said. "The liniment needs time to work. I massaged it in good and deep, plenty of it." He stood up abruptly. "I was fixing a little something to eat. Could you stand some soup?" he asked.

"Yes, I think so," I answered. "And I'd like to get into a blouse." His eyes lighted with tiny pinpoints, almost pixyish.

"Yes, I suppose you would. It's a shame to cover all that loveliness. But I'm a realist," he said, seeing the moment of quizzicalness in my face. "Life is a thing of moments. You come upon them, enjoy them while they last." He gestured to where my bags stood. "I put your blouse inside the top one," he said, and I watched him disappear into what was obviously a tiny kitchen, the end of a sink top visible at the nearest corner. I swung from the couch, felt chill of the night air on my breasts as I moved away from the fire. I slipped into the blouse and returned to the couch, curled up with my legs under me. Even the small effort had made itself felt and I was glad to sit again. Liam came into the room with a small table he set in front of me, then with two bowls of steaming soup that turned out to be a mixture of leek and potato, a plate of buttered biscuits with it. He sat down across from me, pulling up a straight-backed chair. I felt the soup filter down through my stomach, warming, bracing.

"You're a very lovely girl to be traveling alone," Liam Flaherty said and there was the hint of amused interest in his voice.

"It happens," I commented. "I wanted to be alone."

"Between trains?" he remarked blandly.

"Something like that," I said. I watched him get up to put another piece of firewood on the flame. For all his angular lankiness, he moved with lightness and grace.

"Is my car a wreck?" I asked.

"I'd guess more dents and scrapes than anything serious. But we'll see when I pull you out in the morning," he said. I caught his eyes lingering on the soft curve of my breasts as the blouse clung, outlining and emphasizing.

"What do you do when you're not rescuing young ladies in distress?" I asked, leaning back, feeling very warm and contented.

He laughed, a pleasant, light sound. "I'm one of the Irish rovers, going from place to place and job to job. Right now, I'm combining a little vacation with a little work. I'm only renting this place."

"It's a very nice place," I said, glancing around the room again. "It's very secure."

"That's important to you, security?" he smiled.

"Isn't it to everyone?" I asked, saw his little shrug, a half-smile.

"No, not everyone. Man was a nomad once, a wanderer. That vestigial heritage clings to many people. They have to keep moving, searching. It's a matter of needs, of what drives us." His blue eyes had become almost gray, I saw, a sudden seriousness holding his face. The easy pleasantness returned instantly, though. "What do you do back in America, Patricia Conway?" he asked.

"I teach, lecture, write an occasional article," I said.

"At what?" he queried.

"Gothic architecture and art," I answered. "I live in two worlds."

His smile was touched with wry laughter. "You're not the only one, Patricia," he said. I decided that Liam Flaherty's easy, affable exterior, while not a mask, hid a great deal more than it revealed. I also realized I was suddenly very tired, felt my eyes starting to close, much too tired to explore remarks or answer questions.

"A good night's sleep will do it," I heard Liam say, forced my eyes to snap open and saw him rise, come toward me. "The bedroom's just past the kitchen. I'll sleep out here," he said.

"No, please," I protested. "I'll be fine here. You've done more than enough."

"Nonsense. You'll sleep better in a bed than here, even an old, hard one."

I shook my head. "No, please. I'll do fine here. I fit a lot better than you will," I said. "I'll just wash up a bit and change."

He held a hand out, helped me up, then pointed to a narrow, closed door in the corner. "The bathroom's in there," he said. He turned, took the dishes into the kitchen, and I went to my bags. At home, I wasn't one for sleeping swaddled in nightclothes but I'd brought two pairs of pajamas and a nightgown just in case and now was glad I'd done so. I took out the light blue pajamas, padded into the bathroom with them, slipped out of my things, and put them on. Speaking of vestigial things, I grunted, modesty was one of them, more for others than oneself sometimes. After all, he'd already seen most of me.

When I returned to the living room I saw the pillow at one end of the couch, the blanket neatly spread for me. Liam appeared at the door of the kitchen, his eyes appreciative as they scanned me. "Last chance to change your mind about the bed," he said. "No extra charge."

I stood before him, felt my hand reach out to press his arm.

"Thank you is such an inadequate word," I said. His hand came up to touch my cheek, a gentle gesture, and in his eyes there were little centers of intensity.

"It'll do for now," he said. He turned, walked through the narrow, old-fashioned kitchen and into the room beyond. I returned to the couch, pulled the blanket around me, and stretched out as the fire settled down to a low, half-slumber of its own. Tiredness, the right kind now, swept over me as I lay still. For a brief moment, I was back in the raging storm and the terrible shrieking reverberated inside my head. I half-turned, pressed my face into the pillow, and it disappeared. I fell asleep at once, grateful to be alive. The night wrapped itself around me, deep darkness, a world within the world, a place of timeless hours.

> *Great round chandeliers of thick oak, each with iron cups for a half-hundred candles, each a blazing circle of light. Music and laughter fill the grand and glorious house. The big room is thronged with strong-faced men and beautiful women and they dance minuets and quadrilles and rigadoons. I hear the sound of lutes, fifes, and harps. I am there among them.*
>
> *I dance and warm, strong hands hold me and I know happiness, I know love. Everything is as it should be. Suddenly, the great front doors of the house burst open. A terrible wind sweeps in. The multitude of candles go out as one. I am alone, the big room empty, dark, cold. I do not dance but run, fleeing in terror. I know only fear. Death is my pursuer, reaching for me, so close, so terribly close, so cold, so final.*

The couch shook with my trembling as I snapped awake, sitting up, little drops of perspiration trickling down between my breasts. Had I screamed? I wasn't sure. I thought I had, but I heard only the harsh sound of my breathing now. The fire glowed, the logs veined with tiny lines of flame. I fell back onto the couch, drew in deep breaths.

The same yet different. Unlike others at other times, these were all of a part, a tenuous connection running through them. But nothing clear, contradictions again. The others had been more direct. These frightened in a different way. And always, always one was reduced to searching a shadow play for meanings.

Only sometimes it was too late, sometimes the search too long, at the finish only the bitter taste of guilt. I closed my eyes, let sleep come over me again. There wouldn't be another, not tonight. I knew the pattern all too well.

I slept deeply the remainder of the night, aching muscles restoring themselves, and woke to the smell of fresh-brewed coffee. I swung from the couch, my neck and shoulders only a dull ache now, went to the bathroom, and washed in the old-fashioned tub that stood on short legs. I took a fresh skirt and a turquoise sweater from my bag, dressed, and returned to the living room. Liam was there, standing over a large tray of coffee, crumpets, and black currant jam. He wore a lightweight turtleneck shirt over slacks and his glance was sharp, approving. A bright, cheering sun streamed in from the opened windows.

"Really, you didn't have to do all this. I'm used to a quick cup of coffee in the morning," I said.

"Lovely things are made for spoiling, particularly after bad dreams," he said.

I felt my lips tighten, sat down, and reached for a crumpet. "I'm sorry. I hope I didn't keep you awake," I apologized.

"I'm an easy sleeper," he said. "They hang on afterwards, don't they?" My mouth stayed tight. He was acute, quick to catch nuances. I carefully spread jam on a crumpet.

"Maybe," I said carefully. "I take it you don't believe in dreams. Most people don't. It's not fashionable. It smacks of spiritualism, seances, all that sort of thing. The very word is a dialectic stumbling block. Let's use modern terms."

"Such as?"

"Precognition," I said, biting into my crumpet. Liam's face stayed bland but his eyes narrowed.

"Knowing future events, or having an awareness, a warning about them," he mused aloud. "One aspect of extrasensory perception."

"That's right. Do you believe in the phenomenon?"

He shrugged. "I've heard of people having sudden, unexplained awarenesses of something that does happen later. You think dreams are a form of that?"

"Yes," I said, more sharply than I'd intended. He picked up on it instantly.

"So definite about it?" he smiled. I backed away. I'd said more on the subject than I wanted to already.

"I'm full of opinions, all of them strong," I laughed. "I'm an incurable romanticist and romanticists are always full of strong opinions, didn't you know that?"

"Why?" he followed.

"It's an unromantic world we live in. You have to have strong beliefs, strong opinions to stay a romantic," I tossed back and finished my coffee.

"Another cup?" he offered.

"No, thanks. I'd like to see whether my car is usable," I said. He rose, disappointment, almost displeasure, clouding his face.

"Yes, I suppose we'd best see to that," he said stiffly, and I felt guilty. I reached out, touched his arm.

"I'd like to stay and talk more but I just can't," I said. "I'm very complimented, really."

"Forgive me. I'd let myself have a thought I'd no right to entertain. Come on, we'll see about your car," he said, the pleasant, attractive affableness on him again. I followed him outside and watched as he disappeared around the back of the house. It was L-shaped, I saw from outside, and indeed very isolated. Wooded areas surrounded it, and from the three sides towering rock formations rose to give it a walled-in feeling. Liam appeared in moments, driving an old, paint-worn but very solid Land Rover. He halted it, left the motor running as he went inside, and reappeared with my bags. "Just in case you can take off right away," he said. I climbed into the high seat of the Land Rover and he drove off. "Put your feet down flat," he said. "She bucks a bit on the bumps. Came with the house."

We went around a curve and I felt myself jounced, pressed both feet hard against the floorboard. We climbed a narrow road lined on both sides with beech and oak and behind them, the tall rocks. Another sharp curve and he slowed and I saw the tail end of the little Morris Minor wedged into a crevice.

"You're not as far from the shore road as it seems. This spot is just tucked back from it," Liam said as he wheeled the vehicle to face my car end to end. The spot certainly was tucked away, a huge rock leaning forward just beyond it. I was certain I'd not have been found for days if he hadn't been near. I climbed from the jeep and watched him attach a chain to my car, hook it up to the Land Rover. He returned to the wheel, fed the gas slowly, and the little car came out of the crevice with but a slight scraping sound as it brushed against the fallen tree branch that had wedged the door closed. I walked around it, saw that Liam's guess had been right. It was scraped and dented but it seemed otherwise quite all right. The wheels seemed straight, the tires in shape. I got in, turned the ignition on, and in a few minutes the engine caught, warming itself at once to a steady throb.

Liam had unhooked the chain and he put my bags into the car, gave it a quick inspection. "It's good enough," he pronounced. "A few dents in the fender but the windshield's fine and the hood's not sprung." I felt a tiny inner frown, unworthy, I told myself, and chased it away at once.

"Thanks again, Liam Flaherty," I said. "I'd like to stop back and visit you as soon as I'm settled in. May I?"

"Settled in where?" he frowned. "I thought you were on your way touring Ireland."

"I'm going to Cashelderg," I said. A hard grayness tinted his eyes at once and his face seemed to change without changing, as though an invisible mask had dropped down over it. "Is something wrong?" I asked automatically.

He found a smile but it was mechanical. "Not at all. I just didn't take you for the type," he said, stepping back from the car. "Take care, now," he said, turned, and strode off.

"Wait," I called, but he was climbing into the big Land Rover already, gunning the engine. What type? I wanted to ask him, but the Land Rover was turning, starting down the road, throwing little bits of dirt up after it. I turned away and climbed into the car, frowning. It had been a most unexpected reaction, disturbing, and the frown stayed as I drove off. Liam Flaherty, I felt certain, had saved me from freezing to death. He'd taken me into his little house, administered to me, been a most perfect rescuer. But little things stayed with me, disturbing, and as I thought about it, I realized that he hadn't really told me anything about himself, not what he did, not even whether he believed in precognition or in anything else. He'd charmingly fielded my questions but he'd listened to me with intent sharpness. I'd return here, I told myself, out of curiosity if nothing else.

The narrow road suddenly funneled out and I was facing the water, the shore road running at right angles to me. I turned onto it, stared for a moment at the calm, sunlit blue of the sea that made the sudden, overwhelming fury of yesterday seem inpossible. The dull ache of my neck muscles were suddenly reassuring evidence that I hadn't dreamt it all. I drove north, consulted the map again, and took a little spur road that dipped, rose, dipped again. It executed a wide circle and suddenly I caught my first glimpse of Cashelderg, unmistakable, the huge bulk of it massive yet not without delicacy at a distance. Silhouetted against a gold, sun-swept sky, turrets rising from the corner bastions, the great center keep within them, it seemed a cry echoing down the ages. I slowed, stared at it, knew this was how travelers, knights, friends, and foes saw it as they approached, sanctuary or forbidding citadel, depending on who they were.

A bank of trees rose up and I lost sight of the great structure but I felt excitement tingling through me now. The thought of what great treasures it held, uncatalogued and unexplored, was heady stuff. I swung around a curve and the road straightened. At the far end of it, as if rising up from the sea beyond, was Cashelderg. But first, to the right of it on a small rise, I saw an old monastery, the bell tower crumbled, the rest standing. In amazement, I noted that the front employed the four-centered arch and made use of the ogee curve, evidence that the master architect had had knowledge of Persian influences. The road cut through a sudden collection of huts and shelters, clustered together and leading up to the old monastery. Many were built in the shape of the ancient *clochans,* the unmortered, stone, bee-hive-shaped Irish huts with a stone slab at the top. These, however, were mostly of wood and brick, some not more than square lean-to constructions.

Figures appeared in the doorways of many as I drove by, young people, more girls than boys, I noted. Many waved as I passed, smiled, one, near to the road, an attractive girl with long blonde hair in braids. I glimpsed others entering the old monastery and I saw two young men and a girl raking the grounds behind the structure. It was entirely unlike any of the little villages I'd passed through and I made a mental note to go through some of the research material on the area I'd brought with me.

A little rise in the road lifted the car and then I was drawing up before Castle Cashelderg, slowing to a halt outside the towering wooden doors. Once there had no doubt been a moat in front of them but that was no longer here, the land filled in, and once there'd been a stone barbican guarding the entrance. I saw a few square, heavy stones still in place, evidence of that. I felt the frown as I climbed from the car, surprised at the very poor condition of the outer walls of the great structure. Approaching the two huge, arched doors, fashioned of thick timbers held together by hammered iron plates, I saw that one door was standing ajar. I searched for a bell cord, or perhaps a buzzer, a bow to the twentieth century. I found neither and moved through the open door, feeling very tiny.

Inside, a cold dampness reached into me at once and I shivered, gazed across the entrance hall, empty, silent. My frown deepened. I saw a big gray spider swing from a row of cobwebs that stretched across the inside of the door. Tentatively, I moved forward across the entranceway and to the edge of the main dining hall, the vast room dust-covered, almost empty. A long table and four broken chairs were pushed against one wall, a few stones that had fallen from the wall lying on the floor. A pair of polearms hung crisscrossed on one wall near the stone slabs of a tremendous fireplace. My eyes went upwards, to the great, round chandeliers of oak, each holding iron cups for a halfhundred candles.

I felt my throat grow dry, hands fold into tight fists. I stared up at the distinctive round, oaken chandeliers, exact, absolutely exact, just as I had seen them. I cast out for answers, the comfort of rational plausibility. I had come upon others just like them, I told myself, somewhere in my work, in actuality or in research, pictured or described perhaps in a dusty archive I'd unearthed. They had stayed in my subconscious, surfacing in the dream. It had to be that. The mind does such things, little trickeries of its own.

I pulled my eyes from them, clung to my explanation with instant determination, and turned away, walked down a wide stone corridor to another room, past an alcove that had perhaps once been a sewing room. I halted at the door of a square room where a table sagged down on two of its four legs and the walls were dust-covered, streaked, and flaking. A huge tapestry hung from one wall, a hunting scene, now spotted with bare patches and covered with loose threads that hung down from it like so many long, thin tears.

I was more than taken aback, more than disappointed. I felt torn in two. Cashelderg, for all its disrepair and neglect, was still a Gothic architectural and ornamental treasure house. It remained a wonderful, exciting opportunity for me. From where I stood, hardly into the great structure, I saw wonderful examples of the ribbed vault, the spatial outlook, pierced spandrels of geometric foils, and a dozen other things exciting to me. My reasons for coming here were all before me, waiting, and for that I felt only eagerness. But a crime had been committed here, a terrible crime. The great house had been built with care, love, craftsmanship, and purpose. It had sheltered, protected, been part of the fabric of human existence. Not simply stone and mortar and wood, it was a keeper of the spirit of all who had lived inside its greatness. And now it stood abandoned, obviously so, left to stand until it could stand no longer, or worse, be picked apart by those who would profit from its treasures. I thought of Yeats, of the lines from his *Purgatory,* and felt one with his words:

> to kill a house
> Where great men grew up, married, died,
> I here declare a capital offense.

Such a house, a house killed, murdered, is a place of homeless, displaced spirits, a place forever haunted, Yeats wrote.

> But there are some
> That do not care what's gone, what's left:

The souls in Purgatory that come back
To habitations and familiar spots.

I suddenly felt a coldness pierce through me and I shivered. I turned, slowly walked on down the tall stone corridor, paused at the doors of other rooms. I wanted to find Sir Brian O'Donnell, Lord of Cashelderg, writer of charming letters in medieval script. I glanced at my watch. It would be dark in a short time and it was obvious that I wouldn't be a guest here at Cashelderg. My anticipations in that direction had been so terribly in error and I found myself wondering if Sir Brian O'Donnell's sense of humor was more malicious than droll.

I reached the end of the corridor, a set of stone steps going down to an underground area. Facing the stairs was the entrance to another room, a round room with a circular table in the center of it. I glimpsed a window, noted Kentish tracery and on the walls pikes, gisarmes, and halberds hanging. But my eyes were held by a pair of bronze gargoyles carved over the doorway, half-beast and half-human with long, pointed faces and winged bodies with curled tails. They stood poised as if ready to leap down on anyone entering the room and I stepped backwards, feeling not at all foolish. Their bronze eyes glowed with dark, almost living depths and they stared at me, impossible as it seemed. I felt it, unmistakable, the sense of being stared at, watched, an animal sense retained from ancient heritages. It stayed with me, unnerving, and I wrenched my eyes from the horrible bronze sculptures, turning away to face the figure standing in the corridor, staring at me, as motionless as the bronze carvings.

Startled fright stabbed at me and then I pushed it aside, angry at myself and at the silent figure that had stolen up to stare at me. He was a little man, hardly more than five feet tall, a wizened cartoon of a face with tiny, gimlet eyes, a small nose, and a wide mouth. Straying brown hair poked out *from under* a green cap worn at a rakish angle. He stood tilted to the left, as if he were weighted down on one side, a strange little figure somewhere between a dwarf and an elf, comical yet somehow frightening, a leprechaun drawn by Hieronymus Bosch. He spoke suddenly, abruptly.

"What do you want here?" he barked in a high, tight voice.

"I'm looking for Sir Brian O'Donnell," I answered. The little man only stared at me from his tilted stance. "My name is Patricia Conway. Sir Brian expects me. At least I thought he did," I explained.

"Patricia Conway," the tight little voice echoed. "Patricia Conway." He cocked his head to one side and the tiny gimlet eyes seemed to bore through me.

"I presumed Sir Brian lived here," I said, waving a hand at the dust-covered rooms. "Obviously I was mistaken. I'd say no one's lived here for a hundred years at least."

"You could say a lot longer," he answered. The wizened little face held many more fine, parchmentlike lines in it than I'd first noticed.

"Do you know where I can find Sir Brian O'Donnell?" I asked. "He sent for me."

"Really, now," the little man answered and his eyes continued to bore into me as though I were an insect being studied under glass. I felt myself growing irritated at his manner.

"Who are you?" I asked abruptly. "Can you help me?"

"I'm the caretaker," he said quickly. My glance left his tilted little figure and lifted to the crumbling stone, the dust and desolation of the once-great house. He caught my thoughts with a quickness that surprised.

"You're thinking there's not much care been taken," he said. I shrugged my agreement.

"Maybe watchman would be a better word, then," he said. "Yes, I think it would, better and more to the point. Watchman for centuries, me, my father, and his father before him and on, watchmen keeping a death watch."

The phrase hung in the air, dark humor, a bitter ring to it, appropriate yet holding hidden meaning. "Then Sir Brian hired you, I take it. You should be able to tell me where I can find him," I answered.

"I'm paid by the Bank of Dublin, out of a fund set up for that three hundred years ago," the little man said. I felt irritation becoming an uneasy anger.

"What are you trying to say?" I snapped.

The little man cocked his head further to one side. "What are *you* trying to say?" he tossed back.

The question turned around somehow sent a strange chill along the back of my neck, as though a tiny, invisible dancer with icy feet moved along there. "I'm saying that I was hired by Sir Brian O'Donnell to come here to Cashelderg, and I want to see him," I said with deliberate coldness.

The voice that answered me was deep, resonant, a mellifluous voice full of richness and warmth. "I should like to hear more about that," it said.

I turned, saw the man step toward me from a small side door of the corridor. He wore a short but full beard, a rich auburn with hair to match, his face strong, his eyes an electric blue that seemed afire with an inner brilliance. He had a look of eagles, proud, assured, a tremendous intensity reaching out from him, the vibrancy of it almost palpable. He was more than handsome. That overworked word, *charisma,* had, I think for the first time, real meaning to me.

"I am Adam Rood," he said, the intense blue eyes holding me. The name fitted so magnificently, I thought, the sound of strength, the touch of comfort in it, a faintly Biblical ring to it. "I saw you drive up from the monastery window. I came over to find out what you wanted here at Cashelderg."

"That's for me to do," I heard the high, reedy voice snap. Under the green cap, the tiny, gimlet eyes burned into Adam Rood with unmistakable hostility. Adam Rood's smile was to me, filled with patient amusement.

"Multy and I have some areas of disagreement," he said. Multy, I repeated silently. So that was the little man's name. It fit, also, a pugnacious ring to it. Adam Rood was appraising me with a slow smile. "Now, as to that remark about being hired to come here by Sir Brian O'Donnell, I'm afraid I can't accept that, not even from someone as attractive as you," he said.

The smile, embracing, almost made me say thank you to his compliment but anger had become an inner abrasion. "It happens to be true," I snapped. "I've the letter of agreement with me." I reached into my purse, pulled the letter out, and unfolded it, handed it to the auburn-bearded, handsome man. He took it, read it, and I saw the frown come across his forehead.

"Now will you please tell me where I can find Sir Brian?" I said with appropriate smugness. Adam Rood looked up at me, the little frown staying on his brow.

"You sound absolutely sincere," he remarked, and I felt my temper explode.

"I'm more than sincere. I'm damn annoyed, now," I shot back. "I insist on seeing Sir Brian about this."

"I'm afraid that's rather impossible," Adam Rood said. "Sir Brian O'Donnell has been dead for three hundred years."

CHAPTER FOUR

Simple disbelief first, then surprise, shock, anger. And something more, a fleeting moment of strange, unexplained fear. I heard the warm, mellifluous voice as if from a faraway place.

"Perhaps someone is playing a joke on you."

I shook my head, brought myself back to the moment.

"No, no joke. I haven't any friends addicted to that kind of joke," I said. I took the letter back, let it hang down from my fingers, my mind racing, trying to put together answers.

"Then someone must have sent this letter to me in his name, probably assuming it would be more impressive," I said. Adam Rood's eyes stayed on me.

"Someone?" he questioned. "Who? I've been trying to purchase Cashelderg for some time now and so far no one's been able to track down anyone with authority or recorded ownership to sell it. And here someone suddenly contracts with you in Sir Brian's name? No, I'm afraid not, my dear. Perhaps you've no friends who'd play such a joke as this on you but someone has played a rather malicious trick. The world is full of strange, distorted minds."

"*No.*" I snapped the word out. "I was sent fifteen hundred pounds. That's rather much for a malicious prank, don't you think? The check went through, drawn on the Bank of Dublin." I felt the frown come suddenly as I turned to the little green-capped man. "Didn't you say you were paid from funds in the Bank of Dublin?"

"That I did," Multy said.

Adam Rood's frown was deep, his strong-lined lips above the auburn beard drawn together. "Most strange, indeed," he thought aloud.

"There must be someone, somewhere, of the O'Donnell family who has done this," I exclaimed.

"I've heard that there are some descendants settled in Australia but no one's ever been able to track them down," Multy cut in. "Cashelderg is a giant monument waiting to crumble away."

"No," I protested. "It's a treasure house."

Adam Rood's voice cut in, smoothly soothing. "Whatever it is, your letter is obviously a fake, merely signed with Lord O'Donnell's name, hardly something you'd be able to verify as a signature."

"Maybe that could be done," I heard Multy say, saw his jaw jut out at Adam Rood, and I had to think of a terrier I once saw challenging a Saint Bernard. The little figure turned, started into one of the rooms, snapping his head for me to follow. I glanced at the vibrant figure of Adam Rood and he fell in beside me as I went after Multy. From the rear, with his tilted figure, he looked more dwarflike but he set a surprising pace into a third room. Automatically, I noted horizontal string-courses, rarely used in interiors, entablatures, and the beginnings of curvilinear design. Multy finally came to a halt in front of a wooden chest set into a stone wall in a small room, hardly more than an ancient pantry. He pulled an iron key-ring from his trouser pocket, took one of the three keys on it, and opened the front panel of the wall chest. Reaching in, stretching up on his toes to do so, he drew out a sheaf of old parchments.

"Deeds and land grants, letters, documents, old family records, all sorts of thing like that," Multy said as he pawed through the material. I glimpsed old wax seals, proclamations with illuminated lettering, uncials, and black letters. The little man paused at one, pulled it free, and put it atop the others, turned it so I could see it, rested a bony finger alongside the signature. It was identical to the one on my letter, the ornate, unique handwriting unmistakable in its florid twists.

"There'd be no forging that hand," Multy said. I had no answer and was grateful for Adam Rood's calm reply.

"It would be difficult, but not impossible," he said. "Modern techniques, photocopying, camera impressions, they make anything possible. It's very expert, extremely well done, but a fake nevertheless, I'm afraid."

"And the fifteen hundred pounds that followed?" I queried, and saw his lips purse.

"No answer for that, I'm afraid. But there must be some explanation," he said.

"And I'll find it," I snapped. "But meanwhile, I've been hired to do my work here at Cashelderg and that's exactly what I intend to do."

"Go back home," Multy half-shouted. "Do your finding out from there. Forget Cashelderg."

I stared down at the little man, knew there was no way to make him understand, not now, anyway. To turn away from this fantastic opportunity would be like turning away from myself, turning my back on a very important part of me. Never, I murmured silently. I would catalogue this great castle stone by stone, hall by hall, as the letter in my hands said. I folded the letter, returned it to my bag.

"I'm staying. I'm going to do what I was hired to do," I said quietly.

Multy glowered at me. "It's no work for a girl, poking and climbing around this old place," he said. I held back answering, knowing it'd be merely a waste of words. Multy was a product formed and molded beyond change.

"It's a different world today," I said, meeting the gimlet eyes. He grunted and in the staccato sound was a kind of recognition coupled with disapproval. I turned, saw Adam Rood's eyes studying me, thoughts forming behind their vibrant intenseness.

"I think you've made the best decision at that, Patricia," he said, and I felt an explosion of grateful warmth. His smile curled around me.

"That's not for you to be saying," I heard Multy snap, his eyes tiny pinpoints on the big, auburn-haired man.

"I'm saying it and that's final," I said. Multy turned, half-threw the ancient manuscripts back into the wall chest, and my glance went to the huge rooms that followed each other back to the main corridor, barren and dusty. I had expected a very different Cashelderg, a place to stay while I worked, and I realized that sweeping pronouncements are easier made than kept. I certainly couldn't stay here, I knew. Dismay is the mischievous imp of the emotions, always popping up when you don't want it to, and Adam Rood saw it touch me.

"Dreams of glory are often shattered by the bread and water of reality," he said and smiled, and I almost managed to smile back. "Perhaps I can help," he went on.

Multy's high-pitched anger intruded, almost a snarl. "It's not your business. Nothing here at Cashelderg is your concern."

I felt surprise at the intensity of the little man but Adam Rood ignored him, kept his smile for me. "I'll be at the old monastery you passed on the way up here. Please stop by when you leave," he said and I felt warm, secure, welcome, the electric blue eyes that seemed to see right through me not at all disturbing. He turned, strode away, and it was as if a light had gone out, the room suddenly flat, emptied of vitality.

I turned again to Multy, saw him staring after the receding figure of Adam Rood. The dwarflike little man practically throbbed with hatred. I could feel the simmering fury in his frame. I wondered why, certain at once that, whatever his surface reasons were, there were others, deeper ones rooted in what he was, in the subliminal depths of his psyche. He turned abruptly, caught my eyes watching him, probing, and the wizened little face grew crafty. He spat out words that were spears, penetratingly accurate, and I felt suddenly quite naked.

"You're thinking it's envy, aren't you?" he barked. "Ugliness hating beauty, the ugly duckling hating the swan. You've made your quick reasons."

"No," I said lamely, then, hating my own dishonesty, "All right, the thought occurred to me."

"Well, you're wrong," he snapped, a sly smile coming into the craftiness of his wizened face. "And now you're surprised I could see into you."

"Yes," I admitted. He grunted.

"Good whiskey can come in a funny-shaped bottle," he flung out. Emotions played leapfrog inside me, surprise, shame, and now a sudden warmth, wanting to start over again.

"I think we've gotten off on the wrong foot," I said. "I am going to go ahead with my work here and I'll need your help. I'll need certain equipment, ladders, ropes, things I expected would be here."

The little man couldn't stand straight, but he could look as though he were ten feet tall.

"No. You'll get nothing from me to keep you here. Go home. This is no place for you," he said. He turned, quick as an elf, and vanished into a doorway.

"Wait, please," I called after him but he was gone. I couldn't even hear his footsteps and I felt a deep sigh escape me. I walked slowly back to the vast corridor, taking in the architectural banquet waiting for me even as I wondered whether I should stay. I pushed that thought away quickly. Moving toward the tall, timbered front doors, I thought about the letter in my bag. As Adam Rood had said, it had to be a fake and forgery. Certainly there was no Sir Brian O'Donnell with a droll sense of humor. But someone had sent it to me. Who? And why? God, why, I asked myself. A malicious joke that was also a wonderful opportunity? It made no sense at all. Unless the sender expected that when I reached Cashelderg I'd just turn back, crushed and disappointed and frustrated.

Was someone trying to make a fool of me? Had someone expected me to return to the university with hat in hand, the naïve dupe? It would make me something of a laughingstock in academic circles, I admitted. I felt slightly soiled just giving room to the thought, yet I had been around long enough to learn that the halls of academe had more than their share of viciousness. Indeed, it was a tight little world subject to intense pressures, conceits, rivalries, and jealousies as thick as the ivy on the buildings.

Suspicion is a wild horse that, once mounted, runs away with the rider. There were those who disliked me, who envied my position in the field, those who resented me as a woman. Anything was possible, I told myself, anything. Certainly the little dwarf-like man wanted me to leave here. Because he'd been party to the hoax? He would almost have to be, I mused. And yet his anger bore a different quality, too deep for just that, nothing I could pin down yet. I walked down the long, high corridor and decided to look into the letter itself while I did my work here. I hadn't the envelope but it had been plain, ordinary, and I'd tossed it away. But an analysis of the letter might well be a starting point. I reached the doors, halted, looked back at the great main hall, at round, oaken chandeliers with their hundreds of iron cande cups. Not just in my dreams, I murmured silently. Somewhere else, it had to be. I felt cold suddenly, my skin clammy. Self-deceit is a corrosive offering, doomed to eventual rejection. But it clings, oh, indeed, it clings. Especially to those who know fear. I turned away, hurried outside into the sun.

The old monastery was within easy walking distance, just over the little rise, but I decided to drive. The little huts and shelters looked like so many pebbles spreading out from a rock. The thought was more approproate than I realized then. Turning onto the short road that led to the old building, I passed a knot of three girls and three boys seated on the grass, an opened book in each lap, and received friendly waves. Another, smaller group, two boys and a girl, were on a rock seated in a semicircle holding hands. My curiosity, always present and always sizeable, pushed away other thoughts for the moment and as I halted in front of the monastery I saw that the twentieth century had been brought to the ancient structure. I noted an electric light bulb just inside the arched entranceway and cables that trailed discreetly along the side of the building to what appeared to be a small generator just behind it.

The big, auburn-bearded man appeared in the doorway as I swung out of the car, the magnetism of him immediate, startling in its power.

"Hello," he smiled, and once again I felt warm, secure. "Did you make peace with Multy?"

"Hardly," I answered.

"Don't let him upset you. He's a narrow, shortsighted, insensitive, and rather dense little man," Adam Rood said. No, I almost answered aloud, not so insensitive, not so dense. That much I'd learned about Multy in those few sharp, spearing sentences.

"Why is he so antagonistic to you?" I asked the handsome, auburn-haired man.

"Probably many reasons. For one, he's afraid that if I were to gain ownership of Cashelderg his family job would come to an end," Adam Rood replied. It was a real enough reason to fear and to hate for, one that hadn't occurred to me, I reflected.

"Are you still determined to go ahead with your work at Cashelderg?" I heard Adam Rood ask and I nodded quickly.

"Absolutely."

"The bread-and-water of reality again," Adam Rood smiled. "You'll need someplace to stay, close to your work. Why not right here? This is where we have our facilities for new arrivals."

"New arrivals?" I echoed. "New arrivals for what, if I may ask?"

His smile grew broader, curled around me, warming, embracing. "Our little community," he said. His hand took my elbow, a strong, reassuring touch as he half-turned me toward the gently sloping grounds where the little huts and shelters were spaced. "We are a community come together to find the realities and the reasons for our existence. We're a spiritual community. Our root and our rock is the Bible and its treasures. From it, we are forging the answers we all need."

"You're a minister," I said, biting my lips for sounding so surprised. Adam Rood's quick laugh held no austerity.

"Some insist on titles. We don't like them here. I am Adam Rood."

"But you lead the community. They are your followers," I pressed. His smile wore patience.

"I suppose that is true enough, but we are all searchers together," he answered. "I don't like labels any more than titles. Follower and leader are comparatives too often misapplied. We are called the Disciples of Light because there is a distinction between follower and disciple. The first is faith, the second acceptance. One is a handshake, the other an embrace."

He gestured with a sweeping arm to the little huts and I felt the vibrancy of Adam Rood sweep around me, an embrace of its own.

"The young people built those shelters. Work is a form of worship," he said. "Those you see out there are not, except for a few, from here. Actually, most are American but some are English, Dutch, Australian, New Zealanders, German. We have gathered from many places. We have found answers, the keys to happiness, I think."

He turned from the doorway, his hand dropping from my elbow but the warmth staying. "There's nothing I like better than talking about what we have here but let me not get off on that. We have your practical problems to solve yet. You can stay here, be our guest as long as your work keeps you here. But my offer has strings attached to it, I should warn you."

He saw my quick frown, chuckled. "You are obviously an authority in your field. I will be eager to know your day by day progress at the castle. But I want you to give lectures, as often as possible, on your field and what you find in Cashelderg. We will all participate through you." He paused, the intense blue eyes waiting, dancing. "A bargain? Our facilities for your erudition?"

It was my turn to laugh. "Some bargain. It's like asking a musician to play for his supper. Of course, I agree," I said.

"Wonderful," Adam Rood exclaimed. "And while you're here you can learn more about us. Perhaps there will be other things we can give you, an added exchanging, so to speak."

The charisma I'd felt at the first moment with Adam Rood had not been a fleeting thing. The mind was pleasured just in listening to him, but not the mind alone. The senses were made warm, livened by that indefinable quality that sets apart those who lead from those who follow, despite his objections to the terms.

"Yes, perhaps there will be. That'd be good," I said. "Thank you, Father." I saw his quick smile and wanted to bite my tongue.

"You're using titles again, Patricia," he chided gently.

"I'm sorry," I said, reddening. The term had been automatic, falling from my lips by itself. "Force of habit. A good Catholic background."

"Don't apologize for that," Adam said. "Some of your past is part of us. All of the Bible is here. That's why we use no titles. There was no Father Peter, no Reverend John or Rabbi Moses, no Bishop Matthew. There was Peter, Paul, Thomas, and Isaiah, nothing more. That is how it is here."

"I'll remember, Adam," I said, liking the sound of it on my lips, the simple strength of it. He took my arm, guided me to the doorway.

"Let's get your things in from the car," he said. I went happily along. The shock, the cold disappointments and the unexplained things that had waited for me at Cashelderg had been at least balanced by the strength and warmth of Adam Rood. He took some of my bags and I managed with the rest, followed him back into the old monastery, down the long length of it, a center corridor with rooms branching out on both sides, most with relatively new doors added to them. I glimpsed a large dining hall as we went back inside with round tables in it. Three young girls in their early twenties, each carrying a Bible, came from a room as we neared.

"Welcome and bless you," they sang out to me as they passed.

"Assumptions are endemic to the human race," Adam smiled to me. He halted at a door at the end of the long corridor, pushed it open, and I saw a small room, a bed, a table and lamp, and a chair inside it. Obviously, in a time long past, it had been one of the many cells used by the old monks but a full-length window had been put in in place of the little barred aperture once there. It looked out toward Cashelderg and a ridge of heather.

"We don't go in for fancy rooms," Adam said. "There's a bathroom for your use just down from here. Don't expect more than warm water."

"It'll do beautifully," I said.

"Dinner is in the big dining hall at 6:30. We have table groups. Most everyone attends dinner. Breakfast is more casual," Adam said. "I'm sure you've a lot more questions. We can talk more after dinner."

My hand went out, an automatic gesture, resting on his arm. "Adam, thank you. I appreciate this more than you know," I said. His eyes, the intense blue of them that speared with fire, softened for a moment.

"See you at dinner. At my table, of course," he said, turned, and strode away. I pulled the door closed, leaned back against it for a moment, and could still feel the electricity of Adam Rood's presence. I moved from the door, lifted one of my bags onto the bed, and started to unpack. A portable clothes closet was set into one corner of the room and I began hanging my things inside it. The arrangement was perfect, I reflected. I would be close to my work and that was important to me. If I wanted to recheck something I could easily do it. Besides, the days would be full and long, the evenings spent in correlating material and writing my notes. I stacked the notepads and the technical books I'd brought with me, finished unpacking, and surveyed the little room. It was already beginning to take on a lived-in warmth.

The evening chill seeped through the stones and I suddenly shuddered, changed into a deep pink sweater and a gray skirt. At 6:30, promptly, I was at the dining hall and found the chairs at each round table were already filled. Adam Rood rose from a larger table at the front of the room, beckoned to me, and I made my way to him. Cheerful greetings followed me at every table I passed, smiles, an open, quiet kind of happiness rising up from the assembled groups. Adam sat me at his right. There were seven others at the table, five girls and two boys, and I sat down to a chorus of "Bless you." I was introduced to Judy, a smallboned girl with a small face, Joan, a very typical American midwestern type, Barbara and Fran, both short-haired with round faces and filled with bubbly enthusiasm, then Randy, a dark-haired non-descript young man, and Joseph, thincheeked with sad eyes. The last was Beth, a long-haired blonde. Hers was the only smile that was not brilliant, full of warmth. Her greeting was polite, almost guarded compared to the others.

Some of the community acted as waiters and waitresses, I saw, and the food was simple: mashed potatoes, corned beef, and fresh peas. "We grow most of our vegetables," Joseph volunteered. "Any good work is well-pleasing to the Lord." His smile was a shaft of quick brilliance.

"Adam told us of your work here," the girl called Judy said. "Is it true that the Gothic period was really an expression of man's upward thrust for God?"

"Religious thought and Gothic architecture were closely allied, entwined concepts, materially and philosophically," I answered. "The flying buttress, the ribbed vault, the cathedral ceiling, and all the other elements of Gothic architecture were all geometrically designed in imitation of the Lord's perfect design of creation. A leading poet and recorder of the spirit of the time, a man named Geoffrey of Vinsauf, wrote in describing the new architecture, 'As above, so below.' "

"Then it's doubly meaningful that you should do your work here among us," Adam Rood said. "Perhaps even prophetic." His smile held a touch of tongue-in-cheek humor in it and I laughed back. Inwardly, his words rattled about disturbingly. I had my own sensitivities to prophecy.

"Obviously, Gothic man reflected his concern for the spiritual in his art and architecture," I heard Adam say.

"While he was busy inventing some of the most terrible devices for torturing his fellow man," a girl's voice cut in and I turned to see Beth, her lips tight, her eyes on Adam Rood. "How can you reconcile those opposites? How do you reconcile the brutality of the Middle Ages with a spiritual philosophy?"

Adam's voice was low, not without wry humor in it as his eyes touched mine. "Every tree bears some bitter fruit," he said.

"How do opposites exist side-by-side without one being hollow?" the girl insisted, her eyes suddenly sharp with anger, surprising to me.

I saw Adam Rood focus his eyes on the girl. His smile stayed and his voice revealed no displeasure, yet I felt it was there. "Questions or rejections, Beth?" he said, not ungently.

"Questions," the girl said, and I saw her meet his eyes boldly. Suddenly I had the almost overwhelming feeling of another presence in the room, something dark and dread, something totally evil. It was as though a curtain had been ripped open for a brief instant, gone as quickly as it had come. Yet it had been there, a chilling instant.

"Beth only wants answers," I heard a voice say, looked to the next table where a blond-haired young man sat, pale blue eyes in a long face. My glance went back to Adam Rood as I felt his eyes find me.

"Beth and Peter want a syncretic faith," he smiled. "All opposites pulled together."

"No," the girl said sharply. "Just answers that recognize contradictions, rather than ignore them."

I heard a small sigh in Adam's voice. "Accepting is made of depths that must be reached," he said, and I suddenly felt that I was quite without depths.

"All things are possible to him that believeth," Joan and Judy chorused, almost in unison.

"We love Beth as the Lord loves her and she will understand," another young man said from a table nearby.

"Of course," Adam said, his tone pleasant, yet the two words seemed a subtle command, the topic closed. The other tables rose and Adam stood up, his hands outspread. I heard the others murmur in low voices yet with a quiet eagerness.

"Whatever we do, we do in His name. Whatever we think, we think in His name."

A low sound of murmured conversation followed, the open, eager pleasantness returning to the room. I found myself the center of eager questioners, many of whom seemed as determined to assure me of the blessedness of my work as to ask about it. Adam Rood finally appeared at my elbow and the others drifted away. I cast a quick glance about for the girl, Beth, found she had gone.

"I'm sure you've questions," Adam said. "Drop around to my quarters about nine. I'll be finished preparing my material for tomorrow's classes then. We can have tea."

"I'd like that," I agreed.

"My quarters are at the other end of the dining hall. You'll see the light." He pressed my arm and walked away. I watched two young women and a man join him as he strode from the room and once again I felt the embracing, vibrant power of Adam Rood. In his words, he was but a teacher, yet he was obviously more. I'd caught the way some of the others looked at him, their eyes holding something beyond respect, even beyond adoration. It was more than reverence yet bordering on it, I mused, seeking words. Dedication, I found myself murmuring, that was closest to it, a gaze of utter dedication. It was not hard to understand. In the short time I'd known him I had felt his strength, the reassurance he exuded. They felt it to a depth I could only imagine as yet. Most of them, I corrected, thinking of Beth and the pale-eyed young man, Peter. The exchange she had precipitated had been completely out of keeping with the open, eager pleasantness that seemed the climate here. As I started to walk back to my room, still thinking about the exchange, I wondered about that sudden, chilling moment I'd felt then.

I wanted to dismiss it, but I'd long ago stopped dismissing such things. I pushed it aside, though, wanting no further complications now. Reaching the room, I closed the door and put the little lamp on, sat down, and prepared a list of the things I'd need to start work. I also set down a little schedule for myself, made a note to find time to do something about the letter that had brought me here. Finished, I put my head back and let thoughts drift on their own, found myself thinking about Adam Rood and his community and of my own religious background. It had had none of the eager, evangelical climate that was part of the Disciples of Light. It had been traditional, pre-Vatican II, full of rules and restrictions, dos and don'ts, rewards and punishments. As I grew older, I came to see its strengths and weaknesses. That's what I told myself, anyway. We pick and choose our compromises in life, and justify them with the sweet syrup of rationalization. Perhaps I'd done no more than that, but it had been done and I was able to enjoy faith from a more distant place. Yet despite all the rigidities, the overstructured manmade rules, the superfluous encrustations of centuries of theological nitpicking, I had learned, caught hold of a core, a truth, and for that I was grateful.

I'd never known a great deal about communities such as Adam's, evangelical in nature, except that faith always seemed to be a mass exercise with them and I'd always felt it a very private, personal thing. Faith was not worn outside but inside, to me. You believed not because all was answered but because so much was unanswered. Perhaps it was time to learn more, I mused. I looked at my watch, saw that time had flown, and I rose, opened the door, and stepped into the long corridor. A lone, dim light burned at the far end, the corridor a tunnel of shadowy blackness and silence, and I moved down it feeling very alone and uncomfortable, glad to near the light at the far end near the now empty dining hall. I rounded the corner there, saw the wedge of yellow from the doorway partially open, and hurried to it, knocked gently.

"Come in," I heard Adam Rood's rich voice answer. He was in shirtsleeves, a lamp lighting the room giving his auburn hair and beard an added richness. The walls were lined with books and there was a desk and a leather sofa in the room, along with an old wooden cabinet against one wall. Another room adjoined it and I glimpsed the foot of a bed there. The intense, blue eyes speared into me. "Welcome, Patricia. I've been waiting for you. Have you made a list of questions about us?" he asked.

I shook my head and he reached out, took my hand, and led me to the leather sofa. He stood over me, looking down at me. "I suppose many people have told you that you're a beautiful young woman," he said. "Too beautiful to go poking about in musty old houses."

"Beauty is a word I seldom use and never about myself," I answered honestly. "Everybody's definition of it is personal."

"I still like that given by St. Thomas Aquinas," Adam said. *"Id quod visum placet."*

I frowned, drawing on my Latin. "That which gives pleasure on sight," I put together.

"Exactly. It applies equally to all God's creatures." Adam smiled. He pulled a leather hassock out and sat down on it opposite me. "After all, aren't we all seeking beauty, of spirit, of mind, of being?"

"Is that what all these eager young people are seeking here?" I asked.

"Essentially," Adam said. "They are here because they have been wounded emotionally, intellectually, spiritually, and they have found no answers elsewhere for those wounds. My task is to show them how to find the answers that are there for those wounds."

"Does one join the Disciples of Light as one would join any church?" I questioned.

"No. The first step is a total commitment of one's self. Everything that one has becomes part of the community, all material things, goods, income, allowances," Adam said.

"Is that how you exist? Does that cover the communal costs?" I questioned again.

"Of course not. We have other sources of income, investments, funds left us, inheritances," Adam said. "We just finished with a case in court over a very large sum a fine woman bequeathed to us and some of her relatives attempted to contest. I'm afraid greed is endemic also. But right triumphed, as it always does eventually. The turning over of all material things is really a more psychological than practical rule. It gives substance to the word commitment. It is the first step."

"Of what?"

"Of relearning why and how one exists, of rearranging our inner lives."

"It is resisted, sometimes, apparently," I smiled.

"You refer to Beth," Adam said.

"And her friend, Peter. He defended her quickly," I said.

"Peter is only an echo. He is still role-playing," Adam smiled. "He still clings to personal commitment, to individuals rather than concepts." I turned the words in my mind, set them aside for additional clarification. "Beth still has her problems," Adam went on. "The giving over process is always a difficult one."

"Giving over?" I queried.

"Yes, giving oneself over completely to something other than oneself, something bigger than oneself. Call it giving oneself over to the word of God, to the Holy Spirit, to a greater will ... call it anything you like ... but it is giving oneself over to a way of thinking, feeling, seeing, being. It is a divestment of one's former self, a shedding of inner as well as outer skin, and that is always a difficult process."

"And when it's done?"

Adam's smile encircled, warm, confident. "Ask the others for yourself. I think they'll tell you of new heights of happiness and new depths of peace."

"I'll do just that," I laughed, covering up annoyance at myself. Little questions kept prodding me, questions I felt ashamed of even entertaining. "How did you choose this place to settle in?" I asked, taking refuge in ordinary questions.

"We have been in other places, in America first, in fact." Adam replied. "But spiritual development requires a contemplative climate. This is a land steeped in yesterday. It is conducive to redefining the origins of believing. We have been here almost two years now. But I want to expand our physical facilities. That's why I was interested in Cashelderg. It could become our own cathedral."

"I suppose it could," I mused.

"But you wouldn't approve," Adam said and I almost winced at the quickness of his perceptions. He was right, of course. It was another way of killing a great house, and, like Yeats, I flinched at that. But it was also something more.

"I'm a purist, I guess. I believe that function and design are really inseparable. I feel that a converted house is like a transsexual, it loses what it was and never fully becomes what it tries to be," I answered.

A thin, whistling sound interrupted and Adam rose. "I put the tea kettle on. Be right back," he said. He disappeared into the other room and I sat back, surveying the office. It had once been a receiving room perhaps, for new penitents, or the abbot's quarters, and it carried intimations of internal bay design. I was idly glancing about when Adam reappeared with two mugs of tea, hot and strong brew with a tang in it. He lifted his mug in a silent toast and the questions stabbed at me again, embarrassing, refusing dismissal. Adam Rood was at the heart of them, himself a contrast. His presence was not only of strength and intenseness but a highly magnetic, sensual one, terribly in contrast to the spiritual emphasis here. How did they fit, one with the other, the sensual and the spiritual? The questions prodded and I chose words carefully.

"You spoke of Peter as still being committed to an individual rather than a concept. I take it you discourage personal relationships then," I said. I thought I saw laughter inside the brilliant eyes.

"Just how do you mean that question?" Adam asked and I realized I hadn't chosen words carefully enough, silently kicked myself.

"I just wondered about it," I said and there was no question of the laughter in his eyes now. He was letting me flounder, deservedly so for impertinent questions.

"It all depends on what surrounds the relationships, the framework around them," Adam said. I took refuge behind the mug of tea, sipping furiously. "You are a young lady of great curiosity," he added, not ungently. "Curiosity is always a good thing. It is important to you in your work, I'm sure."

I felt a surge of gratitude at his understanding. "I've a dirty mind," I said shamefacedly. Confession was good for the soul, I'd been taught. Adam laughed, a rich, deep sound.

"In Timothy 1, it is written that God giveth us richly all things to enjoy," Adam said blandly. The words were layered with meanings. I took hold of the most appealing one, tucked it away for further analysis. There'd be time for that, I was certain. I finished the tea and put the mug down.

"I should be getting some sleep," I said.

"But we'll talk more tomorrow," Adam said, almost as if reading my thoughts. I nodded, realized I was improperly happy at the thought.

"Thank you again for helping," I said and he took my hand in a warm, firm grip, walked to the door with me. I felt his eyes watching me as I went out into the dark corridor and I heard the door quietly close behind me. I rounded the corner under the single, small light bulb and started back up the long, tunnelled corridor that grew almost black as I neared my room. I'd nearly reached the end when I heard the sound, faint at first, a scraping sound. I halted, felt my skin grow cold with sudden fright.

"Who's there?" I called out.

The sound came again, then the voice. "Please, I must talk to you." The figure emerged from the darkness against the wall, long blonde hair, the girl Beth. "I can't talk now. I'm taking a terrible chance just being here," she said, and I heard real fear in her voice.

"What is it? What's the matter?" I asked. Her eyes darted past me, then back to my face again.

"Tomorrow, all you have to do is listen," she said, whispering words. "I'll find a time, a place. Just promise me you'll listen."

I hesitated, saw the near-panic in her eyes. "Yes, of course I'll listen. But can't we talk now?" I said.

"No. Tomorrow," she said, her eyes darting past me again. She started to back away, turned, began to move down the corridor along the wall.

"Beth. Wait, please," I called. I saw the long blonde hair shake in answer and she turned back for a moment, one finger held up to her lips, then hurried on, silent as a cat. I watched till she disappeared at the far end of the long corridor, turned, and went into my room, closed the door behind me. I undressed, the incident provoking, leaving a patina of uneasiness over the evening. Why was she taking a terrible chance just to be here, in her words, I wondered? Was discipline here such a rigid and all-powerful force? Or was Beth an emotionally unstable young woman given to overly dramatic remarks? Probably the latter, I mused, turning the lamp off, slipping under the sheets. I'd disdained the pajamas tonight, quite certain there'd be no need for them here.

I lay in the blackness of the room, having drawn the brown drape over the window earlier. Hundreds of years ago a monk had lain in this little room just as I did now, and he pondered the meaning of yesterday and tomorrow, of God and man and of existence itself. I lay here with meanings to ponder also, but the difference between him and me was made of more than centuries, more than anatomy and heritage. It was made of desire. He wanted to ponder his meanings, to search out and explore. I was most willing to push mine aside. But that was no more possible for me than it had been for him, I knew, and I turned on my side, closed my eyes. More tired than I realized, I slept quickly, soundly at first. I half-woke once in the night, tossing, turning, feeling my body grow tight as I heard the faint shrieking sounds and felt the storm lashing at me. I saw shadowed shapes hurtling and then it all passed and I was plunged into deep sleep again, totally unaware of anything, wholly immersed in silence. It had to have been hours later when suddenly I was no longer unaware yet not awake, suddenly in that half-world again.

> *I am dancing, whirling this way and that way. Laughter and gaiety surround me. The round, oaken chandeliers of candles blaze and the great house is filled with light and music. I am happy, warm, secure.*
>
> *Suddenly there is a terrible wind, and light and music are no more. The great front doors are open, everything else swept away. I shrink back from a shadowed figure. I know only stark terror and the sound of my scream.*

I sat up, my hands knotted into the bedcover, my skin cold with perspiration. I pulled covers close around me. The same, I murmured, breaking off at the exact same point. A meaning, a message, something. It had to be. I lay back, drained, feeling as though I'd run a marathon race. Too many unexplained things needing answers. Did they connect? Or was I building fears out of the past? I turned my face into the pillow, refusing to swing aboard that carousel which only went in circles. I'd been there before and knew the frustration of it. I would seek answers only for the solid, practical things, a fake letter, a frightened girl. That was enough for now.

I pressed my eyes closed and drifted into sleep once again. Dimly, I thought I heard a mocking laugh.

CHAPTER FIVE

The bright sun managed to filter through the drape as I woke. I swung out of bed, pulled the curtain back, and let the morning into the little room as I dressed, putting on work clothes: jeans, a blouse, and a wool work shirt over it. I put my note pad and a magnifying glass into the little leather shoulder bag that served as my tool kit. A small stone chisel and a little hammer were already inside it. The larger equipment I'd have to pick up somewhere, all the things I'd expected to find waiting at Cashelderg.

Hurrying from the room, dressed finally, the bag over my shoulder, I found the dining hall with the tables pushed to one side and a long breakfast table set up with fruit juice, hot oatmeal, Irish soda bread, tea, and sweet rolls. Some eight or nine others were standing about finishing breakfast, four of them young men. Everyone sang out a cheery "Bless you," as I entered and I saw two of the girls who had been at Adam's table, Judy and Joan. I glanced around for Beth, saw she wasn't there, and poured a cup of tea for myself. A pleasant young man nodded to me, darkhaired with even features, his eyes holding the same ingenuous, almost childlike brightness that seemed a hallmark here.

"Joe Rydell," he sang out to me cheerfully. "We give thanks for another beautiful morning."

"We do," I said, being able to think of nothing better. I wasn't used to such all-encompassing totality of thinking. Giving thanks had always been reserved for deeper things. But perhaps

I had a lot to learn. Certainly everyone here seemed filled with a kind of eager happiness. Almost everyone, I corrected myself once again. I finished the tea and went outside, taking a sweet roll and wrapping it in a napkin and putting it into my bag. I paused just outside the doorway, saw a large group, twenty or so I guessed, seated in the sun on a gentle slope and Adam standing before them. He saw me from the distance, waved, and returned to his class. I stayed for a moment longer, walked slowly to the car. If Beth were watching she'd have ample opportunity to see me. I slid behind the wheel and rolled slowly away, over the little rise to where Cashelderg stood waiting, telling myself again that I'd walk the short distance from now on.

Halting at the tall timbered doors, I climbed from the car, stood back from the great structure for a moment. It was a rarity, this Cashelderg, a castle replete with outer bastions, an inner bailey, and keep, yet without the heavyhandedness of most such architecture. It had obviously been built by architects and masons who worked on the great cathedral structures and attempted to incorporate some of the advances in form. It was, I saw, a kind of architectural herald embodying many of the elements that were to find full flower in the great Gothic cathedrals and monasteries. It was also further proof of how the influences of different lands combined to create the Gothic style.

I started to circle the exterior, halting every few moments to make notes, sometimes stopping to use my little chisel to take scrapings from the stones. I found preliminary evidence of the use of linseed oil and resin in the mortar, a common practice to preserve stone of dubious weathering quality. Moving along the right side of the great structure, I found additional horizontal string-courses, a recessed area with stone entranceways of pointed arches that obviously held multiple shafting and at a series of windows I saw extensive use of the ogee curve and diaper patterns. Continuing my preliminary survey, I reached the rear of Cashelderg to find with surprise that I faced the sea, looking down from the edge of a rock-and-soil steep slope that crept to the very walls of the castle. A narrow path led down to a strand of sand and rocks and the sea rolled in to erupt in little explosions of spray against the larger rocks.

I decided to take a break from my work for a moment and started down the narrow path, found it steeper than I'd thought. Once down on the firm sand I drew in deep breaths of the bracing salted air, looked up behind where I stood to see Cashelderg rising up over the shelf of land. A few stubbles of beach grass grew in spots as I walked down the narrow strip of white sand. I moved through narrow passageways between towering rocks and felt very tiny and, somehow, an intruder. The sandy soil rose up at my right, became covered with a dense, thick, dry brush, a form of yaupon it seemed to me, and higher up, flat shalelike rock.

I'd just emerged from one of the narrow pathways between two rocks when I saw the figure, bent over, pushing aside the clusters of brush, searching through the dry hardy leaves, tall, spidery, all arms and legs. "You won't find any seashells there," I said.

He turned, the affable face registering surprise, a slow smile spreading across it after a moment. "Well, this is a surprise," Liam Flaherty said.

"Why?" I asked. He looked uncomfortable for the briefest moment. "I just thought you'd be with the others, getting acquainted and all that sort of thing," he said.

"You shouldn't jump to conclusions, Liam Flaherty," I said. "I didn't come here to join Adam Rood's community." His eyes deepened with curiosity, waited. "I came here to record the architectural treasures of Cashelderg," I said, and then, unable to keep ruefulness out of my voice, "at least, I thought that's what I'd been hired to do."

"Meaning exactly what?" he asked and I saw that the mild, genial eyes had taken on pinpoints of sharpness. Perhaps because I felt indebted to Liam Flaherty, perhaps because I still didn't quite comprehend it and talking about it helped, I told him everything that had happened. He listened without comment till I'd finished, then surveyed me reflectively.

"Any thoughts on who would pull a stunt like that?" he asked.

"Not really. Only wild guesses, someone who wanted to make me appear a fool in academic circles, perhaps, someone who chases off after any old thing," I mused aloud. "It's not going to work, though, if that's what it was, thanks to Adam Rood."

Liam Flaherty's eyebrows lifted. "Adam has given me a place to stay so I can do what I came here to do. When I'm finished, I'll have a storehouse of priceless information gathered and catalogued," I said.

"He encouraged you to go through Cashelderg?" Liam said.

"Yes. That surprises you. Why?" I questioned.

The disarrayed geniality flooded back into Liam Flaherty's face, almost as if on command, I thought.

"Surprised? No, why should I be?" he replied mildly.

"You seem to disapprove of Adam's community. I saw it in your face when you thought I was on my way here to be a part of it," I pressed. His smile was bland, contained.

"Now who's jumping to conclusions," he chided. He chuckled so pleasantly that I wondered if I had indeed misread his expression yesterday. I was still on edge, I told myself with some annoyance.

"Are you really going to try to have the letter analyzed?" Liam asked.

"Definitely. It might at least point me in the right direction," I said.

"There's a druggist in Drumglas, that's just south of here, but I doubt he does that kind of thing. He might know where to go with it, though," Liam said. I felt my eyes narrow as I regarded the tall, lanky figure in front of me, thoughts from yesterday rushing back. I was on edge, unquestionably, and I'd had enough of strange and unexpected things. Perhaps I was going out on a limb but suddenly I felt angry enough to do so.

"Why the masquerade?" I snapped.

"What's that?" he frowned back.

"The masquerade," I repeated. "Your soft brogue is lovely, but you're not a native Irishman. It's not druggist, not drug store here, it's *chemist's*. Even I know that."

"I didn't think you'd understand what I meant if I'd said chemist," he answered quickly.

"Nice try," I snapped. "The same consideration goes for yesterday? You said windshield when it's *windscreen* here. A native Irishman wouldn't say fender and hood. He'd say *bumper* and *bonnet*. No, you're not one of the Irish rovers at all, Liam Flaherty, if that is your name."

His lips pursed and I saw little pinpoints gather in his eyes as he appraised me. "You're very quick, very observant," he said, and the soft brogue was gone from his voice.

"Occupational disease, observing things," I said and saw his smile broaden.

"You're right, of course," he said. "I'm an American. I'm here getting material for a book on national customs and practices. I thought I'd do better if I made myself part of the country. I guess I need more practice," he concluded ruefully, drawing a long breath. "Sorry, I didn't mean to make you angry. You do have a temper that snaps. And the name is Lee Farrell."

"I guess I'm on edge, myself," I apologized. "What with fake letters and sudden storms and unexpected receptions."

"Any more dreams?" he slid out, his glance quick, sharp.

I stopped myself from wincing at his remark. He was acute enough, also. "Maybe," I allowed. He put out a big hand, took both of mine in it.

"Friends again?" he asked and I nodded. "Will you come visit me soon? I'd like to hear about all the things you've found."

"I promise," I said, feeling very much better.

"Good. I'll be waiting," he said. He turned abruptly, hurried on down the beach. I watched him go, all arms and legs, looking like a very large sandpiper stepping its way along the water's edge. There was a most likeable quality to Lee Farrell, I decided, masquerading or not masquerading. I turned and made my way back to the steep little path that led up to Cashelderg, still thinking about him and I realized he'd never said why he was poking around in the bushes. He had a disconcerting way of always leaving something hanging. I grunted and was annoyed again.

Reaching the top of the path, I moved to the other side of Cashelderg and began going over that section. I noted a set of the same gargoyles I'd seen in the room inside yesterday high along the edge of the corner turret. The stones on this side were in better condition, I noted, obviously not taking the full brunt of storms that swept in from the sea. Continuing on, I finished the morning and went into early afternoon before arriving back at the front of the old castle. As I rounded the last corner bastion I halted in surprise. In front of the tall, timbered front doors I saw ladders, buckets, ropes, heavy chisels, and hammers, all set in a neat pile. I approached the material, stood staring down at it when the voice cut into my wonderings, high and reedy.

"You'd find a way to get them, anyway, I decided," it said. I turned to focus on the little tilted, green-capped figure.

"Thank you, Multy," I said. "I'm glad you've changed your mind about me."

"I've changed nothing," he shouted. "Go home. Go from here before you get yourself killed."

"What kind of talk is that, Multy?" I chided. "I've done old houses before. I know what I'm doing."

"Cashelderg is a cursed place," he half-shouted. "Leave it alone." Arguing would be useless, I decided. His reasons were made of many things apparently, all running deep.

"I'll really begin work inside tomorrow. You could help me a lot," I said.

"I'll be here," he grunted, the little gimlet eyes burning. "But don't take reasons to yourself. You'll be wrong." He moved, slipped inside the castle, and was gone. Pride and fear, I wondered? Or just a strange little man living in his own half-world? No, I decided. There was something more inside that tilted little body. I'd not learn by asking, I knew. I'd learn by watching, catching him at unguarded moments. I turned to the car, climbed in feeling warmed. I'd have help tomorrow and I could really get to work.

I drove over the rise to the monastery, slowed, halted, and got out, sat down on a grassy hillock overlooking the sloping land and the *clochan* like little shelters. I took out the sweet roll and consumed it, watching young men and women move about below where I sat. On a distant slope I saw a half dozen tending a small farmed plot. I wondered about Beth. I'd expected she would have tried to contact me before this. I glanced at my watch. There was more than enough time for me to drive to the little town Lee Farrell had mentioned and return before dinner and I rose, clambered back into the car. I drove slowly down the road, watching to see if I could glimpse Beth at any of the little shelters but I didn't find her. Speeding up, I drove through a narrow road, saw the sign for Drumglas and turned to follow a tree-lined road past a peat bog. The little town was typical, charming as a picture postcard, the *Chemist's* easy enough to find on the single street that ran through town.

I went inside a shop that seemed made of shelves holding apothecary jars of every size and shape. A spectacled man in shirtsleeves and a waistcoat came around a small counter and I handed him the letter and told him what I wanted. He examined it with something that resembled a jeweler's glass.

"It's not something I can do here, not this kind of analysis," he said, looking up at me. "But I've a good friend, Professor Toolan, at the Dublin Museum. He'd do it for me quick enough. I could send it on to him. In fact, I've a package going off to him tonight."

"Would you? That'd be wonderful," I exclaimed. "I'm especially interested in finding out whether that special parchment-like paper is made here or in America."

"Well, he could tell you if it's from Ireland, I'm sure. Most papers carry a watermark and other identifying characteristics," the chemist said. I nodded, gave him the letter and a deposit in advance. "I'll keep checking back with you," I told him, deciding it would be best that way.

I drove back to the monastery feeling satisfied. I'd begun the process of getting answers. There was still light in the day when I parked, walked slowly down along the old building, turning at the rear of it and wandering up along the edge of a row of beech trees. I sat down in the deep shadows at the edge of them along a sloping rise and waited. I'd certainly given Beth another chance to see me if she were looking for that. As it began to grow dark, I rose, walked back along the front of the building, and finally wandered back to my room. The girl's fearful urgency of last night had faded with the day, it seemed. Yet the near-panic of her eyes had seemed more than a passing thing. It just didn't fit right. I grunted as I started to change. Nothing seemed to fit right here so this was entirely in keeping. I freshened up, changed into a skirt and sweater, and went down to the dining hall.

Adam rose as I entered, beckoned to me and I saw the place at his right waiting again for me. I also saw that Beth wasn't at the table. My eyes scanned the adjoining tables. She wasn't at any of those, either, and I saw the boy, Peter, dark circles under his pale blue eyes. I had already decided not to ask about Beth, an instinctive feeling, when Adam spoke up.

"I'm told that Beth isn't feeling well today," he said, and I heard the sigh come into his voice. "Judy feels it's more of the spirit than the body."

"Beth gets moods," Judy said brightly, and I felt my lips tighten. It was entirely possible, of course, especially if Beth was an unstable person. Yet the desperate fear in her eyes continued to stay with me.

"How did the first day go, Pat?" Adam asked.

"Fine. All preliminary work, of course," I answered. His warmth dispelled all other stray thoughts as sunlight dispels the dark and in moments he had me talking about those things that came most easily to me, my work, my thoughts, things I anticipated finding, and dinner was finished in minutes, or so it seemed. He drew me aside as we rose.

"By now you've more questions, I'm sure. Come visit me again later," he said and his eyes danced. I nodded agreement. If I hadn't any questions, I'd think up some. Adam left a quick smile with me and went off to where four young men waited for him. I started to walk back to my room. I'd almost dismissed Beth entirely when I felt the tall, thin form at my side.

"Please keep walking," he said in a whispered voice. "You haven't seen her, have you?"

"No," I said.

"She said she was going to talk to you," Peter told me.

"I know. But she never did," I said. "Which hut does she live in?"

"Number five," he said.

"They said she wasn't feeling well," I remarked. I felt his pale blue eyes turn on me, looked up to meet their stare. He seemed to look right through me.

"You don't believe that, do you?" he asked softly. He turned and began to walk away just as someone called to him. I forced myself not to stare after him and I walked on, but his question, draped in chilling accusation, hung in my mind. Alone in the little room, I told myself to put aside the brief exchange, to wait and see what the next day would bring. I sat down and began to organize the material I'd taken down during the day. After half an hour, I halted. Peter's pale blue, accusing eyes, his question, all refused to stop dancing through my mind. I closed my large notebook, rose, and went out into the silent dimness of the long corridor. I hurried down it and out into the coolness of the night.

I walked down the road, the little round huts on both sides dark mounds with slivers of light coming from them. I paused at one, found the little number to the right of the door and walked on, halted at the next one. It wasn't number five either and I crossed the road to those on the other side. The first two were not the one I sought. I was just approaching another shelter when the door opened and two young women came out. I saw that one was the girl from the table, Judy, the other a tall, severe-faced girl with short, dark hair.

"Hello," I said. "I just thought I'd stop by to see how Beth is doing."

"I'm afraid that's not possible," the tall, severe-faced girl returned.

"She's sleeping," Judy said, smiling pleasantly.

"That's better than visitors, I guess," I commented.

"Yes," Judy said. "I'm sure she'll be up and around tomorrow."

A third girl appeared from inside the hut, short, a trifle pudgy, with an expressionless face and curly brown hair. She took up a position blocking the door. "This is Ruth," Judy introduced. I smiled at Ruth. Her face stayed expressionless.

"Beth will be better soon. She's in the best hands," Ruth said. The tall, severe-faced girl only stared at me and Judy maintained her pleasant smile but said nothing more.

"Tell her I stopped by, won't you?" I said, turning away. I wasn't welcome. I felt it as strongly as if it had been put into words. Walking back up the roadway, I half-turned, glanced behind me. The tall, severe-faced girl and Ruth still stood at the doorway guarding the entrance and I walked on, frowning. It had been a strange, hostile protectiveness. Was it because I was an outsider? Was the community so tightly knit together? Was taking care of their own part of their community discipline? Or, and I felt a twinge of shame at the thought, was Beth being purposely kept from me, a prisoner of sorts?

As I neared the old monastery building I saw Adam's figure in the doorway and he waved to me. "Restless tonight?" he called out.

"A little," I said, halting in front of him. "I thought I'd see how Beth was feeling."

"How was she?" he asked. I scanned Adam Rood's face, saw concern in it.

"I didn't see her. I was told she was sleeping," I said, suddenly unwilling to give voice to the thoughts that I'd carried back with me. I had no right to them, not yet, not on the basis of my own highly subjective reactions and the plea of a possibly overemotional young woman. And I suddenly wondered if perhaps there were things happening within the community that Adam knew nothing about. If so, it was even more important to wait, to be sure, before voicing thoughts to him. I put aside questions, not at all difficult as his vibrancy swept around me and his hand took my arm, a strong, comforting touch.

"I thought we'd celebrate the start of your work," he said. "I've some fine brandy for such special occasions." His smile, warm and mischievous suddenly, curled itself around me. "You're relieved to find we are not total puritans," he laughed.

"And bothered to find that you're a mind reader," I said.

"Wine maketh glad the heart of man, it tells us in Psalms 104," Adam chuckled as I sat down on the old sofa again. He brought a fat-bellied bottle out of the wooden cabinet and then a large goblet with two handles, one on each side. Silver, it struck little glints of light as he held it up.

"What a lovely old piece," I murmured admiringly.

"It predates Christianity," he said, pouring the brandy into it and swirling it about. "It once was a wassail cup." He lifted it to his lips, sipped from it, and handed it to me. I did the same, the brandy a stream of soft fire running down through me.

"When Christianity replaced the earlier pagan rites, the wassail bowl was one of the customs that stayed on, changing emphasis, of course. Instead of being a drinking bowl for simple carousing, it took on a religious meaning. It became a symbol of shared gifts, shared beliefs, fraternity, and a common bond. The old monks renamed the wassail bowl the *poculum caritatis,* the loving cup, which is what we know it as today."

He sipped again, handed it back to me, and I took a deep draught, felt warm and deliciously comfortable in moments. "Have you formed any further thoughts about our little community?" he asked. I paused, selected words.

"Only that most everyone seems very happy, very open," I said.

"They are," Adam agreed.

"Because of what you teach them?" I asked.

"Because they have given themselves over to something greater than their own selves," Adam said. It was the phrase he had used before and I heard answers coming from me out of past teachings.

"Isn't believing different than giving oneself over?" I queried.

"Not if you really want to find happiness. The ancient mystics knew that, the old monks realized that," Adam replied.

"Unusual people can do unusual things," I said. "Is that kind of totality possible for the average person?"

"Of course," Adam said, his vibrancy reaching me with encompassing force. I couldn't shake inner skepticism, though.

"I wonder," I mused aloud. "Doesn't the human factor prevent that? Right here, for instance, haven't they really given themselves over to you, to Adam Rood, the teacher and leader?"

"No, I am merely a vehicle. They have given themselves to What I teach, not to me," Adam said. His smile, warm and patient, made me feel a cynic, yet cynicism, like a limpet on a sea rock, clings tenaciously. I kept remembering how Joan and some of the others had looked at him. It had been far from abstract. But dedication is never abstract. Nor is fear, I reflected, thinking of Beth's eyes in the corridor last night.

"Yes, giving oneself over is entirely possible," I heard Adam go on. "The first step is realizing that we are not sufficient unto ourselves. That error is at the root of all our neurosis, our unhappiness, our constant turmoil. If we would find happiness, we must first deny the self as important. That is demanded of us."

The statement jarred. "Demanded of us?" I echoed.

"Absolutely. It is the sole condition imposed, reiterated again and again in Holy Scripture," Adam said. The vibrancy of his strength was encompassing but I found myself thinking of the Scriptures, of how they spoke of trust, of faith, of believing, but nowhere of giving oneself over, of denying the self as important. But then Scripture was a thing of highly specialized interpretation and I was certainly no Bible student.

"It is not only demanded of us, it is what we all seek," Adam went on, his voice softening. I frowned again and he reached forward, took my hands in his. "That's right. We all want to give ourselves over to something greater, something more than we are. Scripture demands of us what we really want to give." He paused, laughed, a low, rich sound. "You still rebel at the thought," he said, and I shrugged.

"I guess so," I replied honestly. "Maybe I've just never thought enough about it."

"Consciously, you mean," he laughed. "Tell me, have you ever thought about why the medieval ages attracted you so, why you were pulled to go into this field of study in depth? There are always reasons within reasons, Patricia."

I felt myself stiffen, forced my smile to stay. There were indeed reasons within reasons and I wondered how acute, how deeply, his insights could peer. But I wouldn't give voice to those things, not yet, not till I knew Adam Rood better. So I told him of the other reasons, all part of it and all true enough.

"Yes, I've thought about it. It just attracted me, ever since I was a little girl. As I grew up, other aspects attracted me. First, there was the romance and color of the era, and then, as I grew older, the threshold quality, the expression of philosophy in substance. The Dark Ages were only dark in certain respects. There was a closeness about those times despite the hardships.

In a good fiefdom, the people were not mistreated but their needs taken care of in every way possible for the times."

"There was strength," Adam said.

"Yes."

"And security."

"Yes, a kind of togetherness. Even a kind of self-sufficiency within each great castle's domain, sometimes within its very walls."

"And something more," Adam smiled.

"More?" I frowned.

"Yes, being a part of something bigger than oneself," Adam smiled. "You really seek that, Patricia. That's why you have this affinity for those times when one was born given over to something beyond oneself. The thought may not ever have occurred to you but it's there, deeply rooted inside you. You intellectualize your attraction for that period but it's not intellectual at all. It's a matter of need. The great castles and their walls with their protective strength are symbols to you of that need inside you, the need to give yourself over to something beyond yourself."

His insights startled, tore open new avenues for self-exploration. "I daresay the need is so deeply rooted it affects you even in your most personal relationships," he added.

His words suddenly were reaching into bruised places with uncomfortable accuracy. I hadn't ever been aware of wanting to give myself over to anyone or anything, yet how often had I sought just that in the men I'd known? How often had I wanted to find one I could give myself to completely, without regrets? How often the subconscious searching, and how often the disappointment?

"I'll have to think more about all this," I heard myself say. He would see it as a retreat, of course. He couldn't know all the reasons I hadn't voiced, reasons that would offer far different conclusions to him. He smiled, drew his hands away, and I almost protested.

"You can start your little after-dinner lectures tomorrow," he said. "And I want a personal briefing on what you've done each day, what you're planning next, everything. I'm really interested."

"That's nice. It's good to be able to share things that are exciting to you with someone else," I said.

"And it's good to have you here. An exchange of gifts, remember. My work here is a calling, my mission in life, and I've a personal commitment to each person here. Yet you can bring an added dimension to it," he said. I felt more than complimented and shamefully anticipatory. His vital, electric warmth made one want to be a part of whatever he was doing. I rose, not wanting to leave but knowing it was time. "Sleep well, Patricia," Adam called after me as I headed down the darkened corridor, and his vibrant warmth stayed with me. Reaching the room, I closed the door, left the light out and the window drape pulled back, the night outside a deep, inky void. I undressed and slid into the narrow bed, the sheets cold against my skin, and I stayed huddled in one spot till I grew warm. Adam had spoken words that both jarred and intrigued, things which had reached into me. I'd take the time to sort them out. The brandy was still with me and I felt sleep drawing itself over my eyes almost at once. It was welcome and I pressed myself down into the pillow and let the night rule.

Rays of yellow warmth woke me, pushing in through the tall window. I sat up feeling good, my sleep uninterrupted for a change. I slipped on a robe, went to the bathroom, and anticipated getting an early start at work. Finally, clad in jeans and a blouse, my wool work shirt over my shoulders, I went down to the dining hall to find I was not the only early riser, the room quite filled, buzzing with cheerful conversation. Adam was at the far end, talking to five young men, and he waved at me as I entered, then returned to his earnest conversation. I had tea and a biscuit, nodded to the tall, severe-faced girl I'd seen at Beth's hut. Her eyes acknowledged me and she turned away. The hostile protectiveness I'd encountered at the little hut came back to me, still disturbing in its intensity. I finished my biscuit and hurried outside, began the short walk to Cashelderg.

I was a few paces beyond the building when the three girls came around a low bush, walking arm in arm. I saw Joan, Judy, and Beth in the center.

"Hello, Beth. How are you feeling?" I asked, unable to keep surprise out of my voice. I saw Beth's eyes turn to me, wide, round, terribly direct.

"Fine. Just fine," she said. "I had troubled myself and that was wrong, but I've come to know that now."

"That's good," I said, hearing the emptiness of the reply. I searched the eyes that had held panic, had pleaded with me. They held nothing now, no hidden plea, not the glimmer of a message, a silent moment of communication, nothing but that direct, open, pleasantness. It seemed almost a kind of wall, I thought, and was ashamed at the thought.

"Troubled thoughts bring troubled bodies," Beth said, and her smile was bright. "I'm happy, now."

"No more questions to reconcile," I commented, watching her eyes. They only smiled back at me, almost sadly.

"Questions are not happiness," Beth said.

"Beth knows that now," Judy added with cheerfulness. Beth's glance had left me and she stared out into space, her face totally composed.

"What is happiness?" I questioned, feeling unaccountably irritated.

"Being in His hands. Knowing He answers all things. Accepting, waiting, obeying," Judy answered with affable pleasantness.

"I'm glad you're feeling well again, Beth," I said, trying to pull her eyes back to me. She turned and I searched the round orbs again quickly, found nothing but the wide directness.

"We must get on. We're expected at the morning conscious-ness session," Joan spoke up. I nodded, stepped aside as, arms linked again, they hurried on. I turned and walked on, strangely bothered. It was an unwarranted reaction, I reprimanded myself. People do change their attitudes, undergo inner decisions. After all, this was a place of inner decisions. Beth certainly seemed cheerful, albeit the kind of bland, cheerful conformity that was part of the climate here.

I crested the little rise, started down the other side toward Cashelderg, caught the sunlight glinting from the corner tur-rets. I had almost reached the timbered doors when the tall fig-ure appeared, striding toward me and I halted, waited. Peter's pale blue eyes held a deep fire and his hands clenched and unclenched.

"You saw her. You saw what they did," he gasped out.

"Beth?" I frowned. "Yes, I saw her. She seemed quite all right."

"*No!*" He tore the word out, his voice tight. "It isn't her."

"She does seem to have changed her attitude, if that's what you mean," I agreed.

"It isn't her," he almost shouted. "She was going to leave. We both were. We had a plan. But they got to her."

"What do you mean? Why would you need a plan to leave? And who are *they*, how did they get to her?" I asked.

"Didn't you see?" he exploded, and I stepped back from his rush of anger. "Didn't you see what they did to her? I thought she could stand up to them, not let them brainwash her again. I thought she could hold on until we could get away."

"Aren't you being a bit overdramatic, Peter?" I frowned. His pale blue eyes stared at me.

"You don't see. Or maybe you're too friendly here already," he bit out. "Maybe you set them onto her. Maybe you told them she had come to you."

"What are you talking about?" I demanded, growing angry myself. He stepped back, started to turn away, paused to fling words back at me.

"I'll find out. Somehow, I'll find out. If it was you, I'll make you sorry for it," he said.

"Now, just a minute," I called out but he was striding away, not looking back. The threat in his words hung in the air, angering and frightening. He was obviously a very upset young man, perhaps a deeply disturbed one. I decided I'd mention the incident to Adam later. Turning, I headed toward the tall doors when the little green-capped figure appeared in the doorway, standing in his tilted way, regarding me with the gimlet eyes.

"Trouble in paradise," he grunted. I ignored the sarcasm in his words. "Go home," Multy said. "Leave here."

I ignored that, too. "I'll need a pail of warm water and some kind of cleanser, something strong, if possible," I said.

He stood before me for a moment longer, than stepped aside as I went into the old castle. He had disappeared and I walked into the great dining hall, my eyes going to the round, oaken chandeliers despite myself. If I closed my eyes I could see the great hall filled with music and laughter, women in long gowns dancing the minuet and the quadrille. I refused to do so and saw it anyway, and shook away the vision with anger. I'd start here,

I told myself, falling back on the safety of practical things. The great hall first, then fanning outward into the other rooms in wheelspoke fashion. I began in the right corner and was into my second page of observations, notes, and sketches when Multy returned with the pail of water and a cleanser strong enough to send sharp odors up to my nostrils.

"I'd like you to scrub the stones down in each corner of the hall," I said. "Just the lower stonework, no higher than your head and going back about four feet from each corner."

He nodded, carried the pail over to the entranceway, and immediately set to work. I moved into the outer corridors adjoining the main hall. The stonework was uniformly excellent, I'd already noted, though the corridors were cruder in workmanship. Inside the great hall, the structural theory of piers and arches with the necessary end abutments was very much in evidence. The inner stones had been treated with preservative also, I noted, lime-washing and linseed oil. I was immensely excited at finding a small room just off the main hall that held a large, wooden platform on which was an equally large slab of plaster of Paris. It was, I recognized at once, a tracing-floor, the very meaning of it proof that Cashelderg had been constructed by a master architect, one who drew out his plans, made formative tracings, and used geometric precision. Many Gothic structures, including the great churches, were built by men who directed their laborers directly from the conception in their minds, men so learned in their work that they could construct great edifices out of their precise knowledge, such as one Master Simon, described as "setting out the work already conceived in his mind, not so much by his measuring-rod as by the yard-stick of his eyes."

As the science of architecture grew more advanced, the master builders took more to drawing out their conceptions on such as the tracing-floor. The medieval architect was most often designer, mason, and often carpenter in one and only later, in the fifteenth century, did a real line of distinction become evident between the architect and the builder, the designer and the craftsman.

I was sketching and measuring the tracing-floor when Multy poked his head in to tell me he'd finished and I went back into the great hall with him. I sought out the cleansed stones, found what I searched for on a large keystone near the main entranceway, the words carved into the stone, visible now that the centuries of encrusted dirt had been cleaned away.

Raymundus fecit hoc opus, I read, a cry of pride from down the centuries: This work was done by Raymond. I knew now the name of the master builder of Cashelderg and felt somehow closer to the great empty halls. It was indeed a capital offense to kill a house such as this.

Returning to the little room, I finished my notes and examination there and, as always happens, became totally plunged into my work, exploring, scraping samples, making sketches, until the tiredness came over me and I realized that the day was almost gone. Multy had been helpful, scraping stone, moving ladders, holding me in place as I arched backwards to measure a corner curve.

"I'm sorry," I apologized to him. "You should have stopped for lunch. I get caught up when I'm working."

"I don't often eat midday," the little man said.

"You've been most helpful. Where do you live, Multy?" I asked, putting things into my tote bag.

"Down the south road about a half mile, a little coteen with my sister," he replied and walked to the front door with me, his gimlet eyes peering up at me. "You're good at your work," he said matter-of-factly.

"Thank you," I said formally, certain that compliments didn't come often from the little man. He stepped outside and I followed, saw that the end of the day had grown thick, the air clammy.

Multy paused, looked at me. "Go from here. Go before it's too late," he said.

"A cursed place?" I smiled. "I lead a charmed life."

There was no answering smile. "Go from here," he repeated, turned, and hurried on down a narrow road along the top of the cliff, his tilted little walk seeming precarious so close to the edge. A strange little man, full of ancient myths and modern angers. I turned toward the little path that led down to the sea. The day had time left in it to stand by the sea for a few minutes and I made my way down the narrow, steep path. I buttoned the wool shirt as I reached the sand, the air damp and the smell of the sea strong. A bank of mist moved toward the shore like a great gray-white blanket. The tide had only just receded, the sand wet and I saw fresh footsteps there, a man's footprints. Curious, I let my eyes follow them, strolled after their trail. They moved to the thick brush that bordered the steep hill, moved in little half-circles along the line of brush. Idly, I followed along, wedging through a narrow place back of one of the tall rocks that rose up from the sand like so many druidic monuments. The footsteps continued to move, then make little half-circles, now at a section of rock that mixed into the brush. They went on, then seemed to pause again at another area. I halted my little game of following, peered down the beach, and felt the lines press down over my eyebrows. I watched the distant figure going down along the sand, tall, spidery, the long, loose-jointed walk unmistakable.

Lee Farrell had been poking about among the brush and rocks again and my frown stayed as I turned, started back to the little path that led up from the shore. He'd obviously been searching for something, as he had when I met him yesterday morning. I would definitely pay Lee Farrell a visit, I decided. Climbing back on the little path, I reached the top and paused, Cashelderg rising up massively, a forbidding ominousness to it for the first time. I glanced back, saw the blanket of gray-white fog had rolled closer, blotting out the sea behind it completely. I walked quickly back to the long, old monastery building and to my room, washed off the dust and dirt of the day's work, and changed for dinner.

Adam's table was full except for my place when I arrived, and I saw Beth seated between Joan and Judy, Randy and Joseph flanking the two outside girls. I sat down, let my glance move to the nearby table, and met Peter's stare, surprised that pale blue eyes could hold so much fire. The tall, severe-faced girl was serving, I saw, along with the pudgy girl, Ruth. As I glanced out across the room, I felt a subtle excitement in the air. The earnest conversations seemed just a shade more animated, the decibel level a few notches higher. I wondered if perhaps I was imagining things, shrugged inwardly, yet the feeling persisted. I looked at Beth, caught her return glance. Automatically, I looked for some personal instant of communication but her eyes sent no quick message, no unspoken asides. But the round, direct eagerness of the morning was gone from them, also. Instead, I saw a dullness, almost blankness in them, as though she were terribly fatigued. Judy and Joan, on either side of her, were engaged in a bright, animated conversation with Randy on the many meanings of joy. Beth stared down at her plate and I kept the frown from my face. It stayed inside me, though, and I wondered if perhaps Beth was just simply a very moody young woman. I found myself glancing at Peter, rehearsing his words as he'd flung them at me this morning, once again putting them aside.

I turned to Adam for the rest of the meal, content to watch his handsomeness and bask in the charismatic warmth that so effortlessly flowed from him. He rose when the meal ended, tapped his glass with a spoon, and the murmur of conversation died away.

"We are fortunate to have Patricia as our guest and doubly blessed that she has agreed to talk to us about her work here and her vast knowledge of that unusual period of history we call the medieval era," he said. I rose and saw more eager, attentive, interested faces than I usually saw in my classes. I began by outlining the origins of the Gothic style. I could, here, dwell more than I usually did on the very defined relationship between Gothic architecture and religious thought.

"The building of a house was considered a work of great value, the medieval man linking the practical and the artistic together and binding them both with religious meaning," I said. "Geoffrey of Vinsauf claimed that the writing of poetry was indeed a meticulous enterprise, so much so that he likened it to the building of a house. 'He who would build a house sets no rash hand to work, but metes it out with the measuring-line of his heart,' Geoffrey wrote. The medieval builders felt that the mind must encompass the material, that the building of a great cathedral had to involve philosophy, thought, and the measuring-line and compass, each interdependent upon the other. Medieval iconography often showed the Creator holding a pair of large compasses in his hand and measuring out the universe. Geometry was considered basic in religion and in everyday affairs. Creation was a geometrical truth, a grand design, perhaps too vast for man to comprehend, but completely apportioned. Man's works had to reflect this."

They listened with an intentness that was gratifying but I decided that brevity was in order. I went into a little of the geographic relationships in design and finished to applause. Adam rose, stood very straight, and was terribly attractive, I observed. He extended his hands outward.

"Good night. Love each other," he said in rich tones. Everyone rose, the murmur of voices lifting instantly, and I felt the note of controlled excitement touching the air again. My eyes found Beth as she started to leave with the others. She was silent, her face set. The hostility I'd seen in her that first night was not there but the open cheerfulness of morning had definitely vanished. I watched Peter move toward her, pause at her side as she looked up at him. I saw his lips move quickly, a hasty exchange, and then Judy had her arm, hurried her on.

I heard Adam's voice at my elbow, turned quickly. "Now I want my own detailed report on what you did today," he said. "The privilege of rank." His hand at my elbow steered me from the hall to his quarters and I walked beside him feeling very warm and contented. He sat and listened with the kind of interest and attention I seldom found as I told him how I'd finished the great hall and three of the smaller adjoining rooms and of the exciting things I'd uncovered, exciting to me, that is. He managed to catch some of that excitement and I was grateful for his empathy. Those who labor in esoteric fields are always grateful for interest.

"I only wish I had the time to work along with you," Adam exclaimed.

"I'd like that," I agreed.

"Meanwhile, you keep telling me everything. I'm really very caught up in your work," Adam said. I wanted to stay there in the circle of his warm strength but he rose, reached out, and pulled me to my feet. I barely managed to keep disappointment from my face.

"We'll have more time to talk tomorrow night. I've some new applications I must go over carefully and answer tonight," he explained. I nodded, managed a bright smile, and turned away. He stepped to the doorway with me, his eyes bright fires that seemed to know so much more than I wanted to reveal. I went down the corridor that grew increasingly dark as I neared my room. Inside the room, I lay down on the bed in the dark. I was tired and yet I felt restless. The thick fog rolled against the window like billows of steam from a Stygian sauna. I tried to occupy my mind with specific thoughts, starting with the letter from Sir Brian and conjectures about who might have sent it. The attempt only irritated and I turned off the subject, tried to think about some of the things Adam had said last night, of giving ourselves over, of what Scripture demanded of us, demands that were only what we sought in the first place. The idea still jarred while it intrigued but the thoughts were too weighty for my restlessness, too profound to grapple with now. The fog seemed to invite exploration and I rose, put on a heavier sweater, and returned down the corridor and outside.

The billowing night engulfed me at once, the smell made of the sea and the slightly musty odor of thick, damp air. I stood for a moment, letting the swirling eddies drift past, looked back at the doorway to anchor my bearings, and then moved on. I let my footsteps act as eyes, finding the right edge of the road and following its slow curve. The fog immersed me and I strolled through a strange, silent void, a vacuum, it seemed, as though I were suspended in swirling space. Or awake in a dream. The fog parted slightly, trailing away like a tattered scarf, permitting brief glimpses of forms and shapes. I saw a sliver of light, glimpsed the round shape of two of the little huts, and then the fog rushed forward again as if to chastise me for peeking behind its curtain. I walked on a few paces when I heard the girl's voice, gasped little sounds, rising, rhythmic. I halted, listened, heard another voice, another girl, a soft cry of pleasure. The fog toyed with the sounds, swirling them to me from one side and another. The first girl's voice rose again, gasping sounds unmistakable, soft, sweet moanings. I walked on, heard a man's voice, laughter, then hurried exclamations, sounds also beyond questioning. A door opened somewhere not too far away and the soft cries of ecstasy came from it, muffled voices, then the sound of it closing again.

I turned, letting my feet find the road edge again, started back, my mind thinking only of the subtle excitement I'd sensed earlier. I hadn't imagined at all, it seemed, but the implications were sharp-edged, uncomfortable. The fog shredded itself for a moment and I saw the long, dark outline of the monastery, hurried to it, and slipped inside the door to stand quietly in the darkened entranceway. I saw a wedge of light reaching out from Adam's quarters just beyond the corner but I heard no sound. I waited, listening, continued to hear nothing. Was he there? I wondered. Or was he outside somewhere, participating in what was obviously a night of festivities? Had the applications he spoke of going over simply been an excuse to get away? I continued to stand still, not exactly a voyeur yet something more than an eavesdropper. Finally, the shoddiness of my behavior spearing into me, I moved down the corridor to my room.

I was bothered, more than I'd any right to be, I admitted as I closed the door of my room and undressed. I tried to sort out mixed emotions that jostled each other like so many unruly children. It wasn't what I'd heard that disturbed me, I told myself, trying to be honest. It hadn't been the reality of it. Adam had hinted as much when he'd spoken of all things given us richly to enjoy and I'd been improperly pleased at that. No, it had been something else, the quality of it, a night chosen, a time appointed, an almost druidic ritual atmosphere. Was that, too, part of the process of giving oneself over, a logical extension of a concept? Had the night really been chosen, I wondered? I thought of Adam's words at the end of dinner: *Good night and love each other.* A spiritual exhortation, I had thought, yet apparently much more than that. I reined in thoughts that raced. Had Adam chosen this night? Or did the night have some ancient religious significance? Did it make a difference? I asked in answer to my questions. Wasn't it still adherence to the concept in total?

I shook off the questions. They asked answers I couldn't supply yet. But they demanded a talk with Adam, out of my own curiosity, if nothing else. But there was more than curiosity, of course. I felt a warmth and strength here with Adam Rood that was no doubt entirely too personal. Yet I was unable to help that. I was a highly personal individual, my likes and dislikes always drawn in bold strokes. Perhaps that was one reason why the giving oneself over entirely disturbed me. But I would find out more before accepting or rejecting anything. I was all too aware of how little we know about the forces that lie deep within our own selves and surround us from outside. I let the whirling questions slowly lose themselves in drowsiness and the fog rolling by the window soothed in its own way, closing out the world and all its uncertainties. I slept, finally, and the night, like a huge black cat, moved on with silent steps.

Consciousness can leap at you, frightening in its vehemence. Or it can creep up on you with little nudges of awareness. It chose the latter path, a sound first, filtering through sleep. My eyes opened and I lay still. The sound came again, something hitting against the window. I sat up, blinking sleep from my eyes, focusing on the window. I heard the sharp, sibilant sound of my breath being drawn in. Two hands seemed pressed against the glass, disembodied by the thick fog that swirled about them.

The hands, palms outspread, flattened against the glass, began to slide downward. I sat transfixed, then leaped from the bed, yanking on slacks and a sweater as the hands disappeared behind the billows of fog.

I thought I heard a cry, muffled, and I raced to the window, flung it open wide. The night rushed in to embrace me with cold hands. "Who's there?" I shouted, leaned forward to listen. There was no answer, no sound at all, and I swung myself over the low windowsill to stand on the damp ground. "Who's there?" I called again, listened, not breathing. Something sounded through the thick fog, a rustling susurrant sound, and I strained my ears. I thought I heard it again and called out once more. There was no sound then. It could have been a puff of wind moving leaves, branches rubbed together. I felt myself shivering, turned, and swung back through the window, closing it after me.

I lay down on the bed, clothed, pulled the covers over me until I stopped shivering. My eyes stayed on the window. waiting, but only the banks of fog pressed against the glass, blotting out everything but its own pink grayness. I pulled off the sweater and slacks, finally, and crawled beneath the covers. Had I imagined it? Had I been dreaming, wakened with the dream still imprinted on my mind? It was certainly possible, that momentary line between the dream and waking often no line at all. Dreams often carried over into the first few split-seconds of waking.

I knew about dreams, those conjurers of the inner mind with their silent bagful of tricks. Beth had been in my thoughts ever since that night when she'd come to me in nearpanic. The strange suddeness of her change had been accommodated more than truly accepted. Then there had been Peter's dramatic outbursts. Her original plea had never been explained and so it had clung inside the mind, all things made for the sorcerors of the night. It could have been that and no more, I told myself. But

I felt the grim line touch my lips. Dreams were always more, I reminded myself, always more.

My breath had returned to normal and I closed my eyes. I had enough questions to answer. I'd add no more, dismiss anything that was remotely dismissable. Certainly this bizarre little moment was that, a sudden apparition in the night, the stuff of dreams and sudden wakings. I turned on my side, lay very still, and let sleep finally find its way back to me.

I woke again to the morning light, a thin, gray light, and I rose, holding a sweater to me to stand at the window. A diluted mist had replaced the fog but trees and bushes were visible, the towering turrets of Cashelderg rising up in the distance, softly eerie in the mist. I turned away and dressed, made my way to the dining hall. I'd gazed out the window looking to see something, yet not knowing what I sought and, of course, there had been nothing. The strange, fleeting moment stayed a thing of the imagination But the earlier part of the fog-shrouded evening remained very real and I entered the dining hall to find only a few figures there sipping tea. The morning after, I heard myself comment inwardly and felt guilty at the edge of thought. It was almost as though I disapproved and that was not right, it wasn't disapproval at all. But it was something, I admitted, an inability to reconcile the things I found here, perhaps. The pudgy girl, Ruth, stood beside a dull-faced young man. Her skin was blanched, pasty in color, and her eyes were circled, and again my mind insisted on its wonderings. I had two cups of tea and a sweet roll, hurried back to the room to pick up my tote bag, tools, and note pad. I was just returning to the front door when Adam appeared, his smile flooding the entranceway with warmth. I drew a deep breath.

"I do hope we can talk tonight," I said.

"Do I detect new questions?" he asked at once.

"I guess so. Old and new. I took a walk in the fog last night."
Adam's bright-fire eyes took on pinpoints of quiet amusement.

"I see," he replied slowly. "And you were surprised?"

"That's not the precise word, Adam," I said.

"I hope not. Meanwhile, let me give you a key word to think
about during the day," he said. "Framework," he pronounced.
"The structure in which we do the things we do. It does not
change what we do so much as the nature of what we do, the
importances that surround what we do."

His smile widened and I stared up at his auburn handsomeness. "Till tonight," he said and brushed past me quickly. I walked
into the gray morning, saw the sun trying to push aside the layers
of thick air. I walked over the little rise to Cashelderg, Adam's
words revolving inside me, not veiled, yet addressing themselves
to new horizons of human relationships. I put them aside as I
reached Cashelderg, stepped inside and saw, not Multy's little
figure coming down the wide hall, but Judy. Randy and Joan
stepped from the room to the right, just off the main hall.

"Good morning," Judy sang out. "We thought we'd take a
closer look at Cashelderg after your lecture last night."

"You're very early," I said, still surprised.

"We didn't want to be underfoot when you started working,"
Randy said quickly. His smile was pleasant but it wasn't echoed
in his eyes. They held the expressionlessness of someone terribly tired or terribly strained. Judy, I saw, had no morning fresh-
ness to her, either, her hair hanging in long, damp strings, her
light green blouse wrinkled and clinging damply to her body. I
glanced at Joan, saw that her skirt was streaked with smudged
dirt, her eyes bloodshot.

"May the work go well," Randy said and went past me, the
two girls hurrying with him. I waited till they'd disappeared
out the big doors, then turned away. They'd been lying. They'd

not paid an early visit here, not the way they looked. The meaning of the night rose up again at once. Had they spent it here in Cashelderg, a *ménage à trois?* It was not unheard of, of course. Life and literature was full of such trios, more so than ever in this era of the sexual revolution. But here, in the framework Adam had spoken of again, even a *ménage à trois* no doubt had an added dimension. I would hold back further comments for now. But Cashelderg had indeed become a place of strange questions, I mused as I walked to the room with the bronze gargoyles.

Prophecy recognized can shake one. Prophecy unrecognized can be shattering, I was to learn.

Multy hadn't appeared yet so I started by myself and I'd just finished the room when he appeared in time to brace the tall ladder for me as I prepared to climb it for a detailed examination of the bronze gargoyles.

"One of the ewes foaled a kid," he said. "I had to stay about. We keep a few dozen sheep. Bridget tends them, mostly."

"As soon as I'm through here, I'll start on the next floor," I said, climbing up to the gargoyles. Even now in the dispassionate atmosphere of scholarly investigation, they seemed to hold a malignancy, their horribleness hardly lessened at all.

"Do you know of any special meaning these had to the O'Donnell clan?" I called down as I balanced myself and made close-up sketches of the figures and examined the workmanship of their casting, undoubtedly using the *cireperdue* method, the wax molds that were of themselves lost in the process.

"The O'Donnells originally came from Moher," Multy called up to me and I felt my lips tighten, the terrible storm flashing before me at once. The dread women of Moher again, those half-bird, half-human harpies, scavengers of the storm taken as a family symbol.

"A strange choice, I'd say," I returned.

"Everything fits," Multy said flatly. The two words held a quiet chill in them, spearing into the dark places of the soul. Does it, I asked silently, shaking away thoughts, concentrating on my work, once more grateful for the preoccupying power of mundane things. I finished, climbed down the ladder, and, with Multy, pulled my equipment up the steep stone stairwell inside the keep to the floor above. The workmanship was cruder here, the window arches rudimentary in construction. These rooms were used by the armorers, carpenters, and other workmen. The last one was apparently the falconer's area with the original perches and chains still in place. Here an arch of windows had been painstakingly constructed, almost a triforium with a small balcony set outside which again showed the talent of the builder. It had obviously been used by the falconer in training his birds. After doing all the interior examinations, I saw that the exterior of the arched windows was interesting enough to warrant more time.

"We'll rig up a sling tomorrow," I told Multy. "I'll need one anyway for my other exterior work." I saw the distaste in his little eyes. "And I'd like to go through the material in that wall chest downstairs tomorrow morning," I added.

"There are no plans or anything like that," Multy barked.

"I'd just like to see what's there for myself," I returned. His tilted body stood still, staring at me.

"Haven't you had enough? Why don't you go home now?" he asked.

"Why are you so anxious to have me go home? What are you afraid of, Multy?" I asked, trying not to sound harsh. "Is it anything about the fake letter that brought me here?"

I watched the gimlet eyes grow hard as marbles, become tiny agates that glinted in the half-light. "Those that won't listen deserve what they get," he snapped out.

"Are you so possessive about Cashelderg and your family job here? Is that what it really comes down to?" I pressed. "Nothing I do here will hurt you or Cashelderg."

The wizened little face regarded me stonily. "There are those that hurt by wanting to and those that hurt without wanting to," he said, words that struck deep, surprised again by their wisdom. He turned quickly, was across the room in a half dozen strides, and gone. I put my things into the tote bag and went down the steps, the sound of my shoes loud in the silence. Thinking about the letter decided me to drive to Drumglas before the day ended to see if the chemist had heard anything. I walked to where I'd left the car near the old monastery, glimpsed Adam hurrying into the building with Randy, looking unusually stern, it seemed. I drove down the slope, saw a cluster of ten figures in a half-circle, Bibles open in their laps, in what seemed to be meditation. Beth wasn't among them, I noted.

The drive to Drumglas was pleasant and relaxing and I halted in front of the little chemist's shop. The proprietor came out to meet me in his waistcoat, neatly creased trousers, and stiff-collared shirt. I caught the excitement about him at once.

"Miss Conway, I'm glad you stopped by. Professor Toolan called only an hour ago," he said. "That letter of yours is the real thing, all right."

"What do you mean?" I frowned.

"It's at least three hundred years old," the little chemist said. "Absolutely authentic, it is."

CHAPTER SIX

I felt cold, a terribly iciness wrapping itself around me. I heard my voice as if from a faraway place. "No. That's impossible," I gasped out.

"But it's so. They analyzed the paper first, nothing fake about it, handmade it was, carbon dated back to about 1600," the man went on.

"No, it can't be," I repeated, felt my hands clenching into fists, the nails digging into my palms.

"Chemical tests on the ink verified it, iron salts, oakgall and gum, dated back to the same time, it did," the druggist said. "It's real, all right. He's sending it back by special post."

"Yes, thank you. I'll pick it up from you," I said, mumbling words, turning away. I moved to the car, seeing only vague shapes, the coldness a congealing, strangling garment. It was impossible, of course. I'd received a letter from a man dead three hundred years, written three hundred years ago. Impossible, yet it was so.

I wanted to tell myself they'd made a mistake at the Dublin Museum but I knew better. They'd have checked their findings. Everything fits, Multy had said. So much more than he knew, I murmured inwardly. I leaned my head against the roof of the car and felt weak, pressed my eyes closed, and tried to make the weakness go away but it refused.

"Hey, what's the matter?" the voice said dimly, distantly. I gathered in a deep breath, lifted my head, focused on the tall figure, made it take shape, saw long arms and long legs, the affably disarrayed face filled with concern. "Patricia, what is it?" Lee Farrell repeated, moving to my side. I was glad for the support of his arm.

"Something ridiculous. Something stupid," I said in a half-whisper. "That's what it will seem to you." I let him half-turn me so that I leaned against the fender of the car.

"You're white as a sheet," he frowned. "What the devil happened?"

I shivered. "I don't want to talk about it here," I said. "I'd like to sit down someplace." His arm lifted mine, pulled me up, and I went along with him.

"You're in no condition to drive," he said. "We'll come back for your car later." I saw the Land Rover across the street and in moments he was half-lifting me into the seat, sliding in beside me. I put my head back, closed my eyes as he started the car and rolled from the curb. "I'm glad I picked today to do my weekly shopping," he said and I nodded, let my eyes stay shut. The trip back to his rented cottage was a kind of suspended time period, a world with sound and movement in it yet one that seemed to stand still. I found myself inside the warm, secure room again, sitting tensely on the worn sofa.

"Drink this," Lee Farrell said, giving me a shot glass of whiskey. I took it, grateful for the harsh fire of it. "Now suppose you tell me what this is all about?" he said. I was still wrestling with my own, very private shock waves. They still surged inside me like waves against a shore, refusing to be put aside, battering and crashing relentlessly. So much had exploded, burst open, too much to hold back any longer, Shakespeare's too-full cup running over. Words tumbled from me, the things the druggist had told me first. I paused, searching the intentness of his face as I finished.

"That's not all of it, not just the letter alone," he said carefully. "There's more, a lot more."

"Yes," I said, almost defiantly.

"Such as dreams?" he pressed.

"They're part of it. I don't know where anything fits, except that it fits someplace, somehow," I said. "I guess dreams are as good a place as any to start."

"Dreams that are more than dreams," he said.

"They're always more. I'm convinced of that," I answered. "Prophecies, visions, messages, riddles of the subconscious mind. I saw death, twice, and no one believed me. I guess I didn't believe myself the first time. It was a cousin, a young girl. I dreamt of her being taken ill."

"And she did take ill and she died," Lee finished. I nodded solemnly.

"Then I had dreams of a fire once and a man I knew involved in it. I told him about it and he laughed at me. He lost everything he had when his home burned down following a party soon after. But the worst was an old friend, Ted Ehrens. I kept having this dream about him but I couldn't interpret it. I couldn't uncover the meaning of it no matter how hard I tried. It was made of disconnected bits and pieces. When Ted was killed in a private plane crash it was suddenly all so terribly clear."

"But it was too late."

"Yes. I was terribly depressed for a long time after that. I couldn't help feeling responsible for not having been able to interpret the dream."

"Dreams, prophecies, they put people to death for such things at other times," Lee said, pursing his lips. "At least we don't do that anymore."

"But we still fear, we shy away from those who predict such things. It's a love-hate attitude, we are drawn to them but we fear them. I know, I've felt both reactions in people," I said. "And I know all about those other times, too."

I paused, saw Lee's pleasant face holding a frown, his sharp gaze questioning. "I can quote statistics. I can tell you that in Essex, England, there were 111 persons prosecuted for witchcraft between 1580 and 1590 and 63 prosecutions between 1640 and 1659. There were 50 persons indicted in the County of Surrey, 91 in Kent, and 299 in Essex between 1560 and 1700. The accused were tried in civil and in ecclesiastical courts. Some of the offenses were being a sorceror, soothsayer, forediviner, healing by magic, possession, and bewitching. Calling the vicar a witch was punishable by death."

"You didn't come upon all this while researching medieval architecture," Lee said. "You had a personal interest."

I nodded agreement. "In 1587, Elizabeth Pilligram and Mary Godfrey were prosecuted as witches in Hatfield Peverel. Both were ancesters on my mother's side, as was Anne Moore, indicted in Rayleigh ten years later. When I first began to understand the meaning of the things I dreamt, I started looking back into old records, especially during a teaching conference I attended in England."

"You think such things are hereditary?" Lee asked. I could only shrug.

"Perhaps not hereditary in the true genetic sense, yet even medically we recognize a predisposition to certain ailments."

"But you believe very strongly in your own dreams today," he pressed.

"I have no choice. There are forces we do not comprehend. I believe that very strongly. Medieval man feared unreasoningly that which he did not understand. Modern man simply rejects what he does not understand. I sometimes think that the chief product of the scientific age is arrogance. Modern man arrogantly rejects anything that does not lend itself to empirical explanation."

"And you?"

I managed a half-laugh. "I told you, I live in two worlds, the intellectual rationality of this one and the emotionalism of the medieval one. I live in both and I believe in both."

Lee Farrell rose, paced back and forth for a moment, his face lined with thought. "You're too much the modern man to accept all this," I suggested. "At least in these terms. Try seeing it in the terms of parapsychology, psychophysical phenomena, extrasensory perception, and all those terms."

"I can accept some of it, dreams as visions of a kind, messages, even prophetic. But a letter, three hundred years old, sent by someone dead three hundred years, that I can't accept."

"But it's not a fake, we know that now."

"There still has to be some explanation, some logical, identifiable answer. It came to you via the mails, stamped and postmarked. I can't see an ethereal force stamping it and dropping it into a mailbox," Lee answered, his reasoning so perfectly normal and rational it made everything seem like such ridiculousness. Yet it was always that, logic and illogic, the rational and the irrational, two worlds and I could not dismiss either.

"Find an answer," I flung out at him.

"One you'll accept?" he countered.

"Oh, no. One you'll accept," I returned.

"You've made your acceptances," he said.

"In part. I accept those forces I do not understand. I accept strange workings. It isn't the letter alone. Those great, round chandeliers in the main hall of Cashelderg, I saw them in my dreams, in every detail. I tried telling myself that I'd seen them in some previous research but I was just lying to myself. It comes easy when you're afraid. I hadn't seen them anywhere before, not in this conscious, rational world of yours."

"In some other world? You're going into preexistence now?" Lee frowned.

"Perhaps not preexistence. Let's just say the existence of knowledge not gained from this life. We are only learning the secrets of the double helix, the Morse code of DNA. We don't know what may be stored there, what messages are printed in those genetic codes. Until recently, we had no idea that they existed in the way they do. Perhaps we do not come into existence as a sheet of blank paper on which only this life writes its words. Perhaps there is much that is already written for us if we could only become aware of it."

"Maybe," Lee conceded, his eyes probing into me, catching unsaid thoughts. "And there are other forces besides those, aren't there?"

I nodded, added nothing more, wanting to go no further out on precarious, inner branches. But the talking about it had helped, releasing tensions, airing fears and wonderings. I felt much better and let out a soft gasp as I looked at my watch.

"I've got to get back," I said.

"We'll pick up your car," he agreed and I hurried beside his long strides to the Land Rover. He took little short cuts back to Drumglas and the chemist's where the little Morris Minor waited.

"Thanks for listening," I said. "It helped."

"What are you going to do now?" he asked.

"Go on with my work," I said.

"Why don't you go home?" he questioned. "Get away from here."

"It wouldn't work. There's too much that needs to be answered now. It will be. It'll make itself known somehow," I

said. "And I want to finish my work here. That's terribly important to me."

"Mind if I look for answers my way?" Lee asked, and his
hand touched my cheek. "Damn, you've got me into this now, to
say nothing of being concerned for you."

I felt warmed. Concern is a gift impossible to turn down. "I'll
try to stop by in a few days," I said.

"I'll let you know if I find any answers," he said, and I swung
behind the wheel of the car, switched the engine on, and sent the
little Morris Minor rolling back toward Cashelderg. Lee would
look for answers, I was certain, the practical, rational answers
he was convinced had to be there. I really very much hoped he'd
find them. I'd had too much of shadowed things. The clear, defin-
able, reasoned answers would be more than welcome, almost a
kind of freedom. Meanwhile, I'd seek the answers in my own
way. I looked forward to talking to Adam. Suddenly, I wanted
very much to explore those things he had only outlined. Perhaps
there were answers of another kind for me there.

I drove fast but the night reached the old monastery before
I did and as I parked, hurried to my room to leave my things, I
realized that in my shock and all the talk of the letter, I never did
ask Lee what he'd been looking for again along the rocks below
Cashelderg. I washed, gave my hair a few hurried brush strokes,
and went down to the dining hall. Dinner was in progress and
Adam's eyes were concerned as I sat down beside him.

"I wondered what happened to you," he said.

"We'll talk about it later," I said. My glance paused at Beth's
place between Judy and Joan. Another girl sat there, small boned
with wide, brown eyes that focused on me with a doll-like quality.

"This is Carol," Judy introduced. Carol's smile was almost
automatic.

"I enjoyed your lecture last night," she said. "Bless you."

I managed to hold back being abrupt. "Beth isn't feeling well again?" I asked casually. My quick glance found Peter sitting very stiffly, staring down at his hands. I heard Adam's voice answer.

"I'm afraid it's more than that," he said. "Beth has left us, left the community."

He nodded gravely as my eyes turned to him. "She came to see me and we talked. We both decided it was the best course. She was not happy here. The hostility she brought with her never left her. Not everyone can be reached. There are those who resist out of their own guilt complexes. Randy helped her pack her things and drove her to Ballygort. There's a bus there that goes to Donegal." His eyes grew reflective and he paused. "It always saddens me to see someone fail," he said.

"Fail?" I blurted out.

"I see it as that. And their failure is my failure. I did not find a way to them. I did not reach Beth," Adam said.

"Rejection is a sin," Judy spoke up, a quiet adamancy in her voice.

"To go in falseness is a sin," Joan added with the same adamancy.

"Poor Beth," Adam said. "We can pray for her, each of us."

I stared down at my plate, finishing a last bite. I was more than surprised. I was bothered, sorry now that I hadn't had a chance to ever talk to Beth. I saw that moment of panic in her eyes again, but I also thought of how her moods had seemed to change so swiftly, always a sign of inner problems. I shot a glance at Adam. His eyes were still reflective, troubled, obviously thoughts of the girl still clinging. Judy, Randy, and Joan had begun a quietly pleasant conversation, I saw. They were indeed a very close trio, I thought, recalling my meeting with them in the morning. I heard Adam rap on a glass for quiet and I rose to deliver my second lecture. I held to the craft organization of Gothic construction, the very ordered positions of those crafts-men who turned concept into reality. Under the architect, the chief—sometimes one and the same—was the master mason, in charge of all stone work. Then came the master carpenter, the master plumber, the master smith, the master joiner, and the master glazier. In their charge were the mason-hewers, the woodworkers, the hodmen and basket carriers, the painters, tile makers, and weavers, the rug makers and ordinary laborers. I explained a little of the interrelationship of their work, much more so than in today's compartmentalized construction meth-ods, and ended by telling some of what I'd found in the day's work.

Once again I kept the talk brief, but they were so attentive I was tempted to go on. Finished, I waited for Adam as he took Randy aside for a moment, spoke to him in serious-visaged con-ference. I strolled into the hallway, sought out Peter, but he was nowhere to be seen. Adam came, took my arm, and steered me to his quarters. His eyes were pinpoints of quiet amusement as he faced me on the old sofa yet there was no irritating condescen-sion in them.

"Have you been thinking about that word framework?" he asked.

"Not really. Something came up that filled my thoughts," I replied. His eyes held a moment of curiosity but he didn't press further.

"It's really not complex," Adam went on. "Your somewhat unsubtle probing the other day addressed itself to that physical side of the community." I winced inwardly, felt myself coloring, and he chuckled. "No, don't be embarrassed. I told you then that curiosity is always a good thing. You were right to wonder. There are physical needs. The body as well as the spirit must be served.

You said that surprise was not accurate to describe your reactions to last night. Perhaps disturbed would be more so?"

"I think so," I admitted. "But not because of it. I think the feeling of a ritualized bacchanalia bothered me more than anything."

Adam smiled. "Interpretation evolves from conditioning," he said almost wearily. "You saw it as that when actually it was quite different. Again, that framework I spoke about, that structure which surrounds what is done. Giving oneself to the pleasures, the senses, can be very different when one has given oneself over to something else first. Another way of seeing, responding, enjoying, colors one's surrender to the senses. To love properly, even to enjoy the bodily pleasures properly, one must first learn to love as God loves, for the beauty of loving rather than by mere personal attraction."

"But human relationships are, by nature, personal."

"Love is a thing of many levels. I'm afraid, as practiced usually, it is on the most primary level. It is possession, not love. We do not discourage personal preferences. We surround them with a larger discipline and definition which removes possessiveness. Then the true enjoyment of the senses is possible because it is not confined by possession."

I thought of Randy, Judy, and Joan at Cashelderg in the morning, almost mentioned the meeting, and decided it was uncalled for. "All this doesn't lend itself to other kinds of excesses?" I asked instead. Adam frowned back. "An impersonality of human relationships," I added. "Isn't that a negation of love?"

"No one wants impersonality," Adam answered. "It is almost impossible to explain what I mean by our definitions and approach to this area of human relationships. All the pieces fit together, each bearing on the other and you must understand the meaning and importance of each. Remember as a start that the first step is the giving over process. That of itself establishes another kind of emotional discipline."

"I guess I'm the product of a possessive world. That conditioning again," I shrugged.

"Of course, but we can all learn ways that will bring us more happiness," Adam said gently. I felt his patience, warmth, and something more, a wisdom of things I had yet to explore.

"All right, no bacchanalia," I said. "I shouldn't have made that assumption."

"No bacchanalia, but a true, deeper enjoyment of the senses," Adam smiled. "A fulfillment, not an exercise."

"On command," I said.

"Not as you mean the word," Adam answered with a laugh. "There is wrong and danger in all excesses. The balance between the needs of the body and the needs of the spirit is a delicate one. They look to me to keep that balance for them, just as they look to me to guide and teach them in interpreting the Word in Scripture."

"And who keeps your balance, Adam?" I heard myself ask.

"I, too, obey," Adam said. "My decisions are done in His will and His way." He halted and a deep sigh escaped him, and I saw sudden tiredness cloud the bright fire eyes for an instant, unexpected and surprising, human loneliness flashing for a brief instant. "It is not always easy," Adam said. "One never knows for certain."

I felt the desire to comfort surge through me. Even the strong have needs, I saw. "I'm sure you do the right thing, Adam. You work out of an ordered philosophy, a conceptual base. That always helps," I answered.

His smile came quickly and he leaned forward, took my hands in his.

"There are answers here, Patricia. There are occasional failures, as you saw for yourself, but there are answers. Haven't you seen happiness here? Haven't you seen peace and contentment?" he asked.

"Yes," I admitted. I wasn't being patronizing. Certainly I had seen something very close to those things here. Despite what I didn't understand, despite reservations of my own, I had seen a uniform contented pleasantness, save for Beth and Peter.

"There are answers here, Patricia," he said again and the word hung in front of me. Answers, the very word a siren song, beckoning, a refuge. "There could be answers for you, too, Patricia," he said, and I felt the intense fervor of Adam Rood flow around me as waves flow around a rock. "You might be very surprised."

"I might be," I said, feeling not at all impersonal. I was both unhappy and relieved when Adam let go of my hands and sat back.

"And what filled your thoughts so earlier today?" he asked pleasantly, sensing my discomfort, and I was grateful for that.

"The letter, Adam. It's not a fake," I said. His intense eyes held me and I told him what I'd done. When I finished his handsome face was darkened with a deep frown.

"I don't understand it," he murmured. "It's beyond all comprehension."

I said nothing of the many things I'd touched on with Lee, all the highly personal, half-confession kind of things we'd talked about, all boxes I wasn't ready to open again with Adam. I watched as he rose, frowning, his eyes narrowed in thought.

"Multy," he said, his voice almost a murmur. "He must know what this is all about. He's the only one." Adam turned, looking down at me, his intense eyes burning. "It must be Multy," he said. "Or he has to be a part of it."

I didn't reply. He was perhaps very right, but I couldn't be sure of anything now. Like Lee Farrell, Adam would pursue logical explanations, but for different reasons. I rose and Adam came to my side at once, his hand touching my cheek.

"No wonder you were upset, your mind filled with thoughts," he said. "We'll talk again of the things we spoke about tonight."

I nodded and turned, started for the door. Adam's touch went with me and I knew I had been comforted more than satisfied. The power, the charismatic, sweeping strength that was Adam Rood gave words a dimension they did not have of themselves. He had turned what seemed to me a kind of bacchanalia into something of deepened human dimensions. There was still so much to examine, so much that I rebelled at but he had made me feel that there was more that lay beyond my vision. I left Adam feeling that I was the one in need of new horizons, someone whose life had been lived under limited ceilings. His intenseness could do that, and abstractly I was aware it could do that, and yet the feeling remained.

I paused at the outer door, stepped outside for a moment. The thickness of the day had dissipated and stars were visible. My eyes peered out, adjusted to the darkness, narrowed, peered again. There was someone standing alone, head bowed, back to me. I moved closer and recognized Peter's long, thin figure. I went still closer, heard Peter's voice murmuring words. He turned abruptly, saw me, the pale blue eyes holding no fire now but a terrible mournfulness.

"I'm sorry about Beth," I said. He didn't answer, his eyes staring at me. "About her leaving," I added.

"She didn't leave," he said, words delivered in flat, expressionless tones.

"What do you mean, Peter?" I frowned. His eyes remained motionless on me, his voice soft, a monotone.

"No one leaves here," he said.

I felt my frown deepen. "Peter, you're upset," I replied. "Don't you think you should talk to Adam? Beth has left. She's not here anymore."

"No one leaves here," he repeated in the chilling monotone. "They're watching us right now."

I felt myself glancing quickly about, a reflex action, automatic. I saw only the night.

"You won't see them. But they're watching," Peter intoned.

"Peter, go to Adam in the morning," I said. I saw his eyes take on little dots in their centers, the expressionless stare subtly changing.

"It's your fault. You shouldn't have told them she had come to you," he said.

"I didn't tell anyone anything," I flared, but he was turning on his heel, casting a quick look at me that suddenly bore hatred, then striding into darkness. I stayed for a moment, my eyes scanning the dark as his words lingered. I saw no one, not even movement, and I turned and went back to the building. Peter was obviously a very disturbed young man, perhaps dangerously so, I mused. I'd talk to Adam about him tomorrow, I decided. The long, dark corridor to my room was suddenly an uncertain place as I hurried along its stone floor. Peter's words, of course. I should have been able to shrug them off, I told myself, but my own private tensions had made me a captive of shadows, susceptible to every unexplained incident. I found myself thinking of the hostility I'd felt when I tried to visit Beth, of how I'd been turned away and of how she had been utterly changed the next morning. All little things, all explainable enough, yet they clung, cinders of the mind that irritated. I reached my room and closed the door, shaking away thoughts and wonderings.

I felt terribly tired now and pulled off clothes, climbed into the narrow cot, and drew covers over me. I refused to let questions push at me and I fell asleep almost at once, a heavy, deep slumber, a time for restoring the body and refreshing the spirit. The night had moved past the midnight mark when sleep became more than sleep, waking less than waking.

Laughter and sounds of happiness, the great hall ablaze with light. I abound in warmth and love, swirling in time with a hundred other dancing figures. There is only gaiety in the great castle and then the tall doors are flung open. Once again the wind sweeps in and all is plunged into darkness and I tremble in terror.

It broke off again, everything the same, and I sat up trembling. Always the same place, the sweeping cold wind, and then only terror. I let the trembling stop, drew deep breaths, and swung out of bed, pulling on just slacks and a heavy sweater. I had to try. There were ways to move closer to the unknown, to open up the channels of receptivity. Like a radar screen that rotates to pick up signals, I had to try to achieve a kind of psychic tuning and there was but one way to do that. I took the big flashlight, the heavy-handled one, and moved into the dark corridor, hurrying in silent, barefoot steps. I slipped out the door, the night a silent world. I didn't need the light crossing over the rise. A thin moon had come out to strew a meager band of light across the ground but it was enough for me to pick my way along. As I reached the top of the rise, Cashelderg loomed up, suddenly an awesome, frightening monument, and suddenly it seemed to be waiting for me.

How long? I asked myself. How long had it waited for me? Three hundred years? And did it wait just for me? Had circumstances conspired to fall upon me, or had I been chosen in ways unknown, at times unimagined. I pushed the timbered doors open enough to enter, stood for a moment in the total blackness and silence, then moved into the castle. I flashed the light on and moved to stand inside the great hall, letting the light swing upwards to bathe the round, oaken chandeliers in gray whiteness. I moved the light down, scanned the hall with it, and stood very still, snapping it off. Silence can fill the air, did you know? As thoroughly as roaring sound. I continued to stand motionless and I began to feel the tiny vibrations along my skin moving up my spine, like a cold feather being pulled along.

I was not alone here in Cashelderg. I was not alone. I switched the flashlight on, swung it in an arc around the great hall and into the corridor. I saw only the stone of the walls and the layers of dust. But I was not alone. Was someone here, a person pressed against one of the walls? Or was it something else? I couldn't be sure. I moved forward into the corridor and then into the next room, letting the light scan each wall. I found no one, went on to the next room with the same results. Finally I turned back, made my way to the great main hall again. I moved to the very center of the huge room and switched the light off. I was not alone here in Cashelderg, but I felt no person here with me, no living soul. I closed my eyes and the Stygian blackness seemed a palpable thing, wrapping itself around me like a shroud. My fingers holding the flashlight began to cramp and I relaxed the muscles in my hand. Hardly breathing, I stood motionless, waiting, not knowing for what, only that there was something.

This was the place of dreams, the great hall, the place of blazing chandeliers, of music, love, and terror. This was the place of riddles and contradictions, the place I knew yet could not have known. This was the place of my yesterdays and todays and perhaps tomorrows. I heard my voice whispering words of prayer and desperation.

"I am here. I have come. Tell me more. I have listened but I do not know anything. Give me a sign, something I can understand. Please tell me, somehow, someway."

My voice trailed away and there was only the silence and the blackness again. I remained absolutely still, waited. I began to grow cold in the deep chill of the drafty old structure, but I stayed on, determined to wait. Then, suddenly, I was alone, really alone. I had come in vain. It hadn't worked. It had been close, close enough to feel, but the channels had remained blocked. I would know nothing more, not this night, at least. I snapped the light on and walked from the great hall out into the night. I hurried away from Cashelderg and felt its towering massiveness brooding down upon me, casting itself over my hurrying figure. I knew a fear that had no name yet, a fear that still gathered itself and I did not look back. The long, low monastery building appeared and I slipped inside, crept back to my room, closed the door behind me, and threw off slacks and sweater.

I lay in the narrow cot with a consuming weariness holding me. All that had happened drifted across my mind like a film in slow motion, not to let me see more clearly but only to mock my searches. I finally slept again, shutting out thoughts of a letter beyond belief yet beyond disbelief.

CHAPTER SEVEN

The morning sun made the great castle look less forbidding as I reached it with my things. I'd breakfasted early, waved to Adam as he appeared just when I hurried out, and now I climbed to the falconer's room, set things down, and began to prepare a sling for myself. I was finished and Multy still hadn't appeared. "The sheep again," I muttered as I stepped out onto the ledge of the three-part arched window arrangement. I tied one end of the rope that was wrapped around my waist to a narrow column at the right, tied the other end to a similar column at the left. There was ample slack as I stepped from the ledge, braced my feet against the outer wall, and began to work my way along, window-washer fashion. I'd used this kind of rope sling before on other outer wall examinations and moved with practiced ease, a little tool bag hanging from my waist.

The stones along the outside of the triforiumlike arches had been carved with a falcon and leaf design. There was evidence of exterior deterioration and as I edged my way along the outer wall, pushing my feet against the stones, I took the small chisel and hammer from the tool bag. Using the blunt end of the chisel, I began tapping the stones of the carvings every few inches. To the trained ear, it was like looking at x-rays, each sound carrying its own messages about the construction and care in the building of the castle. Tapping good hard blows, I listened for changes in the sounds that would mean stone-fill or rubble had been used behind the carvings, the condition of the interior of the stone, even whether the carvings had been done in place, *in situ*, or done elsewhere and set in place afterwards.

I was just concluding that a degree of stone-fill had been used, but that the major carvings had been done in place, when I heard the sound, sharp and sudden, followed instantly by the accumulative sound of stones hitting against each other. I looked up, an automatic, reflex reaction, saw the stones toppling loose from the wall directly above me, at least five or six of them. They were falling directly toward me, breaking loose some thirty feet up along the wall. I drew my legs in, let the rope holding me swing in, and slammed against the carved wall as the first of the falling stones hurtled past me. Another brushed against my back as I grabbed at a carving to avoid swinging out again. I felt the rush of wind as others plummeted down only fractions of an inch from me. Two others hurtling down apparently struck each other, one instantly deflecting inward. I glimpsed it coming out of a corner of my eye, tried to lean away as I clung flylike to the carvings, but it came down on me, hitting my upper arm just beneath the shoulder. I heard my cry of pain, felt the skin break open beneath my work shirt.

I clung for a moment more, waiting for the sound of any other loose stones toppling over. Finally, I lifted my feet up enough to push out, glanced up along the flat expanse of the outer wall. I could make out the slight indentation where the stones had come loose, saw a remaining stone slightly pushed forward. Using my feet again, I pushed myself back along the arched windows to the ledge, wincing at the pain of my arm. Reaching the ledge, I pulled onto it, put one leg over the low edge of it as I unloosened first the left rope, then the right one. I dropped down over the narrow protrusion and into the room, realized I was trembling. I sank down onto the stone of the floor, grimacing again as I lifted my left arm up to unloosen the ropes around my waist. I opened the work shirt, then the blouse underneath it, pulled one shoulder down to look at my arm. The abrasion was taking on an ugly redness already, the tissue starting to swell. I felt the skin around it carefully, gasping out at the tenderness. By morning it would be a large area of discolored flesh and bruised tendons, I saw, a painful abrasion. But nothing more, I sighed in relief. It had been a glancing blow. I'd been lucky, very lucky indeed. If any of the hurtling stones had struck my head, I might well have been killed. A skull fracture would have been certain.

Gingerly, I pulled my blouse and work shirt back up, wincing at every move. I'd just finished when I heard soft footsteps on the stone stairs, saw Multy's green-capped form appear. His gimlet eyes grew sharp at once as he saw me still seated on the floor by the arched windows.

"Something wrong?" he snapped out.

"Not now," I said, getting to my feet. I recounted what had happened in flat, terse sentences, leaning out to peer upwards at the wall as I finished. Pulling my head back inside, I walked along the inner wall of the room to where a small corridor led from the corner to a set of narrow stone steps that rose in almost ladder-like straightness. I heard Multy padding along behind me. He spoke up as I started to pull myself up the steps.

"What are you going to do now?" he barked.

"Have a look at where those stones loosened," I said. "I think these steps will lead me up to the spot."

"Why don't you go home?" Multy snapped. I stared at him, saw the tiny eyes blaze with an almost desperate fury, it seemed.

"When I'm finished here," I said, turned, and continued up the steep, narrow steps. Multy's insistence was less irritating than it was disturbing now, the quality of it undergoing a subtle change, like his little eyes, almost with a desperation in it, I mused. The steps were dim, walled in, and I took each one slowly. They made a sharp, right-angle turn and I kept on, suddenly halted as I came upon a narrow walkway that bordered the outside wall. I could see the daylight shining in where the stones had fallen from a place a dozen or so feet from me and I edged out along the walkway to the spot. Reaching it, I carefully pressed against the stones around the uneven opening in the wall. One was slightly loose, the others all solid.

I felt my lips press together. It could have happened just as it did, I knew, mortar suddenly giving way in one spot, dried, useless, needing only something to loosen the stones around it. I could literally have brought them down on my head. Vibrations such as I'd made with the hammer and chisel traveled in their own paths. They could easily have set off stones already loose and merely resting atop each other. It was entirely possible, yet I found myself wondering about the coincidence of it, the stones loosening at exactly the right spot to come down on me. The thought shocked, sent a shudder through me. I felt soiled. I hadn't any right to it, none at all. Good God, was I getting paranoid? I asked myself. Were inner tensions affecting me that much?

But suspicions are the jailors of the mind, imprisoning, not letting go once they take hold. I knelt, ran my fingers across the stones of the floor, halting as they came upon the small trail of fine, gritty mortar dust and bits of stone chips. I gathered some up in my palm, brought it to the light, and frowned down at it. Had the mortar dust and tiny chips fallen there over the years? If so, wouldn't they have disintegrated or blown away into nothing? Would they still be in a neat, fresh little mound? Or were they the results of someone scraping away the mortar and loosening the stones? I felt my lips draw back in a gesture of distaste at the thought. The mortar could have come down by itself recently enough, deterioration would be uniform, I pondered.

I rose, dusted my palm off. Like everything else here, it lay beyond clear answers.

I turned, made my way back along the walkway and down the steep steps, and found myself wondering about the questions again and of Multy. Where had he been this morning? Really tending the sheep again or waiting by the loosened stones, waiting for me to move alongside the outside wall? Had he been trying to scare me into going home? Or perhaps bent on something more frightening? The terrible thoughts persisted and I almost shouted in anger at my sudden onslaught of suspicions.

I reached the bottom of the steps and Multy was standing by the arched windows, peering out and upwards. He turned as I came back, the little eyes boring into me.

"You're hurt," he commented.

"How do you know?" I questioned.

"The way you're favoring your arm, the way you hold it," he retorted, the sharp eyes shrewd, probing.

"It's nothing bad," I said.

"Tend to it before you're sorry," Multy said and I let my eyes scan the tilted little figure. He wanted me to go home, that was unquestioned. Yet I couldn't see him going to such lengths. I'd seen acute sensitivity in the strange, wizened little man, observations that held astuteness and reactions that held inner warmth. "You should go back and rest the day out," Multy said. I shook my head.

"I'm all right. I'll put some salve on it later. The French peasants have an expression about those who are injured by the tools they work with, a farmer by his plow, a carpenter by his hammer. The craft has entered their flesh, they say. That applies to me now," I smiled. Multy only grunted, but I caught the tiny glints of understanding in his eyes. "I'd like to look at the papers in that wall chest downstairs now," I said.

Multy shrugged, turned, and I followed him back down to where the heavy, wooden chest protruded from the wall in the room that took up the far corner of the main floor. He used his key ring to open the heavy, wooden wall chest, muttering in annoyance as he did so. He leaned against one wall, watching, as I began to go through the ancient documents, making detailed notes about each. I found old deeds, land-grant uses, hunting grants, deeds covering the sale of property held by the O'Donnells in other parts of Ireland. There were birth records of three children, two boys and a girl, born between 1560 and 1567. I paused at the one deed that Multy had shown me with Sir Brian O'Donnell's signature especially bold on it. One document was of special interest and I made copious notes about it as I read it over a half dozen times, the old-English lettering neatly setting down a kind of shopping list involved in the construction of Cashelderg. *Three wagons of lime,* I read, *twenty barrows of corn, sufficient oil, ten wagons of uncut stones, Hamburg timber and boards, fifty wagons contracted for use, extra hay and three carts of wine.* A footnote proclaimed that *cartage rates* were to be figured at 10*d* for every *20 long miles.* Finally, I finished with the last of the documents and closed the door. Multy was there locking up at once.

"Will you be wanting me more today?" he asked, turning to me and I caught the wise little expression that touched the corners of his tight mouth. He was very aware that my arm was hurting more and I'd want to bathe it in hot water.

"No, nothing else today," I said, trying not to sound petulant. "But I'll be starting to examine the outer wall of the right bastion tomorrow, particularly the stonework under the embrasures," I said.

"I'll be early as I can but there's extra work I've got to help Bridget with now," he explained. He started to turn away, paused, and a craftiness crept into his wizened face, the tiny eyes suddenly sharp. "I understand one of them left," he remarked, unable to mask the frown in his eyes, almost a thing of concern which surprised me.

"How do you know that?" I parried. His tight lips seemed to grow even tighter, almost disappear in his face.

"That's not important, now, is it?" he snapped.

"I'm a curious person," I said, holding fast.

He answered with impatience in his tone. "Tim Grogan delivers fresh milk three times a week to their kitchen. They take what comes to a quart a person each time. They cut back three quarts in their order for next week, he told me. That's one person."

"Yes, one of the girls left," I said. "Yesterday morning."

Multy's gimlet eyes were pinpoints, boring into me. "Yesterday morning?" he echoed.

"Yes, on the bus from Ballygort," I said.

His little eyes continued to blaze. "Not yesterday, then," he commented as he started to turn away.

"Yesterday morning," I repeated, and he shook his head, casting a glance back at me.

"The bus from Ballygort to Donegal," he mused aloud and I nodded. "Not yesterday. It only runs on Saturdays," he finished, hurried away, and was gone.

I stared after his vanished little shape and his words skittered and skipped in front of me. I was upset about the accident, I told myself. Everything assumed greater meaning than it had. There was a perfectly valid explanation for the apparent discrepancy. Randy had taken Beth to the bus, put her aboard it, Adam had said. There was an explanation, I murmured silently as I gathered my things and started from the castle, grimacing at the pain in my arm as I raised it. I walked slowly, trying to shut out words that refused to be shut out. Impatiently, I realized how futile it was to even try, the effort doomed to failure, those jailors of the mind again, refusing to let go. *No one leaves here.* Peter's words, chilling, throbbing inside me. *She didn't leave. No one leaves here.* I had dismissed them once and now they had returned, like runaways coming home, dragging behind them all that was theirs, all the other little things that had touched on Beth. I felt an angry impatience spiraling inside myself as I crossed the rise, started down toward the little huts on the gentle slope. Perhaps there were no answers to strange letters from another time but this certainly could be tracked down, I decided. I let my eyes scan the small shelters, the monastery building, pause at small knots of young people on the grass. I halted, waited as a group of some dozen or so emerged from the building, a class ending, each holding a Bible. They walked, not in formation, but with a quiet discipline that bordered on it. My eyes moved on, down to the little round huts. Some girls were hanging wash on small clotheslines, a few young men repairing a roof on one hut.

I squinted beyond to where a small tract of land had been plowed and planted, saw four figures watering and pulling weeds. None was Peter and I shifted my glance to the line of trees that ran behind the building. I felt my breath quicken as the tall, thin figure moved near them, looking very alone and lost. I started toward him, crossing along the rise and then down past the building. Peter was carrying a Bible, I noted, and as I drew close, I saw that the pale blue eyes were dull, almost expressionless.

"Peter, may I talk to you?" I began. He turned to me and his eyes gathered little dots inside their pale orbs. "What did you mean about Beth not leaving here?" I asked.

"No, no questions from you," he said. "Beth came to you and you questioned her and told them."

I held down instant irritation. "Peter, I didn't tell anyone anything," I said.

"It had to be you," he said, backing from me. "But you'll be sorry." He turned, almost ran off but not before I'd seen the hate flash in his eyes.

"Peter, stop. I must talk to you," I called. "I want to help you." He didn't look back, his thin frame rushing across the grass. I stood for a moment watching, became aware that I was not alone. I turned to see the three figures standing just at the line of trees, each carrying their Bible, Randy, Joan, and Judy.

"How do you want to help Peter?" Judy said, moving forward, and her face was cold. Randy and Joan stepped toward me, too, a pace behind her.

"He's said some strange things to me," I answered, suddenly feeling the need to choose words with extra care. Judy's face held the quiet adamancy it had that night I stopped by to see Beth.

"Evil hears only evil," Judy said.

"What is that supposed to mean?" I flared.

"To think falseness is as to go in falseness. It is a sin," the girl returned austerely.

"Just as rejection is a sin?" I parried.

"Yes," Judy retorted.

"And sin must be punished," I remarked. Judy's eyes were without expression as she said the one word, "Yes." Randy stepped forward and his smile seemed strangely out of place.

"Judy is saying that you, as an outsider, cannot understand the conflict inside Peter. Therefore, you do not understand the meaning of the things he says. You can only fall into error, which in turn leads to graver error. There is no good in your trying to help Peter, not for him and not for you."

The message seemed clear. Stay away from Peter. He is in the best of hands. It was a variation of the same protectiveness I'd felt the night I tried to visit Beth. But only that and nothing more? I'd felt hostility, then, and I felt it now. Was I imagining a veiled warning in the calm words of explanation? I glanced at Joan and Judy. Their faces revealed nothing and that very nothing seemed a kind of mask. *Seemed,* that was the key word. I was tense inside, I realized. The letter was more than enough to do that, but there was everything else, the dream that kept recurring with its cryptic, broken message, and now the accident. I was perhaps the victim of nothing more than an overstimulated imagination, yet I could not shake loose of it, not now.

"All right, perhaps you'll be driving Peter to the bus as you did Beth," I said matter-of-factly. Randy's eyes remained expressionless.

"Perhaps," he agreed. I decided it was time to break off the conversation that irritated and disturbed. I nodded, turned, and walked away. I'd talk to Adam tonight, I concluded, but with care and tact. I hadn't enough for more than that.

Back in my room, I stripped off work shirt and blouse and put hot cloths against my arm, as hot as I could stand, then dried and rubbed in an antiseptic salve that was part of a small traveler's first-aid kit I always carried. A large adhesive pad finished my self-medication and I lay down and stretched out tired muscles. I dozed off as the afternoon wore on, woke when there was still day left. My arm still throbbed, I found, but the pain was less intense and I swung from the narrow bed and dressed, decided that there was time to drive to Drumglas and see if the letter had arrived back. I wanted it in my hands, my reasons undefined, perhaps because subconsciously I still hoped it might yield some clues to me, perhaps just because it had brought me here. I went out to the car, climbed behind the wheel, and headed for the village. The sky, tinged with streaks of deep red, prepared for the end of the day, and I hurried, half-skidding to a halt outside the chemist's. The letter had returned and he gave it to me, chattering about its authenticity. I paid him for his services and hurried back to the car. The emotions always translate themselves into overt gestures. I had the letter back but I pressed it deep into the bottom of my purse where I'd not see it every time I opened the bag.

I started back, had left the village, and was rolling along the narrow dirt road when I saw the Land Rover swing in ahead of me from a side road. I speeded up, swung alongside it, and Lee saw me, waved, and pulled to the side of the road. I halted just in front of him and hadn't turned the engine off when he was beside the car, leaning on the window edge.

"How are you?" he asked, the wide, disarrayed face disarmingly pleasant.

"Good enough," I said.

"I've been hoping you'd stop by. I even thought of driving up to pay you a visit," he said.

"Only you didn't want to go to the community," I finished for him. His smile was a brushing-aside more than a denial.

"I did some checking," he said. "Not on the letter, not directly, anyway. I decided to start with that fifteen hundred pounds sent you from the Bank of Dublin. Someone had to make a withdrawal."

"Go on," I said and Lee's disarrayed features pushed themselves into a wrinkled grimace.

"The request came into the account established to pay Multy," Lee said. "It happened, maybe by coincidence and maybe not, that the fifteen hundred pounds is the same as the yearly amount the account sends to Multy. The withdrawal was accompanied by instructions to send it to you. A new teller got it and followed through. They're still trying to trace how the withdrawal slip reached the bank. The initials on it of the bank official who always initials the withdrawals were forged. That's all I've got on that so far."

"A small plus for rational, practical answers," I said. "If the answers come though."

Lee chuckled. "Maybe it's not much but it's more than you have," he said.

"Is it?" I questioned. "We'll see. But thanks for trying. I mean that." He straightened up, his affable face rearranging itself again.

"One of our services," he said. The sky was starting to darken and I decided against saying anything more now.

"I'll stop in soon," I promised. "I've got to get back now." He nodded, stepped back, and I saw him standing, watching me as I drove off. He stayed, his eyes following me, I saw through the rearview mirror, and then disappeared as the road curved away. I chased the night back to the monastery and went into the dining hall to see Adam in his place, his eyes on the doorway as I entered.

His smile reached out to me and I hurried to my chair beside him. Judy, Randy, and Joan were at their usual places, each greeting me with a pleasant smile that belied our previous meeting. The pudgy-faced girl, Ruth, was serving and murmured blessings with each plate she set down. Randy and Joseph, the thin-cheeked young man, were in a discussion on the subliminal meanings of the last Psalm's call to praise God with musical instruments. Adam put in a few comments, then let the discussion go on without him as he turned to me.

"How did the work go today?" he asked.

"Not too well today," I replied. "I very much want to talk to you later."

His eyes took concern from my tone at once. "Of course. Shall we skip your lecture tonight?"

"Oh, no, there's no need for that," I said quickly. No one else gave any outward sign of being bothered by anything. Neither would I. When Adam tapped his glass, I rose, my eyes scanning the room, taking in the politely attentive faces, all so much alike in expression, I heard myself murmuring silently. Like so many well-trained children, I frowned inwardly, the thought an unworthy intrusion which I cast aside at once. I paused for an instant at Peter. His pale blue eyes were watching me, tiny dots of ice in the center of each orb. I looked away quickly, began to address the room.

"I've touched on the fact that Gothic architecture was also the expression of medieval man's religious philosophy," I began. "This belief occurs over and over as we explore the concepts of the learned Gothic man, along with his belief that the world was created as an ordered place. Geometry was thought of as the essential harmonizer of the universe, 'the science that all reasonable men live by.' All man's works were symbols of the Creator's works. Honorius of Autun, in the twelfth century, decribed the parts of a cathedral as such symbols in this way: The transparent windows which keep out the weather and bring in the light, are the learned doctors who keep out the storms of heresy and let in the light of doctrine. The window glass itself, through which the ray of light passes, is the mind of the doctors of the Church, viewing heavenly things as in a glass darkly.' With such a conceptual approach, it is little wonder that Gothic art and architecture were precise, beautifully composed, extremely functional. The same craftsmen built churches, fortifications, and houses, each precisely designed for its purpose, each a reflection of a higher order of things." I drew the symbolism further with other examples and then spoke of the precision I had found at Cashelderg, how the rooms and anterooms, the great corridors and floor patterns, were geometric and in relative proportion.

"That is, of course, only one aspect of my findings," I conlcuded. "I'm now examining the quality of craft work in the construction itself. In the morning, I'm tackling the right bastion.

The turret protrudes and under the embrasures there seems to be a series of supports worth closer examination."

I finished and Adam was standing at my side, his hand at my elbow, steering me toward the door, waiting for the others to file out first. His touch felt good, strong, and reassuring and when we went into his quarters, he pushed the door closed and sat down on the old sofa beside me.

"You're upset," he said, and I smiled at one more example of his intense perceptiveness, that charismatic ability to draw out the things others never suspected.

"A little," I admitted.

"Some brandy?" he offered and I shook my head. I told him what had happened as I had examined the outer wall. That was the easy part and when I finished his eyes were grave with concern.

"I think that about settles it," he said. "It's time you stopped poking about Cashelderg. There could be other accidents like that. You mightn't be so lucky next time."

"Occupational hazards. I'm not stopping till I've finished," I said. His eyes stayed on me.

"You're a very determined young woman," he said.

"I guess so," I agreed as I cast around for words.

"Something else is bothering you," Adam said. "Is it related to the accident?"

"I don't know," I said. I felt all verbal thumbs, drew a deep breath, and plunged. "I wondered if it was an accident," I blurted out, saw Adam's eyes widen.

"Why would you wonder that, Patricia?" he frowned.

"Things," I said, not wanting to sound cryptic. "I wondered if I might have come onto something others wanted kept silent."

"Here in the community?" he asked. I cast around for words again, found none that softened anything, and plunged forward once more.

"I guess what I'm asking is if you really know everything that goes on in the community," I said.

"Such as?" he frowned. I felt almost traitorous, began with Beth's plea in the corridor that first night and then her not contacting me at all. I went on to Peter's first outburst and then my attempt to visit her and the hostility I'd felt as I was turned away.

"I'd have dismissed all of it, even Peter's remarks about no one leaving here, except for the bus," I said.

"The bus?" Adam frowned.

"The bus from Ballygort," I said. "Are you sure Beth took the bus? Were you there? Did you put her on it?"

"No, not personally," Adam answered. "Why?"

"I'm told that the bus only runs Saturdays," I said, trying not to sound triumphant. Adam leaned back, his handsome face grave. He folded his hands against each other, touching fingertips.

"Let me take the other things you've spoken about, first," he said. "Do I know what goes on in the community? Not every little human detail, every little thing that happens, but I know all that is important to know. I know my children here, these Disciples of Light. I know them because they think and feel as I do. They have given themselves over to a greater force just as I have. That is more than enough. It is all I need to know."

He paused and I held reservations inside myself. "As for Peter's wild accusations, you see that he is a very disturbed young man," Adam continued. "He came to us that way and I'm afraid he is in the grip of forces I've been unable to reach. His wild imaginings are nothing more than that, fed by his personal fixation on Beth. Now as to the night you tried to visit her, I'd say you are no doubt right in having sensed a hostility. Overprotectiveness can bring that. We are a tightly knit community and we have often been misunderstood. People resent those who have found answers, a peace and contentment they have not found." He leaned forward, took my hands in his. "Beth was in a very delicate phase, very susceptible to being turned the wrong way by any outside influences. Judy and Joan and the others didn't want to risk that. Indeed, they couldn't risk that and be true to what they believe, what we all believe. I can understand, if not approve, of their attitude that night."

He let go of my hands and leaned back, a sigh escaping him. "As you know, their efforts failed anyway. Beth left. Which brings us back to the bus from Ballygort. Your information is correct. It only runs Saturdays."

I felt my eyes widen. "But yesterday it made a special run with some plumbing equipment we'd ordered. Randy took care of the details and when he told me the bus would be in Ballygort, I decided to make use of it. Beth was so anxious to leave. Randy drove her there and put her on it." Adam leaned forward again, took my face in his warm, strong hands. "So much for your dark thoughts, Patricia," he said quietly.

I sat silently, feeling ridiculous, yet terribly relieved. He moved back and his bright smile flashed, embracing, gathering me into it. "Don't be embarrassed. We are all subject to doubts and misgivings. Thomas doubted, too, remember," he said.

I nodded, quietly happy. His explanation had been ridiculously simple, gratifyingly mundane. Dimly, almost subconsciously, I was aware that it hadn't explained away everything, but I didn't want to even think about that now. I was more than willing to push everything else away. Adam's auburn-haired handsomeness seemed to glow as he sat before me. Perhaps I was te one who reached up, perhaps he leaned forward, I didn't know and didn't care, but suddenly my lips were on his, sweet fire, pushing against his strong, warm mouth. I stayed, tasting, feeling, aware of the fires that flared up inside me, and finally I drew back, suddenly uncertain, disconcerted. I suddenly felt like a little girl who had been too forward.

"What is it?" Adam asked, catching subtleties at once. I shrugged a reply. "Is it because of what I am?" he pressed.

"Maybe," I allowed. He stepped back, his eyes warm with understanding, his words carrying a fervor and power, the deep, sweeping commitment of the dedicated.

"I believe in what I am doing here in our community. I'm certain that what I teach is right, a way, an answer," he said. "If I didn't believe that I wouldn't be here. My message is the message of Scripture. I am only an instrument to bring His Word, His answer to others. In that, I serve a higher goal. In that, I perhaps depart from the average man. But I am nonetheless a man. I told you, we do not deny the senses here."

He reached out, drew me to him, and I went willingly, my mouth opening for his and his strength flowing over me. To love and to be loved, to feel the consuming fires, was not a new experience to me, and yet I felt like a pilgrim, a newcomer experiencing more than I ever had before. The charismatic power that was Adam Rood extended into all that he touched and now he touched me, his hands pressing into me with warmth, electricity. He pulled back, finally, his bright-fire eyes burning into me.

"There are answers for you here, Patricia," he said. "I know there are. We seldom choose the roads that lead us to the answers we want to find. Perhaps this is your road, through me and with me."

Answers, the word beguiling again, a sound of hope. But I wondered how he would react to the things I'd talked about to Lee Farrell, things which branched off into other worlds.

"Perhaps," I echoed. His hands cradled my face, his eyes suddenly soft. "I want you to forget about Cashelderg for now,

Patricia. Just stay here with us, learn more about what we offer," Adam said.

"About giving oneself over?" I smiled.

"Yes, about what it really brings, its comfort and its answers," he said. Answers, I echoed silently, the word beckoning again. Yet I had to hold back, tiny murmuring voices telling me I wasn't ready yet.

"When I've finished my work, Adam," I said. *And when the unexplained is explained, when I've my answers to letters and dreams and inner uncertainties,* I added to myself. His smile was rueful. "Finishing my work is important to me," I said. "I just want a little more time."

"Of course. You must make your decisions," Adam said gently, almost abstractly, and suddenly I felt apprehensive.

"It's not a rejection, Adam," I hastened to say. He stroked my cheek comfortingly.

"Of course not. I understand," he said and I wondered, fleetingly, why I'd used the word. Because Judy had said that rejection is a sin? Because I was unsure if Adam felt as she did? The mind swoops and darts like a swallow in ways that only seem erratic. I didn't want Adam to think I was rejecting him and what he offered, I admitted silently. I searched his eyes and saw only understanding in them.

"We all do what we must do," he said, as if reading my apprehensions. "It is only learning the right commands to obey." He smiled, rose, pulled me to my feet, and his lips found mine again and apprehensions vanished. "We'll find the answers for you," he said after a sweet moment. "Good night, Patricia."

I carried a warm, human side of Adam with me as I returned to my room and undressed to crawl beneath the covers. I found myself thinking back to how I'd dreaded the searching again when I'd ended it with Carter. Perhaps that search had ended before it really began, here at Cashelderg. This had been a place of the unexpected. I only knew that Adam was unlike any man I'd ever known. I had loved and I'd known all the stages, from schoolgirl crushes to purely sensuous affairs and mature relationships. I'd known them all and experienced the flaws of each and now I looked back and wondered if the flaws had merely been an inner knowing that they were not fulfillment for me. Being with Adam made one look back and reexamine oneself.

His charismatic powers added a new dimension and depth to personal relationships. Giving oneself over, the conceptual base Adam felt was so important, returned to my musings. Denying the self, I echoed, and felt myself automatically shrinking back from the concept. I frowned in the dark of the room. Interpretation evolves from conditioning, Adam had said, and perhaps that was more true than I wanted to admit. Yet denying the self continued to be an inner abrasion. Scripture demanded that, Adam had told me. It demanded that we give ourselves over to God. I searched back into my childhood, all those countless masses and catechetical studies, and denying the self still eluded me. Yet how deeply did such studies go, I wondered. Certainly not into the conceptual depths Adam dealt with in preconditioning happiness. Giving oneself over, I murmured silently, the entrance to happiness. Perhaps, I pondered. When had I been happiest, I asked, the answer simple enough. When I'd been in love, before the flaws made themselves known. Wasn't love a denying of the self? Hasn't love been described as that very thing, the giving over of oneself? ... a time when someone else's desires, needs, wants come before one's own?

The thought stayed, gathered validity, and yet I felt myself balking inwardly. Somehow, giving oneself over, as Adam spoke of it, seemed to have the feel of surrendering the self. The reaction was arbitrary, no doubt, I told myself, and tabled it for further discussion on with him. But I was convinced of one thing. I had been brought here to Cashelderg for a reason. Whether or not the letter would finally have some rational explanation, there was too much else. My coming here was not a thing of accident, the result of coincidences. I felt my thoughts fading, tiredness stealing inexorably upon me, and I closed my eyes, slept quickly. It was a heavy sleep that ended only at the warming caress of a bright sun. I woke, sat up to see that I'd overslept, grateful for having gone the night without interruption and annoyed at having slept so late. Swinging from bed, I grabbed a robe, hurried out to the bathroom, and then dressed hurriedly. I slung my tote bag over one shoulder, attached the little tool kit to my waist, and went down to the dining hall.

Only a handful was still there and I was greeted with cheery blessings and pleasant nods. I sipped tea, looked over at the bright faces, open, eager, uniformly pleasant. Their very uniformity seemed somewhat characterless but they seemed unquestionably happy and content. I saw none of the moodiness, the sullen mornings and bored afternoons I so often saw in class. But I saw none of the flashes of vitality and independent thought, either, and I wondered if only pain gave character.

I finished a second cup of tea as the others drifted out, watched one of the girls clearing away dishes, her face serene, entirely composed and content. I set down my cup and went outside. The scene was becoming familiar, the gentle sloping hills, the small knots of figures in earnest discussion, the formal classes moving into the building. It took on the look of those ancient tapestries in which, no matter what was depicted, the figures all seemed serenely detached. I hefted my bag, turned, and started over the rise and down the other side to where Cashelderg waited.

Multy wasn't anywhere and I'd half-expected as much. I went inside and started up the dim, inner stairwell, climbing up to the very top where it opened onto the outer bailey. Another short flight of steps brought me to the top of the turret where the round, protruding bartizan capped the turret. I Crossed to the round edge, halted at one of the embrasures, and looked down at the ground below, everything miniaturized from the height of the bartizan. I wondered how many archers had stood at these embrasures and fired their shafts at others below. Taking my gear from the tote bag, I decided not to wait for Multy. Below the bartizan were the supports which held it out from the bastion itself, supports which could shed valuable light on the inner construction of the entire castle.

I tied the ropes around my waist, allowing plenty of slack, then took both ends and knotted them around a merlon, the stone side of the embrasure opening. I tied a French bowline, secure, made for the kind of work I was about to do. Passing a length of rope from my waist under my thighs, I stepped forward through the embrasure and began to lower myself down the side. I moved down the outer wall of the bartizan, round a protruding construction, continued to lower myself, finally halting when I reached a spot level with the supports. Using the ropes as leverage, I pushed with my feet, swung inwards under the bartizan, reaching out to grasp an edge of one of the stone supports. I pulled myself deeper under the overhang of the bartizan, braced my feet against the wall of the bastion, and reached into the tool bag slung from my waist. I pulled a small but very sharp drill from it, pressed the drill point against the nearest support, and began to bore a round neat little hole into the stone. I pressed in deeply, pausing only to clean away little mounds of stone dust that gathered at the opening.

I sought evidence of iron rods used inside the stone supports. For many years, it was believed that Gothic architecture was purely of masonry, but then there was the discovery of extensive iron reinforcements laid within the stonework. Iron was used for cramps, dowels, stays, tie-rods, and general reinforcing in many structures. Prodigious amounts of hand-made iron nails were also used in places. I drilled deeply but came upon no evidence of hidden iron reinforcements in the first support and shifted myself on to the next, resting my arm and shoulder muscles for a moment, then commenced drilling again. The drill met only stone and I made a second hole farther down along the support where an oblong, triangular space was formed where the supports joined the bastion wall. It revealed nothing, either.

I moved on to a third support, made two holes again at different places and from different angles with the same results. I got a hand over the triangular space and rested there, slid the drill back into the tool bag. Three supports were enough. If iron reinforcements had been used in the building of Cashelderg, they'd certainly have been placed in the bartizan supports. Cashelderg had obviously been crafted by a master builder who rejected the use of hidden reinforcements.

I started to work myself along a little further under the overhang of the bartizan when suddenly I felt my skin grow cold. I halted, hung in midair for a moment as a sudden sense of danger swept over me, unexplainable yet undeniable, so strong that little beads of perspiration coated my skin as if by magic. I was alone and yet suddenly I was not alone, I was threatened, the scent of death suddenly so strong I could almost feel it. Suddenly I had to pull myself up to the top of the bartizan, the command a silent scream. I kicked out, started to swing out from under the overhang, pulling myself up along the rope when I felt the taut rope suddenly grow slack. In split seconds it started to fall loose in my hands. I heard my scream as if it were someone else crying out. I twisted, kicked with my feet, swung in under the overhang with the last tautness still left in the rope and then I felt myself starting to plunge down as the rope fell loosely around me.

I flung arms out, felt my fingers slip along the stone support, catch hold of the edge of the triangular opening at the spot where the support joined the wall. I twisted, managed to get my other arm up, a second finger hold. Gasping, I pulled, pulled again, suddenly aware of the strength beyond strength that the will to survive can generate. I got a hand along the edge of the support, reached into the triangular opening, drew my arm into it, and clung there for a long moment as my breath came in great gasped draughts. I brought the other arm up, linked it around the opening, and hung there, the ropes that had been tied around the merlon hanging down from my waist. They had come loose, only they couldn't have come loose, not with the bowline knot I'd tied, not of themselves. Someone had crept up to the merlon and loosened them.

The thought shattered, almost as totally as I'd have been shattered on the ground below. I wanted to dwell on it, incongruously fascinated by the horror of it, but I had to put it aside, my arm and shoulder muscles warning that their aid was a limited, tenuous thing. As a newborn infant must breathe before it can act, I had to survive before anything else. I wasn't lying on the ground far below, broken and beyond repair, but I had bought only a tentative reprieve. Death, like the gargoyles of Cashelderg, still leered at me. I clung with my precarious arm-lock like an insect wedged into a corner of a spider's web, alive but helpless. The edge of the overhang was too far away to reach, even if I could find a fingertip hold there. One mistake and the would-be killer's objective would be realized. I clung, looking out at the bottom of the protruding bartizan as a drowning man looks at the shore beyond reach. I needed the length of the rope that had held me secure to even reach there and I winced in pain as my arm muscles began to protest. The face of death is a shattering immensity that sends shock waves through the system, jarring the mind, turning reason into a benumbed ally. Abstractly, I looked down at the ropes that hung down from around my waist, staring at them as conscious thought slowly gathered itself.

Frowning with the effort, letting the numbness start to wear away, I shifted my grip through the triangular opening, reached down with one hand and gathered up first one, then the other strand of rope. I slipped one end through the opening between the support and the wall, did the same with the other, pulling them tight and then, slowly and carefully, using one hand only, I tied another French bowline knot. I tested it, grunted grimly. It wouldn't give way, any more than the first one had slipped loose.

I unlocked my grip and swung down from the support, hanging for a few moments while circulation returned to my arms. Pushing against the bastion wall with both feet, I swung myself out, caught hold of the lower edge of the bartizan, held there for a moment as I checked the amount of slack in the ropes tied to the support. There was just enough, I hoped, and I started to inch my way upwards along the outer bartizan wall toward the nearest embrasure. It was but a short distance but I had to inch my way along flylike, fingertips finding crevices between the stones as I cursed the craftsmanship of the builders of Cashelderg. My nails were broken, my fingertips pained and bruised, when I reached the embrasure, got a hand through the opening and pulled myself up. I was halfway through it when the ropes tightened around my waist, the slack in them used up.

I hung there, letting breath come back, then slowly edged my way backwards, just far enough to allow a little slack again. Hanging on the narrow opening of the embrasure, more out then in, I worked the ropes tied at my waist loose enough to push them down over my hips. Wriggling forward again, I pulled back deeper into the embrasure, kicked legs, and felt the ropes sliding down across my thighs, over the knees and then fall loosely away. I flung myself forward, toppled head first onto the flooring of the bartizan, and lay there, gasping deep breaths. I could feel myself starting to tremble, an after-shock beyond control, and I lay there shaking as if in some kind of fit until, slowly, it subsided and I lay still. The sun was warm, I thought incongruously, then decided that the thought was not incongruous at all but a recognition of the warmth of life.

Slowly, I pulled myself up, stood holding onto the merlon, gazing down over the round side of the bartizan. My hand moved across the spot where I'd tied the knot and the ropes had been secured around the merlon. Someone had crept here, untied the bowline to plunge me to my death. I shuddered, unable not to and angry at myself for it. I turned away, aimlessly walked to the other side of the bartizan. I could see down to the sea and the rock-studded narrow strip of sand and I stood very still, my eyes focusing on a small figure receding down along the beach, far away now, yet the loose, disjointed walk unmistakable. A furrow pressed into my forehead. I turned away, went back to the spot where I'd tied the ropes. I stared down at the merlon as though in some mysterious way it could give me a clue, an answer to the thoughts that now raced wildly through my mind. Only one thing was absolutely certain to me. The ropes hadn't come undone of themselves. I knew that my life hung on that knot. I'd tied others before, each time knowing the same thing. They had never slipped before and they hadn't this time. No more than the falling stones of the wall yesterday had been an accident. I knew that now, also. No coincidental happening, no accident, but planned, deliberate.

The realization defied belief and I said it again to myself, as though the saying of it would make it less horrendous. All yesterday's questions came rushing back, along with new ones, new suspicions dancing gleefully along with them. The answers with which Adam had explained away yesterday's questions were suddenly surrounded with uncertainty. With startling clarity, I heard Adam's explanation again, the one fact standing out above all else. He hadn't seen Beth get on that bus. My uneasy suspicions of yesterday had returned like unwelcome vultures to hover overhead. Suspicions couldn't be wrong and right at the same time. Or could they? Facts and truth were all too often very different, I reminded myself.

I turned from the wall, looked down at my fingers that were red and bruised and aching, felt the muscles of my shoulders pulling in pain. I wanted to be alone, to go over every detail, to think out each little thing for myself. I had to do that before saying anything further to Adam. The thin, reedy voice cut into my thoughts, calling out from below.

"You up here?" it asked and I stepped to the edge of the round bartizan, saw Multy emerging from the stone steps that led up to the bastion. I climbed down from the bartizan to face the little figure that waited, tilted to one side.

"Where have you been?" I questioned abruptly.

"Bridget had to go into Drumglas. I tended chores," he said.

"I'm finished for today," I said and saw the gimlet eyes studying me. I searched them for a sign, an indication of surprise, disappointment, anger, anything that might give me a clue. I saw only sharp appraisal. Multy grunted, shrugged, turned away and disappeared down the dark passage of steps to the keep, saying not another word. Just his manner, I wondered, or because he knew words were dangerous, often revealing more than themselves? I moved forward, started down the steps, into the dimness of the inner stairwell. Fear, I quickly realized, clothes every ordinary act in its deep, dark robes. Each step was a thing of caution, taut and apprehensive. When I reached the main floor I was damp with perspiration. Adjusting the tool bag, taking up the larger tote bag, I hurried outside, went down along the side of the castle to the little path that led down to the sea. On the firm sand, I walked a few dozen yards to where a giant rock reared up from the sea and the sand, straddling both with the implacableness of ages, its strength comforting. I sank down on the sand behind it, stretched my arms out, and let the sea roll over my fingers, the cool water soothing, taking the burning ache from skin and muscle.

Finally, I pulled my hands from the water, turned, and lay down on my back on the sand. I forced my churning thoughts to arrange themselves into ordered sequences. I would go over everything, dismissing no one. To do so might be to dismiss my life, I knew now. I decided to start with Lee, perhaps because he was the least likely of all, and instantly saw his loose-gaited stride receding down the beach. I grunted as I reprimanded myself at once for making evaluative judgments before I'd even started. Had Lee been poking about amid the rocks and bushes beneath Cashelderg again? If so, what did he search for with such determination? His visits were too frequent to dismiss any longer as idle exploration along the shore. He searched for something. The question now was whether he had simply been searching again. Or had he climbed up into Cashelderg, to the turret from which I hung suspended? There'd been ample time for him to do so, untie the ropes, and return to the beach to hurry off. The killer wouldn't have waited around to risk meeting someone else.

But killing requires a reason, a motive. Even insane, paranoid murderers have their own twisted reasons. I could assign no motive to Lee Farrell. Indeed, he had saved my life once. Of course he hadn't known anything about me then. He hadn't known where I was going or why I was here. I remembered how, even on that first morning when he learned where I was going he had grown tightlipped. Something about my presence then had disturbed him. I shook my head impatiently. It didn't make sense, not even for murder. But logic is a strict drillmaster. Once one marched to its tune, it permitted no falling out of step. I could dismiss nothing because it didn't make sense, no one because they seemed to have no motive. Not until I knew more than I did. But I put Lee on the perimeter of the circle of suspicion, really there only because I'd seen him hurrying down the beach.

Multy was next. I found, with some surprise, that it hurt to think of him as a killer. The tilted little man with his sudden flashes of sensitivity, his acute perception that caught one off guard, had become an abrasively appealing little figure. Yet now I had to think of him as something entirely different, those qualities meaningless as proof of anything. Many killers were both perceptive and sensitive in their own ways.

Multy didn't want me here, I reviewed. From the very moment I'd arrived he had made that clear. I'd come to take his repeated demands that I go home as harmless rhetoric. Had that been an almost tragic error? Perhaps he resented me more than he did Adam. Perhaps he felt that my work here would eventually pose more of a threat than Adam did to his family tenure at Cashelderg. I thought back to the things he had flung at me. *Cashelderg is a cursed place. Leave here before you get yourself killed. Those that won't listen deserve what they get.*

Warnings all? I'd read somewhere that many killers give their intended victims numerous warnings, a kind of prior justification for their intended acts. Was that what Multy had been doing? Or was there an ancient curse on Cashelderg? Had he told me and grown enraged at my disregard of that? Was Multy as tilted inside as he was outside? His possessiveness about Cashelderg was perhaps more paranoiac than anyone realized.

Did he consider it his mission to make the curse of Cashelderg come true? Rational reasons, understandable motives were unimportant with the paranoid killer. He builds his own distorted reasons for killing, his own twisted castles of the mind, I thought with macabre appropriateness.

Was that Multy? I pondered. He had conveniently been away both yesterday and today when death struck at me. Away, or simply creating his fatal accidents? I felt the deep sigh that escaped me. The strange little man had to be in the center of that circle of suspicion.

My mind went on to Peter and my first thought was not really a thought but a shivering recollection. I saw the deep cold fire pits of hatred that had been in his eyes last night as he watched me. He believed I was responsible for whatever happened to Beth. He didn't believe he'd left and he held me to blame for whatever had become of her. It was more than enough motive for murder, certainly for someone as disturbed and distraught as Peter. I'd be sorry, he had warned me. Had he brooded, let his disturbed, hurt anger turn into action? It would have been easy enough for him. He had been at dinner, had heard me tell of what I'd planned to do today along with everyone else there. Peter had motives and opportunity, the two necessary ingredients. I set him alongside Multy, unable to do more.

I paused, held back thoughts for a moment, let my breath escape in a deep sigh again. This dispassionate culling of the human organism, this reasoned assigning of motives for murder, was a shriveling experience, turning the world into a sour place. But it was a necessity and I went on to others, to Randy, Joan, and Judy. Their involvement depended on the truth in Peter's cry, *no one leaves here.* I had to face the monstrousness of it once and for all. What if those words were true? I thought of waking that night, seeing the hands against my window, hands that disappeared in the swirling fog as I turned to yank on slacks and a sweater. I'd dismissed it as a dream tarrying, sliding into those first split seconds of waking as they so often do. But what if I'd been wrong? What if it had been Beth at the fog-bound window, desperately seeking help, her pursuers right behind her? What if it had been no dream impression at all but stark, ugly reality?

I sat up, the horror of the thought sending a shiver through me. Had I any right to think that on the basis of a disturbed man's words? Had I any right not to, I countered at once. It had been the night before Beth left. She had been terribly anxious to leave, Adam had said. Perhaps in fear for her life and afraid to trust anyone, I pondered. Adam hadn't seen her onto the bus. Randy had done it all, even arranged for the special run of the bus. What if there really had been no special run at all? What if Randy had anticipated someone questioning the presence of the bus and had cleverly arranged the story. The questions pursued one another in a grim rigadoon. To go in falseness is a sin. Rejection is a sin. I heard Judy's words delivered with such chilling absoluteness. And sin must be punished, she had added with equal ice. Beth had done both, rejected the community and its teachings and gone in falseness, a bearer of error. Indeed, more than enough reason for punishment to those who had assumed the role of guardians of truth, defenders of the faith.

It, would not be the first time for such as that. Man had a way of turning the spirit of love into the spirit of hate. Distortion came easily to those things that touched deep. But it never sprang into being full-blown, it grew little by little, nurturing itself on its own darkness, a weed of the soul choking off all else. They would have reached their terrible, distorted pact in stages of convoluted thinking, each a part of the whole. The hostility the night I tried to see Beth hadn't been overprotectiveness, then, but a last attempt to bend her will to theirs. I'd taken her abrupt switches in attitude as signs of a disturbed, confused young woman. Had it been their mind-bending, the brainwashing Peter had spoken about? Had he been right in that, too? Had Randy, Judy, and Joan, and perhaps others, crossed that line between the spirit and the ego, between strength and power?

My lips grew into a thin line as I thought of how I'd met them the next morning when I reached Cashelderg, clothes streaked with dirt, faces tired, tense, and drawn. A *ménage à trois*, I had concluded. Maybe it had been that but one of a very different kind. Had they take Beth to Cashelderg in the night, held her a prisoner there? If so, was she still there? Certainly there was much of Cashelderg I hadn't explored yet. Once again, the stark horror of the thought shattered and yet I couldn't turn away from anything now. The hands at my window in the fog had been the very night before, and when I flung the window open I'd heard sounds I'd dismissed as wind in the trees. Everything shouted out the single word, possibility, and I felt the grim sourness inside me. Everything but one thing, something Adam had said. I rose instantly, consumed with the need to speak to Adam. His answers would provide no blueprint for guilt for anyone, no exoneration, but they could strengthen or weaken the chain of suspicion I'd had to forge around the trio.

I started back to the little path that led up from the shore, thinking about Adam. I had to be careful, to choose words with caution. Adam was a teacher, a guide, as he saw himself. But he was in reality a shepherd and a shepherd protects his flock. I not only understood that but sympathized with the feeling, the sense of responsibility that was his. I could say nothing more about suspicions until I had more than words, more than neat little constructions. But if Randy and the two girls were guilty, they had tried to kill me because they feared that Beth might have gotten to me. Perhaps they had decided to play safe, uncertain whether I was holding back in an effort to trap them. And so, as I climbed the little steep pathway, I tried to choose words, compose beginnings. I reached the top and Cashelderg glowered down at me as I hurried past it before it pulled me into its dim vastness. I would return to search its hollowed rooms again, a very different kind of exploring this time. Instead of seeking beauty, art, and order, I would search for evidence of horror, distortion, and evil.

When I crossed the rise and reached the long, low monastery, two girls emerged from the front door just as I started in. "Have you seen Adam?" I asked abruptly.

"Yes, a little while ago. He was going into his rooms," the taller one said. "Peace."

"A lovely day. We give thanks," the other smiled. Their worshipful cheerfulness was suddenly irritating, undeservedly. I grimaced inwardly at my churlishness. I went inside, marched to Adam's room, and saw that the door was slightly ajar. I paused as I reached it, heard Adam's voice, stern, a note in it I'd never heard before, almost anger.

"But where was he most of the morning? You were told to keep watch on him," Adam said.

"I don't know," I heard the answer come in Randy's voice. "He just slipped away from us. Joseph is watching him now."

"Inexcusable," I heard Adam bite out. "I told you, he's to be watched every minute. Don't let it happen again."

The door was opened and Randy emerged, saw me, and his eyes widened in surprise and then he brushed past me. I saw Adam, his face biblically stern, a disapproving prophet. "I was just coming to see you for a moment," I said.

"Please come in," Adam said, the sternness still with him.

"I'm sorry to interrupt," I offered. "I couldn't help hearing."

"That's all right. I was bothered. I'd given orders to have Peter watched every minute in his agitated state but he slipped away for over an hour this morning."

"Peter," I echoed and felt the rush of thoughts buffering me, my mind clicking off connections. Peter slipping off to murder? I had almost a feeling of relief. Peter's guilt was the easiest one for me to accept. I heard Adam's voice break into my thoughts.

"What is it, Patricia?" his voice asked. I pulled myself back into place. Peter's disappearance was presumptive evidence and nothing more. I couldn't afford the luxury of conclusions.

"A question that's been bothering me, Adam," I began, all my careful words suddenly inadequate. "You said you'd talked to Beth about her leaving. Was that the morning she left?"

I saw the question form in Adam's eyes and he surveyed me with almost cautious amusement. "Why do you ask that?" he returned slowly.

I shrugged. "It'll help me understand something better. I'd just like to know," I replied.

"Still playing with dark thoughts, Patricia?" Adam asked gently. I grimaced inwardly. Not dark thoughts, *murder,* I wanted to shout back but I kept silent.

"I'd just like to know," I said doggedly. Adam's eyes held me with the quiet amusement in them. Finally, with a deep sigh almost of disappointment, he answered.

"I spoke to Beth the night before," he said. "She came to me and we talked and reached the decision. She left with Randy in the early morning."

I felt the leaden weight inside me. I had wanted so for Adam's words to exonerate, to strike away suspicion. Instead, they had only renewed it. He hadn't seen Beth the next morning. He knew only what Randy had told him. That fog-bound night remained the enigma it had become. She could have slipped away, raced to my window. The next morning she was gone, but on the bus from Ballygort, or to someplace else? Peter was no more indicted than the others, despite his disappearance this morning. My question to Adam had brought nothing. I decided to try one more.

"Do you know that fellow that rents the cottage a mile or so down from here?" I asked.

"That writer chap?" Adam queried. "Why? Has he been around again?"

"Again?" I frowned.

Adam's eyes had grown stern once more. "He wanted to live in Cashelderg, write about it, some notion of steeping himself in the feel of the place so he could get it down better on paper. I caught him snooping about twice and finally ordered him off. He became quite nasty. I threatened to put the police on him if I found him anywhere near the place or the community," Adam said.

"I did meet him once," I lied, and found my thoughts taking instant shape. It explained Lee's dislike of the community and of Adam. It no doubt explained other things, too. Adam moved toward me, reached out, and his hands closed around my shoulders.

"What is it, Pat?" he asked gently. "Are your dark thoughts still on the accident yesterday?"

Today, I wanted to shout, today with the shadow of yesterday still in it. But I held silent, knowing again that all I had was theory, neat, careful constructions without solid evidence. Certainly I couldn't go into my fears about Beth and the tapestry of terror I'd woven with Randy, Joan, and Judy at the center. He leaned down and his lips found mine, sweet strength, warm fires instantly kindled, and then he pulled back and his eyes were grave, riveting with the depths of their fires.

"Others have come here with darkness inside them," he said. "Others have come to stand before me troubled, searching. I was blessed by being able to help them. I served and, as in Philippians, He served with me in the gospel. It is why I exist. We all have our appointments. That is mine. Let me help you, Patricia. Let me combine duty and desire, serving and loving."

He stepped back and I felt the intensity and sweep of his feelings wrap themselves around me. "Your work is not all-important. Your happiness is everything. That is what we all strive for. There are roads here for you to take. Some of us have been entrusted with the task to do what is right and good. That gift has been given me. It is a kerygmatic gift. I want to share it especially with you."

He reached out and I was inside the circle of his arms again, more than a physical embrace. I felt unworthy, a violator of trust, with the dark suspicions I held inside me. I reached up, found his mouth, and let the senses push aside all else. When I finally pulled back his hands continued to hold me.

"Forget Cashelderg for now, Patricia. Stay here and take part in some of our sessions. Let me show you how much there is here for you," he said.

I didn't want to refuse again, not with the deep sincerity that I saw in his eyes. His offer was not simply an offer but an affirmation of all he believed in as a man and a shepherd, held out to me. "Maybe," I said. "Let me think about it some more."

"Meanwhile, promise me you'll stay away from Cashelderg. The work seems to be disturbing more than rewarding now," he said.

"I'll see," was all I could offer on that and his smile was ruefully understanding.

"I've a class waiting," he said. 'I'll see you tonight." I went to the door with him, clung to him for a moment longer, took his strength and vibrancy with me as I went outside. The sun made me blink and I halted for a moment to adjust my eyes. I glimpsed the thin figure walking down the far hill toward the huts, Peter, and behind him the thin-faced boy, Joseph. I walked to the car, climbed into it, and turned the engine on, rolling slowly down the roadway. I wanted to get away from Cashelderg for a little while, from the climate of things hidden, unexplained, lurking. Not that I could run, I knew better than that. I just wanted to enjoy the lingering comfort of Adam's embrace without the intrusion of fear.

I drove slowly, found myself on the shore road, wandered aimlessly, and suddenly realized I was abreast of the narrow road that led to Lee's cottage. I turned down it, wondered fleetingly if I'd really driven so aimlessly, whether we really ever do anything aimlessly. One is always drawn back to those with whom inner secrets have been shared, sometimes in warmth, sometimes in regretful bitterness. Confiding is always part pleasure and part pain and, still reeling from shock that afternoon, I'd confided to Lee things I'd never spoken of to anyone else.

He came out as I pulled up, standing in the doorway, his affable countenance registering agreeable surprise. "I was just having some good Irish tea. Now it'll be that much better," he said. The room was a rush of recollection. That night seemed so long ago.

"I've nothing more on the letter, if that's what brought you here," he said, pouring a mug of hot tea for me.

"No rational, practical answers waiting for me?" I smiled. His eyes paused, glinted down at me.

"No, and you didn't expect any, did you?" he replied. "You're still quite certain I won't find any."

I shrugged agreement. "I've found out a few things, though," I remarked between sips.

"Such as?" he questioned, sitting down beside me.

"Why you don't like Adam Rood and his community," I said. "You had words with him over your staying in Cashelderg. It's a personal thing."

I watched Lee's eyes narrow, then his smile come slow with ruefulness in it. "We had words," he admitted.

"And that's why you've been poking around below the castle. You've been looking for a way to get in without being seen," I finished. His eyes continued to hold a quiet admittance.

"What can I say?" he laughed, turning up his hands. "You've called it. I've read that all those old castles have hidden passages that lead outside. I'm sure Cashelderg does and it probably leads out along the shore."

"Probably," I agreed. "The very ancient underground passages were called *souterrains* and were often used as places to hide." I paused, watched his bland and slightly shamed expression for a moment. "So your dislike of Adam and the community is purely personal," I finished.

"Yes, but I don't care much for his kind of thing, anyway. He's got a good thing going for him and he's milking it all the way," Lee said. I felt myself bristle at once.

"That's hardly fair. You don't know anything about Adam Rood," I said.

"Enough," Lee said, and then, his eyes narrowing, he looked sharply at me, a sideways glance. "He's gotten to you, hasn't he? He's got a way with him."

"You make it sound like some calculated effort," I shot back angrily. "Adam Rood is an absolutely sincere person."

"How do you know that?" Lee speared.

"You can feel it, know it just by being around him. It's in his intensity, his strength. It exudes from him. He believes very deeply in himself and in the community," I replied. I found myself growing furious at Lee Farrell's shrug of dismissal. "Sincerity and believing deeply aren't things of importance to you, apparently," I snapped.

"Right and wrong are important to me," Lee countered almost offhandedly. "Adolf Hitler was sincere. The people who burned witches believed in what they were doing."

I felt myself grimace, knew he'd chosen the example with purposeful emphasis. "The comparisons are gratuitous," I answered. "Those are negative things. A belief in serving others, in bringing the message of Scripture, is a very different thing."

"That depends on the message, I guess," Lee returned. His manner was flip, almost as though he were trying to irritate. He was succeeding, if that was his aim.

"I didn't realize you were such a cynic," I said acidly, feeling very bitter at his attitude, as much for Adam as for myself. "I imagine you've had quite a laugh at the things I told you the other day," I sniffed.

"I'm only cynical about some things and some people," he said evenly. I refused to be mollified. I had given him an inner part of myself, shared confidences, and now his attitude seemed a negation of trust.

"I can see why you must have a practical explanation for everything," I tossed out. His smile was infuriatingly pleasant.

"Hell you do," he said mildly. "You're just angry because I don't accept the Messiah."

"Thanks for the tea," I flung back stiffly, setting the mug down. He seemed unperturbed at my obvious displeasure, which of course made me angrier. He followed me as I strode out to the car and slid behind the wheel, his smile pleasant.

"How are the dreams?" he asked.

"What if I told you somebody tried to kill me?" I flung back, wanting to pierce his affable tolerance, his smug attitudes.

"Dreams or for real?" he asked evenly.

"Try both," I snapped.

"I'd say you ought to get the hell away from there," Lee answered, his voice calm, mild.

"I've heard that before," I shot back, switching on the engine. "Let me know when you've anything more on the letter." I sent the little car off with a scream of loose road stones, saw Lee Farrell stay to watch me disappear. I was disappointed in him and angered at his cynical attitude toward Adam. He was a superficial person, I decided, all surface pleasantness but no real depth, not even enough to be a killer. I took him out of the circle of suspicion. His poking about below Cashelderg had been explained and he had no other motive or involvement. My list grew smaller by one.

But a single, grim truth remained. Someone had tried to kill me. He, or they, would try again. I still lived. They had to try again. I had very real suspects with very plausible motives. Death had struck close today and a killer still waited with reasons made of now. Yet there was more, a dream that came again and again, always the same, and a letter out of the dim and dark past. They had a place in this. Somehow, somewhere, someway, they had a place. I found myself thinking of Yeats again, lines that held a special meaning for me. *There are some ... the souls in Purgatory ... that come back to habitations and familiar spots.* How much of death today was made of yesterday? How had I been called here? Those answers, and the others, could come together. Perhaps they wouldn't all be shining and clear, but they would be together, fitting, somehow, someway.

I drove up to the old monastery building and parked. Others were going in to dinner. I went in, walked the long corridor to my room. It seemed a time for being alone.

CHAPTER EIGHT

The day had drained more than I'd realized from me. A terrible tiredness clung as I freshened up and I did everything in slow motion. Strangely, I kept thinking about Lee and how disappointed I'd been in him. I wanted to call back the inner feelings I'd shared with him. He had listened then, not accepting as I did the beliefs I confided, yet listening with respect. Now his attitude had changed completely, an upsetting, disturbing change. I felt betrayed for myself, angered for Adam, by his glib, cynical comments that had sounded almost jealous.

I put aside thoughts of Lee and returned down the hall. Adam's eyes were on the doorway as I entered, concerned, searching, and I felt warm and grateful at once, forced myself to walk to his side. "Sorry I'm late," I said, sitting down. "I'm not really hungry, anyway, tonight."

His glance was sharp, penetrating. "We'll skip your talk tonight," he said and I was glad to agree. My glance roamed across Randy, Judy, and Joan, and I returned their pleasant nods, watched them go back to an animated conversation on Paul's Epistle to the Galatians. I looked past to the other tables, found Peter, his pale blue eyes masked yet staring at me. Was he unable to understand how I was there before his eyes? I wondered. I turned away from his stare. Only Multy was missing, I thought quietly. Was I sitting in the same room with whoever had tried to send me plunging to my death? I wondered. My glance went out across the dining hall at everyone there, their faint murmurs of conversation dancing in and out of hearing like flashes of sound from a distant place. Suddenly I had the shuddering thought that perhaps the would-be killer was someone else entirely, one of the others here, someone quietly masking a deep, twisted homicidal urge. Psychotic killers were often completely unsuspected, revealing nothing of their strangulated emotions. Good God, I was becoming really paranoid, I groaned, extending fears to everyone and everything. Suddenly everyone wore a mask and I leaned toward Adam to feel the touch of his arm against mine. I was being completely foolish, I reprimanded inwardly. It had been no psychotic, unsuspected killer, no motiveless murderer. There were too many other things that were part of it for that.

I shunted further thoughts away and toyed with a piece of meat, gave up, and had some jello pudding for dessert and was grateful when dinner ended. Adam's hand was light on my elbow as he walked with me, steering me to his rooms. "You're still bothered, upset over something," he said as I sank down on the old couch and the door closed behind me.

"I'm tired," I said, falling back on a half-truth. Adam came to sit beside me, his hand reaching out to rest on my cheek.

"There is what we call a reaffirmation session going on tonight. I wish you'd attend," Adam said.

"Reaffirmation session? Why do you call it that?" I asked.

"Because those who have come here are products of our society and the past clings. Old pressures, old wrongs, are held over and they must be guarded against. Jesus went into the desert to let the devil tempt him but his strength is not given to the rest of us. We must constantly renew our commitments," Adam said, in his voice the ringing power of commitment itself. I thought of Lee's ill-tempered remark that Adam had a good thing going for him and felt myself grow angry all over again. I wanted to scourge it from my mind completely.

"How do you bring others to believe as you do, Adam? Do they come believing?" I questioned.

"Hardly ever. It is a process you cannot understand from outside. You must experience it, become part of it. I am a spiritual lamplighter. I only light the lamps. The light itself is not of my making. Scripture is the light."

He reached for my hands, rose, pulled me with him. "Come see for yourself, Patricia. Spend one night that could change your life. Try, for me," he said.

I felt myself nodding agreement, aware that I wanted to try for myself as well. But fear clings with its own tenacity. "Who'll be there?" I asked, trying to sound casual, and wondered if I detected the trace of a smile touch his lips.

"Ellen, Amy, Mary, Todd, and John. You know them by sight, you'll see," Adam said, turned, his arm around me and I pressed against him as we left, went out into the night. The first bite of the air chilled, sent a tiny shiver through me. Adam led me to a hut in the first row, two windows flanking the door. He knocked and a girl opened, dark haired, not pretty, a face I'd seen as I lectured.

"Patricia has come to ask questions and to take part," Adam said. "This is Amy," he introduced.

"Bless you, Patricia," Amy said and I followed her inside, the hut dark, lighted only by three candles. I recognized the others, the young man nearest introducing everyone, Todd, his name, a fairly short, pleasant-faced person.

"I'll come back later," Adam said, pressed my arm, and turned, disappearing out the doorway. The hut gave me an igloolike feeling, making everything turn inward. There were no decorations save a biblical quotation from Isaiah framed against one wall:

Have ye not known? Have ye not heard?
Hath it not been told you from the beginning?

A place was made for me in a circle of straight-backed chairs and I saw three cots against the far walls of the hut. I met pleasant, uniformly bright faces turned to me. Ellen, a mouse-blonde girl, smiled patiently. I drew a deep breath.

"What made you come to Adam?" I asked.

"I was tired of not knowing," she answered.

"Not knowing?" I frowned.

"That's right. Not knowing how to live with the hate and greed in the world and all the other things that didn't make sense. I asked and received nothing. As Job tells us, they cry but none giveth answer," she said.

I looked at Amy. "Did you feel the same way?" I asked.

"There was nothing. The world disappointed. People betrayed," she said. "I looked further and a friend brought me to Adam. He showed me Isaiah. 'Be not dismayed for I am thy God.'"

"Just look around you," Todd spoke up. "Everyone out for themselves, everyone thinking their way is the right way. Trust not in ourselves but in God, Corinthians tells us."

"Commit thy way unto the Lord, Psalms says," Ellen added. The belief was unmistakable in their words and in their faces, but I wished they wouldn't answer everything with a quotation.

"All is well with us when we obey the voice of the Lord, Jeremiah says," Mary offered.

"Our Father knoweth what things we have need of, Matthew tells us," the other boy, John, chimed in. "We simply obey and we are in His grace."

I felt the tiredness rushing back over me, urged on by the realization that my questions would not be answered here. They spoke out of their acceptance, their commitment, and I would not move behind that, I knew. I accepted their acceptances. That wasn't what continued to bother. "I think I ought to go," I said.

"No, we haven't begun yet," Ellen said. "Adam wants you to stay." I felt my lips press together. She was right, Adam did want me to listen and take part and I'd agreed.

"All right, but I am tired," I answered.

"That is even better," Todd said, and I questioned with a glance. "Tiredness opens the mind. It wipes away the diverting mental detritus of ordinary things." He rose, took my hand, led me to one of the cots. "Lie down here, please," he said. "All you need do is relax, put yourself in our hands, and listen."

It seemed harmless enough and lying down was a definitely attractive idea. I stretched out, glanced up as Ellen appeared at my head. Her hands pressed against my head, her fingers moving gently, rubbing my temples. "This will make you feel better," she said. I didn't object. Her fingers felt good, soothing, taking away the edge of a headache. I heard Todd's voice beginning to read.

They wandered in the wilderness in a solitary way;
they found no city to dwell in.
Hungry and thirsty,
their soul fainted in them.
Then they cried unto the Lord in their trouble,
and he delivered them out of their distresses
And led them forth by the right way.

His voice went on, a singsong chant, and I felt myself falling asleep, almost did so when Ellen's fingers pressed a nerve and I came awake. The words filtered through to me, imprinting themselves on my mind as I lay half-awake, half-asleep ... *obey his voice ... for the promise is unto you ... do that which is right and good ... provide for thee ... Whom the Lord loveth he correcteth.* They were good words, appealing, comforting, and I drifted into a kind of sleep in which Todd's voice came into my mind dimly, yet penetrating. I felt myself in a floating, effort-less state, warm, secure, asleep yet awake. His voice continued to drift through to me and I felt myself rebelling, a deep, silent undercurrent of resistance rubbing against the relaxed, comfort-able warmth. Out of what seemed a void, I heard Todd's voice. "Sleep, Patricia, sleep. You will hear me and you will know this is a sign," the voice said. I wanted to sleep, yet Ellen's soothing touch somehow kept pressing a nerve in my temple, just enough to keep me from falling into a deep sleep, enough to keep the channels of the mind receiving. "A sign of that which can be yours always," I heard the distant voice intone. I felt drugged, but from a depth of will power, some wellspring of inner determination, I snapped my eyes open, swung from the cot.

"*No!*" I got the word out, a sharp sound, and suddenly I was thoroughly awake and standing.

"Please lie back," Ellen said. "It's only a beginning." Her round eyes were wide, appealing to me.

"It's enough," I snapped.

"Adam will expect you to be here," Amy said. I speared her with a gaze, saw the open dismay and disappointment in her face. I looked at the others, saw the same dismay echoed in their eyes.

"I'll explain to Adam," I said briskly, moving to the door. "Thank you for letting me take part. I'm not up to anymore tonight."

I opened the door, slipped outside. The chill of the night was welcome, a bracing bite to it. Reactions tumbled in my mind like so many clothes tumbling about in a washing machine as I started up the slope. The dismay in their faces had been real. There'd been nothing evil there. That certainty blazed through my mind but a single word pushed itself at me: *brainwash-ing,* Peter's word. I turned it over in my mind. The session hadn't been that, not exactly, and yet it had had some of that in it. It had been an attempt to condition me, to create a receptivity. It had, as Ellen had said, been only a beginning. What if I had stayed? How deep would the conditioning have gone? How much would I have wanted, subconsciously, at least, that effortless, suspended, carefree state when I'd wakened?

But I hadn't stayed. That fact pulled others along with it I had felt wonderfully warm, uncaring, relaxed, yet I'd fought into wakefulness. Brainwashing, the word poked at me again. The technique was an established fact, it worked, but not with everyone. That was equally known though the reasons were not clear. I was disturbed at what I'd experienced, not for the experience itself but for the propensities in it. The approach to emotional and mental conditioning lent itself to abuses. Had it been abused with Beth? It would explain their isolation of her, the abrupt mood changes I'd witnessed in her, a succumbing, then a struggling to regain independent thought and a succumbing again. Had she been a mental prisoner, then a physical one? How far had they subverted Adam's teachings? How far had they strayed from the spirit of his message?

I reached the monastery, started to turn toward Adam's door, and halted. The session had added nothing concrete, only another possible link in the chain I'd woven, a chain made of *ifs* and *maybes*. It was still all suspicions and they were not enough; I was too tired to fence with words and examine the uses of preconditioning techniques. But that was not the whole thing, I admitted as I turned away and walked to my room. What if I laid attempted murder to Randy, Joan, and Judy, or even implied it strongly, if it had been Peter? The hurt to Adam would be searing, the error perhaps beyond remedy. He would see me as mean of spirit, vicious, someone willing to think the worst with but only suspicion, only constructions of conspiracy. Indeed, could he see me any other way? I refused to cast myself in that role yet, not with Peter's all-too-real candidacy. And there was Multy, not to be forgotten in the shuffling about of suspects. I reached my room, closed the door, and undressed quickly. I would put away further thoughts and meet Adam's disappointment in the morning. Speculation was an unrewarding pursuit, I decided, nothing but a maker of shadows. I fell into bed and was asleep in moments.

I woke to the morning sun, my mind starting to marshal instant answers for Adam's reaction. When I opened the door to go out to the bathroom, I found the small square of notepaper, read the strong script aloud to myself.

Patricia—you must know I am disappointed. We'll talk tonight, after dinner. I must spend the day with some gentlemen from the county assessor's office on property matters concerning the community. I should like you to spend the day away from Cashelderg, as a favor to me. I fear for the strain it seems to be putting on you. Till tonight—Adam.

I folded the note, put it in the pocket of my robe. I'd do as he asked, stay away from my work for today, I decided. I felt I owed Adam that. Besides, I welcomed the time to think, unable to admit that I was more than uneasy about rushing back into the castle. Yet I would go back, I knew that, too, but a day away wouldn't hurt. I finished dressing finally, donned a skirt and a sweater, and sauntered to breakfast late, found I was quite alone with my morning tea and sweet roll. I spent the early part of the morning going over some of my notes, putting them into order and starting to transcribe some others. But it was labored, other thoughts nagging at me, persistent, demanding attention. I put everything away and decided to go down to the shore, hoping the timeless calm of the sea would wash over me, figuratively, at least.

I walked out into the day, saw the sun was high and warm, and headed for the path that led down behind Cashelderg. I was almost past the huge structure when the little green-capped form stepped out in front of me.

"I was waiting for you," he said, thin accusation in his tone.

"I'm not going to do any work today," I replied. The gimlet eyes widened a fraction.

"Your idea?" he questioned sharply and once again I felt the force of the shrewd, acute mind behind that elf-dwarf exterior.

"Partly. Adam thought I was showing the strain," I replied. Multy grunted, a sharp little sound that carried a comment I couldn't discern. His hard, bright little eyes stared at me for a minute more, and then he turned, started off down the edge of the cliff, leaning to one side as though he'd topple over at any moment. I watched him go and wondered if I were watching the one who had tried to kill me. I shivered at the thought and turned away, hurried down the narrow path to the sea.

I lay down on the sand a dozen yards or so down the beach, near one of the giant rocks, fought down the temptation to go over my three areas of suspicion again. It would be merely replowing the same soil with nothing new to add yet. The sun was already moving down toward the latter part of the day. I could, I would, hold out against speculation, I told myself, closing my eyes and listening to the distant cry of the sea birds and the soft sound of a gentle surf. I must have fallen asleep because I heard nothing until the voice cut into my halfway world.

"Beachcombing is looking up," I heard it say, opened my eyes and sat up to see the tall, spider-legged shape standing there. "I expected you'd be at work combing castle architecture," Lee Farrell said.

"I decided to take a day off," I said, trying not to sound snappish. His wide, disarrayed face beamed down with irritating affableness.

"Your idea?" he asked and I felt my frown at once.

"That seems to be the question of the day," I retorted. "Adam suggested the day off might be a good thing and I agreed."

"Mister Sincerity," Lee grunted and I turned an angry glare at him. His genial smile stayed entirely unaffected.

"I had enough of your cynicism last time," I shot at him. He lowered himself to squat down beside me, dismissing my remark with a shrug.

"Speaking of last time, have you told anyone else about people trying to kill you?" he asked.

"Why?" I asked, suddenly cautious.

"I just wondered," he countered casually. "Whether you're sure." His eyes didn't match the pleasant smile on his face, little glints of sharpness in the center of each orb.

"I'm sure," I snapped. His smile widened.

"Enough for yourself but not for anyone else," he commented.

"That's not a new situation for me," I said, no waspishness in my voice now, the statement all too true. I pressed hands into the firm sand, pushed myself up, and Lee rose with me.

"I'd be careful until I'm sure," he remarked almost idly.

"Thanks," I returned. "No more practical explanations of the letter?" I queried, unable to resist the dig.

"Not yet," he answered calmly. Somehow, I had the feeling that he was both gauging me and trying to say something in veiled terms, and once again I was irritated by his attitude. I turned, nodded briskly, and started back to the pathway that led up from the shoreline. I felt his eyes watching me but I refused to look around, climbing up the little path and turning only when I'd reached the top. His loose-jointed figure was moving on along the sand and I watched him, wondering again about Lee Farrell's change from concerned interest to prodding cynicism.

The sun was touching the horizon's edge across the sea, I noted, and I headed back over the rise. I saw Judy and Joan as I reached the old monastery, off to one side in earnest conversation, and grew angry at myself for the moment's flare of suspicion I felt. I went to my room, washed the sand from my hands, combed my hair, and returned down the corridor to the dining hall. Randy and Joseph were at the table as I arrived and Judy came later.

"Joan's not eating with us tonight," she announced. "She's not feeling well." I waited, watching the door, and Adam finally entered after dinner had been served. His bright-fire eyes met mine and I saw a kind of sternness in them and felt chastised immediately. He took his place next to me and his smile was reserved.

"Did you rest and relax today?" he asked and I nodded. "I'm glad," he said. "When dinner's over, before we talk, I'm going to ask some questions here. I want you to listen carefully to the answers." Once again I nodded and realized how much I needed his strength. Without looking, I could feel Peter's baleful eyes, accusing, angry. When the meal ended, Adam tapped his glass and rose. I saw the room of faces turn to him with wide-eyed, waiting attention. He gestured to a thin girl with blonde braided hair. "Jennifer, how have you felt since becoming one of the Disciples of Light?" he asked.

"At peace," Jennifer answered at once. "With myself and with everyone else. I'm not full of anxiety anymore."

"How about you, Richard?" Adam asked of a young man with thick curly hair.

"I'm not afraid anymore," Richard answered. "I'm not alone."

"And you, Leila?" Adam asked a girl with sad eyes.

"Fulfilled. I'm part of something beyond myself. I'm in safe hands," she said.

"Terence?" Adam prodded. A black-haired man half-rose.

"Life has a meaning, to serve God, to follow his word in Scripture as you show us how to do," he said.

"Amy?" Adam asked.

"I feel love," Amy replied. "I feel warm and secure."

"Thank you," Adam said. "Have a good night. Enjoy each other." He turned to me and I watched the others rise, start out, and I wondered if his parting admonition had been planned or a sudden dividend. He took my arm, walked with me to his rooms, and closed the door, turned to face me.

"What you heard just now is the heart of it," Adam said. "It touches on last night, on you, on my existence. Peace, not being anxious or afraid. Fulfillment, meaning, warmth, love. Aren't those the things we all want? Aren't those the goals we all reach to find? Are they something to turn from?"

"No," I answered as he paused, waited. There was no other answer. Indeed they were the things everyone wanted in life.

"I wanted you to gain an insight into the real sense of those things last night," Adam said. "I was terribly disappointed when I found you'd broken away and left the session. I expected you'd understand and stay."

I felt suddenly traitorous. "I'm sorry, Adam. Really, I am," I apologized.

"They were attempting to break through conscious, conditioned resistance, that's all," Adam said. "It's necessary, particularly at the beginning."

"I know, Adam. That didn't bother me of itself," I replied.

"Something bothered you. You left. You ran," he countered. I felt my lips turn in, realized that my answers to that were still unformed.

"I know why, Patricia," he said, his voice suddenly filled with gentleness. His arms reached out, pulled me to him. "You were frightened at how wonderful you felt for a brief moment. That can frighten, the sheer wondrousness of it can be upsetting."

I heard his words, was unsure of agreement. "I think the method frightened me, Adam," I said. "That way of breaking through conditioned resistance." I paused, gathered the question together carefully. "Don't you think it can be abused too easily?"

Adam's smile was slow, full of wisdom. "Can be? Or are you saying it has been?" he asked. "Beth and Saturday buses again? I thought I'd answered that."

I backed away, unwilling to raise objections yet. "You answered it, Adam. I just keep wondering about methods and means of reaching people," I said.

"Giving oneself over takes time," Adam said.

"I'm sorry. I just don't know what that really means, yet. I guess I'm not ready to know. Maybe I never will be. Maybe I'm too conditioned," I said, leaning my head against his chest.

"Nonsense," he murmured into my hair. "You're tired of being alone, of making every decision on your own. You want love."

He touched truths and yet I wondered. Did independence and love have to be opposites? Was it impossible to have them both together? His hands moved, pressed warmth into my shoulders, an electric touch, and I dismissed inner questions.

"A time has come, Patricia, a time for you and me," he said.

"Has it, Adam?" I heard myself ask, await his answer, his deciding for me. It was a new feeling, disquieting yet not without appeal.

"Yes," he whispered, and his hands moved again, slowly, down over my breasts, soft strength that lighted instant fires only waiting to be sparked. I opened my lips for his mouth, pushed myself against his hands, my body suddenly serpentine. "You will know new dimensions of love here, Patricia," I heard him whisper. "I will teach them to you."

Perhaps there would be, I thought, but this was enough, a dimension enough for my needs. My blouse came undone and I felt my hands unbuttoning, unhooking, offering. I pressed my skin against his warmth, clung to the sweeping, embracing vibrancy of him as though I could somehow absorb it through my pores. I saw the lamp go off and the rest was made of wanting, ecstasy, desire made tangible, the word made flesh.

Later I lay with my nakedness against him, drained yet fulfilled. It was never right the first time, usually, not for me. There was always strangeness in the midst of intimacy, a residual foreignness that disappeared only with time. But Adam's encompassing vibrancy, that special gift of his, had swept the usual aside, turning lovemaking into more than a sensual exchange, so much more that I needed time to be alone, to sort out all the new and unexpected things that he had brought to our togetherness. Reluctantly, I moved from his arms, pulled on clothes, and then turned once again to him, folded myself into the warm circle of his auburn handsomeness.

"You can give yourself over," he smiled down at me.

"That way," I admitted.

"That way is a sign," he said. "In all things we serve. In all things we obey. It is a beginning."

I leaned into his chest. I didn't want to examine, dissect, add more to what had happened. Loving to me was still a very personal wanting, visceral not intellectual. I'd given myself completely but I hadn't denied myself. That distinction still held firm inside me.

"Sleep well. Tomorrow will be more than a new day," Adam said, brushing my face with his lips. I moved from his arms, turned, and slipped outside, began the walk up the long corridor to my room. There, I quickly flung clothes off and stretched out under the bedcovers, running hands down along my body where Adam's hands had caressed, touched, held, reliving with the fingertips. It had been more than wonderful with Adam. He had surrounded the sensual pleasures with other dimensions, a comforting, encompassing totality that had extended the senses into the spirit. It had been a new experience for me, a distinction in being comforted. To Adam, all roads led to one place. There was nothing that did not include the spiritual. Perhaps that was the right way. For me, there had always been a division between the spiritual and the temporal and I had to wonder now if that was wrong, a reflection of how we compartmentalize our every emotion and thought in a compartmentalized world. I heard his words again. *In all things we serve. In all things we obey.* I still was unable to make the connections. I loved, and love was neither serving nor obeying. It was a thing alone, of itself a totally singular, unique state which encompassed those things along with a hundred more. But perhaps that was only my conditioning again, old errors that needed reexamination. I was willing to learn, to listen, to sit at Adam's knee, literally and figuratively. Certainly he had brought to others here those deep and basic feelings I had heard catalogued: comfort, peace, fulfillment, love. He had created here a kind of oasis of contentment. Certainly the foundation blocks for that, whatever they were, could not be dismissed.

It made the other shadows that hung over Cashelderg that much more horrible. There was evil here in Adam's oasis. How much of that evil had its roots in the same things that brought others contentment? Did Adam's teachings, his methods, really hold any responsibility? Or, if guilt lay with Randy and Judy and Joan, were they simply distorted aberrations of Adam's work here? I found myself calling back thoughts, putting a rein on runaway conclusions. I still had nothing but suspicions. I could not weave further threads until I knew more. But as I felt myself starting to grow heavy-lidded, I had to wonder why I kept coming back to Randy, Joan, and Judy. Peter could have been the one, alone that morning, off by himself. And Multy, too. I had catalogued all their motives, their opportunities, their abilities to attempt murder. Why did I keep returning in my thoughts to the three Disciples of Light? Somehow it had to connect with something deep down inside myself, perhaps an unreasoned reaction, even a strange prejudice of some kind. Somewhere, it rubbed against something I could not define, a locked-away, instinctual stand. Rationally, they were no more suspect than Peter or Multy, perhaps less so. But then, I answered grimly, nothing here at Cashelderg had been rational.

I turned over, closed away thoughts, and let sleep wrap itself around me. In moments, I was fast asleep and the night held the world. Hours had passed when I snapped awake, the night already on its slow climb toward morning. I sat up with hands dug into the sheets, my skin wet with perspiration, hearing the sound of my harsh breathing. The dream had come again, the very same again, the great hall ablaze with light and laughter and then everything swept away. Only terror remained and I was fleeing death.

I sat for a moment, then swung from the bed, pulling on jeans and a sweater, stepping into shoes. It was suddenly not just clear but terribly defined. I had to go to Cashelderg. I'd gone there once in the night to seek a sign and had whispered pleas into the silent dark. They had gone unanswered. I had been brought here, shown the place. It was enough, perhaps all that could be given. Yet there were answers waiting in Cashelderg, waiting for me to find for myself. The certainty was absolute, beyond questioning, a message too strong to come simply from within my own unresolved state. I took the heavy flashlight and was suddenly made of impatience.

I rebelled at going back down the long corridor and opened the window, clambered over the sill, and down onto the ground. Hurrying across the rise, Cashelderg's massive bulk blotted out the night itself, waiting, implacable. I slipped inside, switched the flashlight on, and moved into the great hall. This time there was no standing in the blackness, no fearful pleas. This time I was like someone who had mislaid something and searched fever-ishly for it. I moved from room to room, the light sweeping back and forth in each, crossing and recrossing the empty rooms I had so meticulously examined, rooms I had come to feel comfortable in, and now I was as if poised to spring, my mind tuned to catch at any overlooked thing that promised a new meaning. It was here, somewhere here in Cashelderg, something that would tell me more Perhaps it would be but another piece of the puzzle, but it would be something. I moved through the dark rooms mutter-ing in impatience and frustration. Perhaps it was somewhere else, a place I had yet to explore, I pondered. Perhaps what I sought lay in the depths of the cellar.

I shook away the thought. The cellar might hold things but not what I sought now. It was here, closer, my certainty too strong to ignore. I moved through another room, found nothing, hur-ried on to another and then still another and finally to the last. It was the room where the wooden chest protruded from the wall and I turned the light on it, froze, heard the gasp of surprise from my lips. The drawer was pulled out, open, and I stepped closer. The old documents I'd gone through inside it had revealed noth-ing but it held something else now. I moved closer, stared down at a thin, leather-covered book, hardly more than a manuscript. It hadn't been there when I'd gone through the drawer before. I'd looked at every piece in it.

I reached in, ran my hands across the leather, saw that the cover was bound with narrow strips of hide. I propped the flashlight up against the edge of the opened drawer and drew the book out, using both hands. It didn't come apart with age but was obviously well preserved. I opened the thin leather cover to stare down at the first page of what I estimated to be not more than a half dozen parchment pages, the same kind of parchment as the letter that had been sent me. The first page bore large, black uncial letters that stared back at me, hand-lettered lines completely legible.

The Curse of Cashelderg
As Recorded
In This
Year of 1351 anno
domini
by
Justus, Chronicler to Lord
Brendan O'Donnell

I felt my lips dry, ran my tongue over them, took the flashlight, and sank down to sit on the stones of the floor, cross-legged, the ancient manuscript on my lap. Using the flashlight as a lamp, I began to read the large, black uncials that began the second page:

What is set down here was witness and attested to by many, including the writer. It tells the events of one single night, and of those things that bore on that night.

It is best and fitting to begin with that night of celebration, a great feast and party for the wedding night of Rory O'Donnell, son of Lord Brendan O'Donnell, master of Cashelderg and all its vast lands. Rory

O'Donnell had, but a few hours before, taken in marriage the very beautiful Mourne Moynihan, the combining of two great houses, indeed. Guests had come from all the counties of Ireland and from the continent for the occasion.

It was an especially happy one for Lord Brendan for Rory O'Donnell had been a trial and a heartache for too many years, a poor gambler, a heavy drinker, and a quick-tempered, selfish horseman. A handsome, charming lad, he had gained a continent's reputation as a rake and had been chased over half of Europe by enraged husbands and irate lovers and had killed at least six men in duels. Only Lord Brendan's wealth and influenece saved him from many a jail.

But he had returned home to settle down finally and after six months, the marriage vows to Mourne Moynihan were announced. The wedding followed quickly and Lord Brendan had arranged a great banquet for the honored guests and members of the O'Donnell clan. He had arranged another party outside for the servants, shopkeepers and tenant farmers who rented land from the vast O'Donnell domain. Only one of these families failed to come, that of Arar Conahey. They even refused to send a gift to the wedding. Aran Conahey, a huge man with a huge family, was a brooding, bitter sort. He had had two daughters, Pegeen and Margaret, both of who worked at Cashelderg as maidservants. Before becoming betrothed to Mourne Moynihan, Rory O'Donnell was said to have often visited Pegeen Conahey, and there were rumors of promises he'd made to her. Then one night, Pegeen never returned home, leaving a note at Cashelderg that she'd run away.

Only a few weeks later, the second daughter, Margaret, followed her sister's example and ran off in the night when the marriage to Mourne Moynihan was announced. Aran Conahey blamed Rory O'Donnell for having broken his daughters' hearts with charm and promises and became bitter as gall over it.

So it came to pass that the wedding night of Rory O'Donnell filled Cashelderg with music and laughter and the rejoicing flowed over the four counties where O'Donnell land lay fertile and rich. The great party was at its peak when suddenly the doors of the castle were flung open. Aran Conahey stormed in, followed by his huge family, each man armed with axe, blade, or lance.

"Filthy, murdering beast," Aran cried out, pointing his arm at Rory O'Donnell. "Spawn of the devil."

Lord Brendan stepped forward to demand an explanation.

"Here's my explanation," Aran Conahey thundered, stepping aside as others swung the bodies of Pegeen and Maggie Conahey to the floor. "They never ran away. I never believed it of either of them. Each night I searched and finally I found them, down in the cellar of this very house. He killed them when he was finished with them, when they were becoming a problem. *Murderer,* he is."

Everyone's eyes had turned to Rory and Aran Conahey's words needed no reply. The guilt was plain to see in the spoiled, selfish face of Rory O'Donnell.

"Cashelderg is a place of betrayal. There will never be anything but death and unhappiness here. That is the curse I leave on you," Aran Conahey roared. With that, he flung his lance. It caught Rory O'Donnell full in the chest and killed him almost at once. A terrible wind swept through the hall, blowing out every candle.

The O'Donnell men rushed forward to attack Conahey and the battle swept out into the night to rage across the countryside. When it was over, many were slain on both sides and the wedding night became a wake.

Even in death, Rory O'Donnell had been true to form. It turned out that Mourne Moynihan was with child before the wedding. She closed the castle to all and had the child who grew up to carry on the O'Donnell name.

I paused as the lettering changed character and hand, obviously followed by another scribe who filled in a kind of addendum.

Mourne O'Donnell's son, Padrig, grew up to carry on the O'Donnell name and the curse of Cashelderg. He married at twenty-one and his bride was killed soon after their first child when a carriage overturned. He married again and was killed by his second wife in a quarrel. The child became Sir Dulin O'Donnell and when he brought his bride to Cashelderg she fell in love with a Captain in the guards and Sir Dulin was slain in a duel. She flung herself from a cliff some years later in remorse though not before a son was born, Brian O'Donnell. His childhood and marriages were plagued by tragedies and he finally left Cashelderg in failing health, betrayed by his wives and scarred by life.

Hereso inscribed, 1601, a.d.

I turned the last page, closed the thin book, and snapped the light off to sit in the inky blackness for a moment. Sir Brian O'Donnell, the last direct descendant to live here at Cashelderg, writer of the letter I had received, I pondered. The old chronicle had given no final answers but it was a sign, a confirmation of the dream, of visions and warnings, imprints of yesterday somehow sent me for tomorrow. How? That lay beyond all answering, as steeped in the unknown as all the other premonitions and extrasensory perceptions I'd had. That was as unknown, as unexplainable to me now as it had been to Elizabeth Pilligram and Mary Godfrey when they were burned as witches. They had no answers for *how*. I could give none now. But *why* remained an answer for here and now, one on which my life hung, I was convinced.

The dream—vision and warning—had begun and continued from the moment I'd decided to come here to Cashelderg. Whether I had come by happenstance, coincidence, or moved by forces beyond our knowing, by coming I had become part of whatever was here. The ancient manuscript in my lap spoke of death and betrayal here. It told of happenings long past, yet it addressed itself to this very moment. But whose death, I pondered? Mine? Or someone else's? *Cashelderg is a place of betrayal,* Aran Conahey had cried. Betrayal of what? Adam's teachings? Of love and happiness? Or of the spirit of life itself?

I snapped the flashlight on, pulled myself up, and started from the castle, clutching the old manuscript to me. As I moved through the cavernous rooms in the silent dark, only the narrow beam of the flashlight cutting a path, I wondered again who had left the chronicle waiting there for me to find. I grunted almost derisively. Who had sent the letter from Sir Brian? I'd let Lee Farrell go on to find his rational, reasonable answers, certain he'd not find the real ones there. Yet now I had to wonder if there just had to be an answer rooted in the ordinary, the mundane. It would be so welcome, clearing away so much that shadowed the soul. I wondered, and wanted it so, and knew no rational, reasoned explanation would suffice.

I'd reached the front doors, slipped out into the remains of the night. A predawn mist had risen from the ground, layering the land with a diaphanous blanket and a halfmoon afforded enough light. I moved through it up to my knees, across the rise and down the other side. I'd go back through the window and I drew near the building when I halted, peered through the gray half-light. Something moved just outside my window. I half-crouched, instinctive movements out of some vestigial animal sense, crept forward, and saw a figure at my window, half-visible in the mist. My hand clenched the flashlight as I took another step forward, heard my shoe dislodge a small stone. It rolled noisily. The figure at the window ducked down into the low layer of mist.

"Stop," I called out, a hollow reaction. The moon reflected from the low layer of mist, giving it an opaqueness it didn't possess. I could see no one as I reached the window, my flashlight upraised to strike. But I was alone. Whoever it was had fled. I stayed at the window, crouched down into the mist, and let my eyes roam across the gray-white top of the opaque blanket. I shifted my glance up to the rise and the black, towering bulk of Cashelderg beyond it. I waited, squinting, and then suddenly I saw movement on the rise, the figure scurrying along, half silhoutted by the moon. The walk was unmistakable, even at this distance in the moonlight, the uneven, crablike tilted movement.

"Multy," I breathed inwardly. Multy hurrying over the rise. Multy here at my window, peering in. Why? To see if I were really asleep? To make certain? Or to do something more? I rose, climbed over the window ledge, and closed the window, latching it. I pulled the drape, and put the old manuscript under the bed, and undressed. Sliding under the covers, I lay still and felt tiredness flowing over me. I had little mental strength left for powderings. There'd be time enough for that in the morning. Aran Conahey had found horror in the cellar of Cashelderg. Was it a place of further horror? Was that the real message in the old manuscript? Was that why it had been left for me to find? Left by whom? The questions only circled each other endlessly. I turned my face to the pillow and smothered them.

CHAPTER NINE

The night was with me when I woke in the morning, impatience pulling me from bed. Messages and meanings raced about my mind like so many undisciplined children in a schoolyard. I had no need for breakfast, not even tea, to help snap me awake. Pulling the drape back, I unlatched the window and gazed out at the rise where I'd seen Multy's figure in the night.

Had he left the old manuscript for me? I wondered. He knew of the curse, had warned me that Cashelderg was a cursed place. The thought arched itself backwards. Could he have, in some way, known about the letter that brought me here? Was there that connection Adam had first been so sure existed? And why was Multy peering in at my window last night? Was he nothing more than a harmless little voyeur, availing himself of an opportunity? The thought was out of place, yet perhaps no more so than anything else here. But one thing stayed firmly in place. I had to see the cellar of Cashelderg. I had to know if that was the meaning in the old manuscript.

I took my tool bag, hung it from my waist, and picked up the big flashlight. I pushed the window open and swung over the sill as I had in the dark of night. I wanted to avoid Adam until I'd seen the cellar for myself. I hurried across the ground and down the other side of the rise to the massive timbered doors, slipped inside the castle, and halted, listening. I heard only the silence and moved down the side hall to the end where the stone steps led down to the cellar. The daylight filtered down only to the first flight where a small landing marked a sharp right-angle turn in the steps. I paused there for a moment, snapped the flashlight on, and started down the rest of the steps. A stone, arched entranceway appeared at the bottom of the steps, a metal door standing open to one side of the arched entrance. I took a deep breath as I went the last few steps. The thought that lurked inside me refused to stay imprisoned any longer. Would I find Beth down here, held a prisoner, perhaps being subject to some form of punishment? The question, freed, hurled the other shattering thoughts with it. Would I, like Aran Conahey, find the terrible face of death down here?

I took another step nearer the arched entranceway to the cellar and let the light hold on the metal door for a moment. I halted, felt my skin grow cold. Something was wrong. The metal door was left open invitingly but that was nothing itself. It could have been left open a hundred years ago. Yet there was something wrong. I saw it before realizing it, knew it before comprehending it. The eye becomes trained, seeing things with instant reaction, as conditioned as Pavlov's dogs. My eyes were conditioned to the search for authenticity, the recognition of true Gothic art and architecture, always alert to the encrustations and deviations of later additions.

Most often, these additions were no attempt to delude but simply the work of other craftsmen centuries later, often in the Gothic style but nonetheless impure and not true Gothic. One had to keep one's eyes open, catching the details that betrayed or authenticated. It became an automatic thing and so my eyes had held on the metal door, reacting instantly to the workmanship at the lock and the strip edging the bottom of the door itself. The open door had been added later, in the 1600s, I guessed, the craftsmanship not true Gothic. With that automatic observation, I noiced the cellar just beyond the entranceway was floored with wide, wooden planks. I also noticed, almost abstractly, that the thick dust of the wooden flooring around the open door of the entranceway had been scuffed and partly wiped away. I let my light probe deeper into the cellar. The rest of the flooring beyond bore a layer of gray-white dust. I brought the light back to the entranceway. The door hadn't been opened a hundred years ago, nor ten years ago, nor a month ago.

I stepped closer to the arched entranceway into the cellar. I could only see directly ahead as high stone sides of the entrance blocked my view to the right and to the left. Grimly, almost unwillingly, I edged as close as possible to the floorboards just past the entranceway. Bracing myself with one hand against the stone side, I lifted my foot, stretched forward, and came down as hard as I could on the first wide floorboard just inside the entranceway. I heard the snap as it gave way in the center where I came down on it and I leaped backwards just as death hurtled from above. Flattened against the wall, I saw the polearms come crashing down into the flooring, four of them imbedding themselves with a sickening thud into the wood. The long weapons quivered there, two halberds and two pikes, I saw as I stood still and the sound slowly died away and the dust swirled upwards in little circular spirals.

I pushed from the wall, edged carefully around the stone sides of the entranceway, around the polearms that clustered together in a towering bouquet of death. Inside the cellar itself, I swung the flashlight upward, saw the thin cords dangling from a wide cross-beam. I swung the light first to the right side of the beam, then back across to the left, following the trail of thin cord. The device had been carefully rigged, medieval in its simple effectiveness. Even the old ladder was still in place against one wall. Someone had climbed it, crawled out on the beam, and positioned the weapons over the entranceway. Then they had run a light string along the beam and down to the ends of the wide floorboard. When the floorboard was broken in the center, it triggered the device. The thin string snapped, releasing the cords holding the polearms, and the weapons hurtled down.

I let the light go over the device again, staring at it. My reconstruction was plainly accurate but a tiny something pushed at me. I couldn't define it and so dismissed it and simply stared now at the long weapons as they stood imbedded in the floorboard. Had I simply walked through the open door, my foot would have fallen through the weakened floorboard, holding me in place as the huge lances hurtled down to rip through me.

The cleverness matched the enormity of it and thoughts rushed forward, clicking off connections. The old manuscript had indeed been left as a sign for me. Whoever left it knew that its story would lead me to search further, to come down here to the cellar, and now there was but a single name that rose up before me. Multy. He had been the one at my window and then scurrying along the rise. He had come here after I'd left and set up the device, first leaving the old manuscript for me to find. He had probably expected that I'd find it in the morning but I'd hurried that part of his plan along a little. The main part had turned out as planned, however, *almost*. Why he'd paused to peer in at my window hardly mattered now. It seemed beyond question that it had been Multy all along. I felt a sense of sadness, a disappointment which I knew I'd no right to feel. He was a strange, twisted little man whose anger at my presence here had been apparent from the very first, a mind distorted with its own aberrant reasoning.

But I felt an anger of my own rising inside me. I wouldn't give him the chance to meet me casually outside as he had the other times and once again hand me hurried explanations for his whereabouts. No, this time I wanted that final statement. This time I wanted him to come down here looking for the results of his handiwork. Beyond that, my anger rebelled at the motive underlying all that had happened to stop me. I had come here to Cashelderg for a purpose and I'd continue to serve that purpose. I was here in the architectural riches of the cellar and I'd continue on as if nothing had happened while I waited to see his tilted little form appear. Routine, that web of repeated behavior, of insignificant little acts to which we become conditioned, is of itself far from insignificant. It is the emotional cement that holds us together and lets us function. I turned and walked on into the cellar, letting the flashlight cut a path for me.

It was a trenchlike place of stone walls, the center flooring of wide planked board and dirt passages extending into arched areas. Using the light, hammer, and chisel, I quickly became absorbed in my work, found that the builders had used a strong mixture of lime-mortar and rubble. Because the foundation went deep, nearing the sea at one side, I saw that deep pilings had been sunk, leveled off. I knelt, dug with a small hoe I carried, verified the construction technique. On the piles a layer of wooden planks had been laid, dowelled into the piles. On this the footings of the stone walls had been put into place. Where solid rock was encountered, it was leveled off and the wall footings placed over it. The trenches and cellar areas were then hollowed out and the concrete foundation stones put into place. I had become so absorbed, carried away, making notes by transferring the light to one hand and scribbling in my pad with the other, that I suddenly realized that I had been at work for hours. Multy hadn't come. I'd have heard any footsteps on the stone stairs. The cellar magnified every sound. He hadn't come to check on the results of his careful planning. Perhaps he was being extra careful. I returned to my work, continued the slow process of making my notes by flashlight.

Another hour passed, then almost another, and I was finished. I had gathered a wealth of valuable material and I'd examined the dirt and stone cellar for a trace of where Pegeen and Margaret Conahey had been buried. I saw one corner fenced off by an iron line of pickets, but I couldn't be sure. And Multy hadn't come, no one had crept down the stairs to make certain of success. Perhaps he was so certain of it that he felt no need to see for himself. I wouldn't wait any longer, I decided. Putting my things into the tool bag, I moved back through the tunnelled arches of the cellar, edged around the polearms, and felt the satisfaction of having cheated death.

I flashed the light up onto the high ceiling beam and the dangling cords once more, felt my frown as I stared up at the mechanics of murder. I lowered the light, shone it on the blades imbedded in the floorboards, and was just about to turn away when something glinted in the light. I bent down to the boards, an inch from one of the halberds, and picked up the button, square, gold with a tiny black dot in the center. It could have come from a waistcoat, a man's jacket perhaps, or possibly a sport shirt. I slipped it into the pocket of my jeans and rose, turned away, and hurried up the steps. At the top, I switched the light off and hurried down the side corridor to the timbered doors and outside. I paused there, made my steps slow and deliberate and expected the little, tilted form to pop out from someplace, gimlet eyes masking his surprise, words offering an excuse for his absence. But he was no place and I tarried awhile longer, then turned and walked over the rise.

The afternoon was beginning to nod to dusk as I neared the old monastery and I saw Adam coming toward me, his face stern, his intense eyes carrying anger.

"You were at Cashelderg," he said. "I suspected as much. I thought you'd agreed to stay away from there."

"I'm sorry, Adam," I began. He cut in commandingly.

"I thought last night was more than an understanding of bodies, Patricia," he said.

"It was, Adam, but I had to find out something for myself," I said. "Please, let me show you." The sternness stayed in his face but he followed me to my room. I reached under the narrow bed and pulled out the old manuscript. He sank down on the bed and read it, his brow darkening as he turned each page. When he finished, he stared up at me.

"Where did you get this?" he asked. "What does it mean to you?"

I told him how I'd found the chronicle, of how I'd gone to Cashelderg in the night, prompted by the dream. Then I hurried words on, recounting what had happened but a few hours earlier in the morning and how I'd seen Multy in the night. When I finished, his eyes stared out into space and he muttered words that seemed as much for himself as for me.

"Multy. It was him, all along. It had to have been him," Adam murmured.

"I guess so. But it doesn't explain everything," I said. He looked up at me, frowned.

"You mean the letter," he said. "I've no answer for that. But the rest was Multy. You've spelled it out yourself. It's plain as the sun, right down to his not showing up today. No doubt he thought it wisest not to come around. He's probably run off someplace for a while."

I nodded, turned, and stared out the window, a frown pulling at my brow. Adam rose, his hands pressing my waist. "You're still wondering about the letter, aren't you?" he said. "You're wondering who sent it to you."

"Who, why, how," I answered.

"Forget about it. It's not important anymore. It doesn't matter now," Adam commented. I pressed lips tight, kept my silence.

Perhaps I could lock it away in a corner of the mind where it would only throb occasionally but I could never forget it. There were too many reasons that were mine alone for that, things I'd yet to tell Adam about. I felt Adam pull me to him.

"And you stay away from Cashelderg until we've put a final end to this," he admonished.

"Yes, what are we going to do about Multy? I don't have any hard proof," I remarked.

Adam's lip pursed. "I don't know. We'll talk about that after dinner. Right now I've a meeting of the community finance committee. I'll see you at dinner," he said, kissed my forehead, and hurried away. I stayed in the room for a few moments, put the old manuscript atop the bed. I felt restless, strangely unsatisfied. I had the important answer, the identity of the one who had tried to kill me, and yet there was so much that remained unanswered. Would it stay that way? I wondered. Would it become one more riddle added to the continuing question for which there was no rational, empirical answer? Would it become one more part of those other visions, premonitions, dreams I'd had before and for which I could assign no reasoned explanation?

I shook my head impatiently, unwilling to accept the thought, pulled the door open, and hurried outside, a kind of frustrated anger filling me with impatience. I was tired of the unfinished, of explanations that always left as much unanswered as answered. If there were to be things beyond answering once again, I wanted them separated from the rational. I would have no overlapping, amorphous endings. Still buried in my thoughts, I walked briskly, turned along the edge of the cliff, and strode on the narrow path there. I watched the sea slowly change from blue to lavender and then to gray as the sun began to slide along the line of the horizon. I'd walked perhaps half a mile when the woman appeared, coming toward me on the narrow path, a stocky, gray-haired woman, her hands in the front pocket of a long apron and a black shawl around her shoulders. She had a face that had known hard years and yet bore no resentment for them. She came to a halt as she neared and I met her stare with curiosity.

"You're her," she said and I frowned. "You're the one who came to Cashelderg. Multy gave me the looks of you."

"You're Bridget," I exclaimed in sudden realization. "Where's Multy?" I asked and felt myself draw caution around me at once. The woman was certainly very different from the little man.

"I was coming to ask you," she said. I felt the frown come to touch my brow again.

"Why?" I questioned.

"He never came home last night," the woman said. "He went out a little before midnight. He was bothered and he said there were some things he wanted to see about for himself."

I picked words carefully, my mind making its own quick additions to the woman's statements. "Did he often go out like that? At that hour?" I asked.

"Often enough," Bridget shrugged. "Multy was always going off on his own at funny times. But he always came back later."

"And last night he didn't," I finished, and she nodded slowly.

"Not this morning, either, not today at all," the woman said.

"Maybe he decided to go away for a few days," I suggested, watching her face intently. "Maybe he went visiting somewhere."

The woman shook her head and her eyes stayed on me. "No. No, he didn't go away," she said.

"What makes you so sure?" I pressed. Her face stayed expressionless, almost set.

"I went looking for him this morning. I went along the beach," she said. I waited, my eyes questioning. She drew her hands from the deep apron pocket, Multy's green cap held in her fingers. "I found this," she said, "wedged into one of the rocks, wet from the sea. Multy wouldn't go anywhere without it, not even around the corner. It was as much a part of him as his skin. Something's happened to him."

She pushed the cap at me and I took it, stared down at it, turned it over in my hands, and felt the dampness in it yet. My throat grew tight as I came to the large, uneven stain at one side around the inner band, red brown, the color of blood washed out with sea water. As I stared down at it, I heard Bridget's low, flat comment. "It wasn't there yesterday."

I continued to stare down at the stain and the little green cap, swallowed hard to relieve the tightness gripping my throat. Did it say all that Bridget feared, and so much more than she suspected? She was right, of course, and I heard her words repeating in my mind. He wouldn't go anywhere without it. Even I knew as much. It had been a part of him, of the tilted little figure, worn at the rakish angle as if it had grown atop his head. The line of it had been visible last night, I recalled, identifying as much as the leaning gait hurrying across the rise. Last night, I murmured inwardly, images leaping forward, suddenly sheathed in new shadows. The little green cap in my hands seemed to come alive, throbbing with a life of its own. What was its meaning? An accident, Bridget feared, but I discarded that at once. Whatever its meaning, whatever had happened to Multy, it had not been an accident, no more than his presence on the rise and at my window had been an accident.

Suddenly all the neat conclusions I'd put in place were no longer neat or in place. Suddenly, all that I'd so quickly put aside was rushing back with new questions riding piggyback atop of old. The red brown stain hypnotized, the portent of it as shattering as the polearms that had almost torn me in two. Did it shout out its own accusation, a cry for vindication? Did it cry out that I had seen nothing correctly, misinterpreted and misunderstood everything that had happened? If so, then his role had been something else, not that of a killer, certainly. If he had been slain, it was because of something he knew. Or, and my racing mind paused, for something he had found out. If he had been slain, if the red brown stain was indeed silent testimony to the worst of suspicions, then I had seen nothing correctly. I had to have time to think, to order thoughts into some semblance of logic, and I couldn't do it here with the woman's eyes waiting. I handed the cap back to her.

"I haven't seen him all day. I can't tell you anything, not now," I said. "But I'll find out whatever I can."

The woman's eyes absorbed. "I'd be beholden to you," she said, turned away, and started back the way she had come. I watched her trudge away, the green cap hanging from one hand, a lonely figure. I began to go back, trying to slow the whirling carousel of thoughts that spun inside my head. By the time I reached the old monastery it was almost dark and the carousel still spun wildly. I went to my room, lay down across the bed in the short time left before dinner.

What did it mean? I pondered with grim foreboding. The old manuscript lay closed, inches from my face, and I stared at it as if trying to will it to reveal its secrets. Had Multy left it for me or had someone else? Had Multy been killed because he had seen whoever put it there for me? Had he come upon the real killer or killers and paid the price? And why had he been at my window? Why had he run when I called out? I pushed myself up to a sitting position, angry at the questions that flooded the mind, too many, too quickly upon each other. I had to examine each one, discard it or assign it a proper answer, and there wasn't time for that now. I'd have dinner first, though I really wasn't hungry. But I'd take the time to slow the mind's whirling. Only one thing stood out with any real clarity. Something had happened to Multy. The cap and the red-brown stain were too indicting. I'd go over it all with Adam after dinner. Perhaps it was time I stopped trying to find answers all alone.

I freshened up, brushed my hair, and went down to the dining hall, to my place at the head table beside Adam. Joan, Randy, and Judy were in their places, as was the thin-faced boy, Joseph. I felt Adam's hand touch mine for a brief instant under the table and I was glad for its comfort. My eyes roamed across the big room, paused at Peter sitting between two young men. Adam was obviously keeping the tight watch on Peter. I felt a deep breath escape me. Was I, once more, sitting in the same room with someone who had tried to kill me?

"I've been asked when you're going to continue your after-dinner lectures," I heard Adam say.

"Not tonight," I answered quickly, saw Adam's eyes flick to me as he caught the moment of panic in my voice. "I'm still too on edge," I added.

"Of course," he said understandingly and his hand pressed my arm. I toyed with my food, ate a few mouthfuls, and scanned the faces around me. Everyone had that open, contented pleasantness I'd observed before, certainly an atmosphere that defied my dark wonderings. Each one was the same, except for Peter, who sat with his pale fire eyes brooding. Had he slipped away again in the night? I wondered. My eyes shifted to Randy, Joan, and Judy, their faces reflecting the same bright pleasantness. Only somewhere, someplace, the same was not the same. Somewhere, horror was masked by cleverness. My eyes turned from the trio, halted, and went back again, focusing on Judy, her blouse, a deep blue cotton with square gold buttons, each with a tiny black dot in the center of the gold square. I stared transfixed at the buttons, traveled down the line of them on her blouse. The third one from the top was missing.

I felt the trembling inside me, pulled my glance away to stare down at my plate, afraid my face would reveal the thoughts racing inside my head. Under the table, my hand crept into the pocket of my jeans, fingers closing around the small, square gold button there with the black dot in the center. I saw myself in the cellar, staring up at the cords and strings that had been part of the device of death and suddenly I knew why I had frowned as I'd looked up at it. Subconsciously, I'd wondered how one man, alone, could have rigged up the arrangement. My glance lifted to the trio across the table. Three, I grunted silently, how much more likely for three. How much more probable.

I looked away, heard Adam's voice asking me a question about what I'd found of architectural interest in the cellar. I answered, finding smiles, smooth words, little masks of my own. When the meal ended, I rose with Adam, whispered words quickly. "Please, we have to talk, Adam." His glance held instant concern and he took my arm, steered me from the room. Moments later, the door closed, I faced him inside his quarters as he appraised me with a frown.

"You're more upset than you were earlier. What's happened?" he questioned.

"I'm not sure," I said, spilling out the story of meeting Bridget and of the stained green cap. He said nothing and when I finished, his eyes waited. "Don't you see, Adam? What if it wasn't Multy at all?"

Patience crept into his eyes and a kind of dismissal that I rebelled at instantly. "Of course it was Multy," he replied. "You saw him last night, yourself. Apparently he had an accident afterwards. He probably ran in the dark, slipped, and went over the cliffside someplace."

"Bridget walked the beach and didn't find him anywhere," I reported.

"At some spots, he'd have gone over into the sea or landed where the outgoing tide would pull him with it," Adam said. "I'd say it's a piece of divine justice."

I rejected his answer. It was too neat, but then, Adam didn't reason out of the net of suspicions I had built. "What if it didn't happen that way?" I asked. "What if Multy wasn't the one? Maybe there are things here you don't suspect, Adam." My hand pressed against the button in my pocket as if to provide substance for my words.

"Methods being abused? Dark thoughts again, Patricia?" Adam smiled. "How many times must we set them aside?"

"What if it were so, Adam?" I persisted. "What if your techniques, your teachings, your methods, everything you have here, were being subverted, twisted?"

"By whom, Patricia? How? What do you have to justify such thoughts?" I felt myself retreat at once, faltering. I had suspicions, fears as justification. "Why do you cling so tenaciously to them?" he prodded. I grimaced inwardly. I clung tenaciously to my own constructions, certainly not to solid evidence. Even the button in my pocket might be explained. Perhaps it had fallen from her blouse on a previous visit to the cellar. I was not yet certain it was impossible. I still needed more to accuse.

"I think something very terrible could be here, Adam," I offered. "A terrible evil. Is that impossible for you to believe?"

"Yes," he answered, his voice ringing out. "And I see you do not understand, yet. There can't be evil here, not within the community, because we are a community of God, formed to do his work, his bidding. If evil exists, it can exist only outside the community. I don't think you grasp the essential meaning behind this, my dear."

"I guess not," I conceded. Adam's voice took on the strength of fervency.

"It is a scientific principle that two material objects, two bodies of any kind, cannot occupy the same space at the same time. It is an absolute that applies to truth and falsehood, good and evil, right and wrong. Just as no two physical bodies can occupy the same place at the same time, no two philosophic bodies can occupy the same space at the same time. Only one can prevail, in mental, spiritual, or physical space. Here, in the Disciples of Light, truth, right, God occupies this space."

"Someone tried to kill me, three times," I said.

"It had to be Multy," Adam replied. "Someone outside the community."

"Or Peter?" I offered. Adam's lips pursed in thought.

"We must consider that possibility," he replied. "Peter is here but not touched by truth. He is essentially outside the community."

Adam believed. He had faith. Against those strengths I had nothing yet. I needed more to make him see differently, certainly more solid evidence than I had now. And, as I looked into his eyes, I realized I needed more for myself as well and I turned away. His arm reached out, encircled my shoulders, comforting, strong.

"Get a good night's sleep. You'll see more clearly in the morning," he said, lifting my face to his. "This is nothing but a passing moment. There is so much more waiting for you." His kiss was quick and he stepped back, led me to the door. "Tomorrow will be a new day, a new light," he said in parting.

I wanted so much to believe that as I walked the dim corridor to my room. I was almost envious of his strength, his unwavering certainties. His positions on good and evil, right and wrong, were ordered strength, philosophic and spiritual blocks that rose up on each other with all the sweep of a Gothic arch. It compelled, drew one to it, and I wondered why I continued to hold back. I accepted physical absolutes but I distrusted absolutes in abstract things such as truth, right and wrong, error. It was an irrational dichotomy, I realized, as I closed the door of my room and pulled the drape over the window. I took the button from the pocket of my jeans and laid it alongside the old manuscript, stretched out across the bed, let my eyes stare at them side by side. I reviewed everything I had put together about Randy, Joan, and Judy. It all still held, more so now, if my original hypothesis was right that something had happened to Beth, that Peter's grim words had held truth. It all hung on that, my first article of unfaith, I murmured with grim appropriateness.

I reviewed Peter's role again, much the simpler. He could have slipped away again last night. Multy could have come upon him setting up the trap. But that brought me back to the old manuscript and who had left it for me. I couldn't see Peter as the one. I. stared at the leather cover. The old chronicle held the key to everything, I was convinced, a message somewhere. I had to start with a premise and work from it, I concluded. Multy had left it for me, I decided. He had left it and, somehow, had been slain for it. Then it had been left to lead me into finding something and not to my death.

I opened the leather cover, began to read the carefully lettered words again. Repetitious. Two things continued to stand out above all else, the curse Aran Conahey had shouted out and the place where he'd found his daughters. He had found horror in the cellar and I had followed that, but as I reread the words I frowned down at them. Perhaps I had been too literal. Perhaps where he had made his grisly discovery was not the message but that he had searched. I felt excitement spiraling inside me. He had searched for something, suspected it was there, and kept searching. Yes, I murmured silently, that's what the manuscript had to tell me, to search, to seek unlikely places. I rose, strapped on the tool bag, tying it around my belt, excitement gripping me now.

Multy had been very interested in Beth's sudden leaving, I recalled. He kept a count of such things through his friend who delivered milk. Why? I wondered. What had he suspected? I paused, adjusted the little tool bag at my waist. I had to return to Cashelderg and search further. But where? I had gone over the castle itself, and the cellar now, also. What was left to search? The word pulsated as I thought about it: search, seek, pursue. But what, and where? Suddenly Lee Farrell's image came to mind, searching along the shore for a secret passageway into Cashelderg. Could he have been searching for something more than simply a way to get inside Cashelderg? I pushed the question aside for now. But his quest suddenly vibrated, a secret passageway. There was one, perhaps more. I was as certain of that as Lee Farrell had been and I had knowledge far beyond his on such matters. I had examined enough of them myself and had become familiar with many more in researching Gothic structures. Even some of the medieval churches had such passages built into them.

I felt the excitement pulling at me, reaching back into my mind. There was a pattern to their construction, even to their place and access. They were invariably on the main floor, almost never placed off the main rooms that might most likely have someone in them. The same held for corridors where attendants or guards were apt always to be present. They were designed to enter unseen and emerge from just as unobtrusively, positioned off a small, more private little room somewhere. I took the flashlight. It was becoming a most faithful friend. Pulling the drape back, I pushed the window open, swung out into the early night.

The wind struck me at once, coming in from the sea, dampness in it, and I looked up at the sky. It was moonless, racing clouds a pink-gray cover. I struck out, head down, for the castle and even as I crossed the distance, I felt the wind increasing, heard the sounds of it through the trees, a quiet wail. Reaching Cashelderg, I went inside, thinking back on all the old castles I had researched. I wasted no time and hurried back to the smaller rooms beyond the main hall and the large corridors. Secret passage access was never near the doorway of a room, hardly ever in corners. Most often, it was on the longest wall of the room where a tapestry or wall-hanging might be, the pivot stones never higher than a man's hand could reach. I began pressing along the wall, using my hands and my body, sliding along the stones. Satisfied there was no secret entranceway there, I went on to the next room, working carefully, pausing to hammer with the chisel, listening for a difference in sound that might spell a hollow. I had reached the very last of the rooms, the one beyond where the old wall-chest rested, when I had success. I felt a stone give way ever so slightly to the pressure of my hand, returned to it, and pressed hard. I heard the scraping sound as a section of the stone wall began to swing back, leaving an opening large enough for a single figure to enter. I slipped through, stood inside the start of the passageway and glanced about, found the handle a foot over my head. I pulled down on it and the panel of stone swung back into place.

I had been about to snap on the flashlight when I realized that I wasn't in complete darkness. Light flickered from down the tunnelled passageway, enough to barely outline the walls. I moved forward, gripping the flashlight but not turning it on, The tunnel widened slightly, grew brighter, and I came to a wall bracket in which three thick candles burned. The passageway led on and grew brighter as more wall brackets glowed with candles. They hadn't been burning since medieval days, I remarked in grim silence, and felt a combination of fear and excitement wrap itself around me. The passage divided suddenly, two tunnels. The one to the right was unlighted and I switched the flashlight on, beaming it down the dark passage. I saw the passageway end a dozen yards on and, in astonishment, the light outlining a rowboat almost against the end wall.

I went down the passageway, halted at the rowboat, no medieval craft but a modern enough boat. I ran my hands along the bottom of the hull. It was damp. The boat had been in the water not too long ago. I moved forward, put my ear to the stone that ended the tunnel, and heard the sound of the sea crashing onto the beach, faint but unmistakable. The tunnel led out onto the shore where Lee Farrell had been poking about. I decided another talk with Lee was a must. Turning back, I walked up the other fork of the passage, turned the flash off as it widened into a small room lighted by a wall bracket of candles. I stood frowning in the grottolike little room, at a table, a long slab of stone with two stone ends supporting it. A long, thin candle stood at one end of the table slab and in the center, a silver cup. No, not a cup, I corrected, a chalice. The table was a crude altar, I realized, and I moved closer, went around one end of it. A flat ledge of rock jutted from the wall behind the table-altar and something lay on it. I went to it, felt my breath start to draw in tightly. I reached down, picked up a passport and, under it, an address book. I opened the passport and Beth's picture stared out me. Whirling fears, suspicions, grim words of warning, everything spun around me, exploding in all directions. Passport and little green cap, they came together in front of me, shouting the same cry. Beth wouldn't have gone away without her passport. Multy wouldn't have gone anywhere without his cap.

Details were unclear but the meaning was shattering in its vividness. Perhaps I should have felt triumph, but I only felt sick. My eyes scanned the altar again, almost numbly. I didn't want to explore its meaning, not now, not alone. I had to go to Adam, bring him back here. I put the passport and the little address book in my tool bag, turned away, and started to hurry up the passageway, realizing that it had led downward much more sharply than I'd noticed. Questions buffeted me as I hurried on, touching on each other in a disordered way. Had Multy suspected this? Or had he other, less horrible, suspicions? He had left the old manuscript for me. Had he sent the letter that brought me here, a letter written three hundred years ago? That continued to offer no explanation, no rational one. I could understand the old chronicle. He could have known about that. But the letter still refused to fit.

I reached the end of the passageway, pulled on the handle again, and the stone panel moved and I slipped out. A pressure against the stone outside and the panel closed again. The wall of the room was an unbroken line of stone once more. Using the flashlight, I hurried through Cashelderg and now its cavernous empty rooms seemed to poise over me with foreboding, its arches frames of terror and not beauty. I heard a wailing sound, paused, realized it was the wind outside, still gathering strength. I shivered, felt terribly cold suddenly, turned as I felt eyes watching me. I swung the flashlight in an arc, froze as it rested on the twin bronze gargoyles over the doorway, the dread women of Moher, their wild eyes burning down at me, their half-human, half-bird bodies poised as if ready to spring. I turned, ran, angry at a fear I could not control. I halted at the tall, timbered doors, made myself draw deep breaths. I was adding the terrors of the unreal to the terrors of the real, I told myself, and heard the mocking reply at once. The real and the unreal, a line that was no line at all. I, of all people, knew that.

Yanking the door open, I ran out, the wind pulling my hair back in a wild stream at once. I half-ran across the rise, glancing back at Cashelderg, and I heard Aran Conahey's shout. A place of betrayal. Indeed, his curse had been right. Adam had been betrayed here, all that he believed in betrayed. I reached the monastery, hurried to the far end and Adam's room. I saw his door open, the light streaming from it, and rushed in with relief. I froze, relief turning to shock. Judy stood there, her eyes masked, surveying my excited, flushed face, answering the question I didn't need to ask.

"Adam isn't here," she said flatly. "He had to go to Drumglas with Barbara, to the doctor there. She's not feeling well. He said you might be looking for him."

"Yes, I had something to talk to him about," I said, finding words.

"You've been at Cashelderg again," Judy said, her eyes going to my disarrayed hair, then down to my hands where smudges of dust remained. "Adam thought you were in your room trying to sleep."

"I'll talk to him later," I said, "maybe tomorrow." I backed out and the girl took a step forward. I turned, half-ran from the room, and out into the windswept night. I halted, saw a figure standing near. I peered, moved toward it, stopped when I recognized Joan, a trenchcoat on, her hands in her pockets. I looked behind me and Judy stood at the doorway. I felt fear, real, unvarnished fear. I turned away, began to stroll toward where my car was parked, bent forward as the wind flung itself at me. I reached the car, glanced backwards. Joan still waited a dozen yards from the monastery and Judy's figure was outlined in the doorway. A gust of wind rocked the little car and I pressed my foot on the gas, turning the ignition on. Nothing happened. I switched the ignition key back and forth, tried again. The motor made no response whatever. It had worked perfectly the last time I'd started it and my eyes went to the two figures standing motionless, waiting, watching.

Tiny, crawling sensations traveled up my skin and I shuddered. I didn't get out and open the hood to peer into the engine. I didn't need to go through the motions. Wires had been pulled out, the car rendered useless. Suddenly I realized that this was a kind of last opportunity for them. Adam away, an accident could be arranged. I had been upset, gone out into the storm, perhaps back to Cashelderg. The stories would be plausible, beyond proving differently. I climbed from the car, started to walk back to the monastery when I saw the third figure moving along the ground, not hurrying, staying back, Randy. Judy stepped aside as I reached the door.

"If you see Adam when he gets back, tell him I've gone to bed," I said. The girl nodded and I met her eyes. They were surprisingly round, open. I shot a glance outside, saw Randy's figure moving toward the other end of the building where my room faced outward. I went inside, started up the dim corridor that grew almost dark as I neared my room and I felt the throbbing, pulsating beat of my heart. They hadn't time to waste, to risk Adam's return. They had been afraid I'd find their secrets as I examined Cashelderg. When they realized that I had doubts about Beth's leaving, they had to move. Somehow Multy had suspected something and they'd come upon him leaving the old manuscript. They'd seen the chance, turned the message left for me into a trap of death. Beth, first, then Multy, and now me. The reasons would be different for each, I knew, but death the same. Judy couldn't see me from the door now and Randy would be positioning himself outside, watching for the light to come on in my room, or just waiting until I was in bed. I turned, darted across the corridor to one of the rooms that led off from the hallway to the right, some used as classrooms, some as guest rooms.

I didn't dare use the flashlight but I gripped it with knuckles white with tension. I crossed one of the rooms, went through an adjoining one and I was on the far side of the building. A window rose up ahead of me and I lifted it at the bottom. It refused to move. Reaching into the tool bag, I took the chisel out, wedged it into the sill, and pushed again, using the tool as a lever. I felt the window give slightly, jammed the chisel in further, and leaned again. The window groaned, rose, and then, as if giving up its battle to stay closed, traveled upward easily. I put the chisel away and climbed out. I hadn't much time. They wouldn't wait long. I headed for the row of trees, disappeared into the blackness of them, and heard their branches bending with the wind. I moved through them, paralleling the road until I reached the bottom of the slope where the road turned to cross my path. I swung onto the road and began a steady trot, pacing myself. The road would lead me to the little turn-off for Lee Farrell's place. It was my only chance.

I ran, wondering stray thoughts as I ran. There were things that fitted nowhere yet. But they would fall into place, I was certain. If I could stay alive. They would have entered the room for me by now, found I wasn't there. I quickened my pace. The head start was all I had now. The wind slammed into me with increasing force, an invisible hand trying to hold me back, and I felt a spray of rain. The dark road was my only guide and I stayed in the center of it as, on both sides of me, trees and brush swayed in the wind and made a hissing, sibilant sound. I could see the sea at my right now, the gray-white spray of the waves as they thundered onto the sand and against the rocks. I had been alone for a good enough number of years. I'd made my own ways in life, but now I felt an aloneness that drove deep into the very marrow of my bones. I kept going and wondered if I would ever want to be alone again.

Another spray of rain came, flung itself into my face, and my lungs were beginning to protest. I kept on, kept going, and the sea flung itself higher now. I saw the break in the road, turned into it. It was where I'd first met the touch of death here. It seemed more than appropriate that I end up here again. I rounded the sharp curve in the narrow side road, saw Lee's cottage, one window lighted. My breath rasped as I pounded on the door, waited, listened, and heard only the rising cry of the wind. I pounded again, waited, and the door remained closed. I tried the knob, felt it turn, and I opened the door. "Lee," I called and there was no answer. I pulled the door closed, went around to the side of the house. The Land Rover wasn't in place and I felt the stab of apprehension go through me. Was he returning any moment?

The rain came again, not a spray this time, but hard, stinging needles that continued to strike. From the distance, from the shoreline, I heard the sharp, wailing sound and the wind whipped around me. I stepped closer to the side of the house, my foot stumbling against something. I snapped the light on to see a tarpaulin lying against the house on the ground, covering something. I kept the light on it, moved my foot out to pull the corner of the tarpaulin back. If I screamed, the sound rose into the air and was whipped away by the wind and I stood in horror, staring down at the uncovered edge of the tarpaulin. Multy's body lay under it, the wizened, elfin face a death-mask. I couldn't move, my feet rooted to the spot, unable to step back, turn, lift. I felt sick, my stomach turning over, and yet I was unable to tear my eyes away. It was more than Multy's lifeless form, more than the horror of it, but the absolute, total unexpectedness of it. Here, the one place I had fled to find safety, Lee the one person I had discarded as having any part in death's pursuit.

I almost laughed, felt my body trembling, my stomach nauseous. I swayed, felt my knees giving way, and a gust of wind drove the rain hard into my face, a storm-whipped spur. I shook the water from my eyes, found strength suddenly, turned, and tore myself away. I had no answers now. I knew only that I had to run again, run, not think, find a place to hide and then start over again. I kept my grip on the flashlight as I raced up the road, the windswept rain slamming into my face, blinding. I didn't see the figure come at me from the side but I felt my arm being caught, pulled, and I was spun around. Randy's face glared down at me and then, beyond him, Judy, her face a white mask.

I screamed and felt my arm twisted behind me. "You've been lucky and clever," Randy said, his voice far away. "Satan has been leading you well."

"Bring her to the car. Hurry," I heard Judy snap. My arm was twisted behind my back, sharp pain spearing into me. I was pushed forward, saw the dark shape of the car that had silently crept to the house as I'd gone around the side. Joan emerged from the front seat and I saw the cord held in her hands. She came around behind me and I felt my wrists being tied together as I was pushed into the back seat of the car. Judy came in beside me and Randy took the wheel, Joan next to him.

"You're sick, all of you," I said. "You can't do this. You can't get away with it."

I looked at Judy, saw her eyes were round, almost sad. "The sickness is within you," she said quietly.

"As it was in Beth?" I probed. "As it is in anyone who rejects?"

"We only obey," I heard Joan say. The car turned onto the shore road and the wind was shrieking now, the terrible scream-ing as it had that night when I first came here. The dread women of Moher had taken wing again, screaming their vengeance on the world. The car shuddered and swerved but somehow held the road and the rain beat against the windows. I thought I saw hur-tling shapes going past as I worked my hands against the cords around my wrists. They moved, but nothing else. Joan had tied them well. The car left the road, took a narrow back way, and I felt it climbing sharply and then, through the rain, I saw the towering turrets of Cashelderg loom up. Randy had circled up behind the trees and driven along the ridge. The car halted and I was pulled out. Rain and wind struck at me and I tried feverishly to loosen the wrist ropes, gave up the thought. Judy held my arm as I was taken into Cashelderg, through the cavernous rooms it seemed I had almost made into a second home. Were they to be my last home?

Randy, using my flashlight, opened the stone panel I had discovered only an hour or so earlier and stepped into the passageway, pulling me after him. I heard Judy and Joan follow. He led me down the tunnel to where it divided, turned me toward the grotto with the altarlike table. He pushed me forward to face it and I saw the long, gleaming saber lain across the stone block. I felt my throat go dry and I turned to him, summoning up questions to delay whatever lay in store.

"Multy knew, didn't he?" I asked.

"Multy knew nothing. He was always prying, a plague of a little man," Randy said.

"But he left the old manuscript for me," I countered. Randy nodded.

"Apparently he was afraid you'd stop looking. It was his way of pushing you on," Randy said.

"Then why did he urge me to go home when I first came here? Why did he persist so in that?" I queried. Judy stepped forward, Joan beside her, and once again I felt surprise that their eyes showed no malice, only a round, calm directness.

"Error begets error. Sin begets sin," Judy said.

"What do you think you've done? What do you think this is?" I exclaimed, finding anger suddenly.

"You still don't understand, do you?" the voice answered, round, smooth, strong, and I whirled. My lips moved but I heard only the whispered word fall from them.

"*Adam.*"

He stepped forward, a deep, purple chasuble all but covering him, gold trim and a gold cross woven into the center of it. His auburn beard glowed in the candlelight and his strong, handsome head was held high. His bright-fire eyes burned into me. "Adam," I cried out again, this time the word torn from my closed throat, a cry of disbelief.

"I am so very sorry," Adam said softly. "You could have been valuable, a real help to me. Your mind is a good one."

He stood before me and I stared at him and felt as if I were in a dream. I tried to move my arms and the cord dug into my wrists, a reminder that I was in no dream at all.

"Why, Adam? Why?" I asked and inside I was emptied, able only to wonder numbly. Everything had changed once again so totally, so shatteringly. Pieces and parts still didn't fit, but more than that, meanings and beliefs refused to fit. Adam turned to Randy and the two girls.

"Leave now," he said. "Go back to the others. Make your rounds. Be seen, then return here."

They turned, left on silent steps, disappearing from view in the tunnel. "The others, they're not part of this?" I asked as Adam turned back to me.

"They believe and they are fulfilled. They know the peace and happiness of Scripture. That is enough," he said.

"And this, this is you, Randy, Joan, and Judy," I asked.

"Every structure needs some form of hierarchy, even a simple one such as this," Adam said.

"You didn't answer me, Adam," I said. "Why?"

His eyes became sad, almost forgiving. "I tried to reach you," he said. "I tried to make you understand. I wanted you to understand."

"Understand what? Murder? Killing? A distortion of everything in Scripture, of the Word itself?" I cried out.

"Distortion? There is no distortion," Adam answered. "If one believes, if one has the truth, one is commanded to carry it high, to permit nothing else. It is as simple as that. What thing soever I command you, it tells us in Deuteronomy, observe to do it. Keep my Word, Scripture tells us. Permit no evil to rule men. Religion today has lost sight of that truth. They are too busy interpreting the words of the Bible, perhaps because those words are too plain. They have replaced faith with tolerance, belief with permissiveness. But truth is not permissive. It cannot tolerate wrong, error, sin. That scientific principle again. Truth cannot occupy the same space with untruth, right with wrong, belief with unbelief."

"And your answer is to kill?" I asked.

"My answer? No, not my answer. I only obey. In Jeremiah we read, I will punish according to the fruit of their doings. They have sinned against the Lord and their blood shall be poured out as dust, it is told in Zephaniah. No, my dear, thy God is a vengeful God. He who turns away from the voice of the Lord shall be put to death, Deuteronomy tells us."

"No," I exclaimed. "No, that isn't all of it. You're choosing to suit your own, twisted conclusions."

Adam smiled; there was forgiveness in the smile again and I felt anger at it. I heard Aran Conahey's voice crying out: *Cashelderg is a place of betrayal.* Adam's teachings hadn't been betrayed, as I'd first thought. It wasn't even the betrayal of my own happiness, of what I thought I'd found. It was a betrayal of all that once before had been betrayed, of love, of mercy, of the spirit of Scripture itself. Adam started around to the other side of the stone altar.

"What are you going to do, Adam?" I asked.

"Only what I must do," he said slowly.

"What you did with Beth?" I questioned. "You did kill her, didn't you? There never was a special bus to Ballygort, was there?"

Adam's eyes were steady, almost sad. "She couldn't be allowed to go to spread falseness, to tell lies about the community," he said. "She had a chance to accept the spirit and she refused. That cannot go unpunished. Scripture tells us that."

"She was a sacrifice of a kind, wasn't she?" I queried.

"Offerings," he said.

"The rowboat, you used that, didn't you? She was held here and then taken out to sea in the dead of the night," I offered. He made no comment. "Where does Lee Farrell fit in?" I asked and saw Adam frown. "Liam Flaherty," I corrected.

Adam's frown held. "Him? He's nothing but a busybody. Of course, if he keeps on annoying us I'll have to take steps."

I held back the questions that rushed to my lips. There was no need for Adam to lie to me, not anymore. But Multy's lifeless form had been under the tarpaulin at Lee's house. I didn't make connections but I was suddenly aware the conclusions I'd made at the cottage had been wrong. Adam reached out, lifted the silver chalice, and I brought my thoughts back to him. He raised it over his head and I heard his voice, low, murmuring. I watched, hypnotized, my eyes flicking down to the long, glistening blade of the saber, then back to Adam. His eyes were half-closed and he was praying for me, conducting his own service. Only the cords biting into my wrist reminded me that I was not watching some strange play.

Adam's murmuring voice continued as he held the chalice up. It would have been easy to dismiss him as simply a twisted mind, a distorted killer, an egomaniac who had encased himself in the wrappings of religion. But it was inaccurate. Perhaps there was some of that in him, but there was more. He was not a simple psychotic. He saw no wrong in what he was doing, not because he could not make distinctions but because he believed, he held to those philosophic, Scriptural foundation blocks that governed his world. Even now, I could feel his strength, his intense, embracing warmth. He could impart comfort, he could show others how to fill their empty, searching lives. He had a charismatic gift because he believed.

He was not the first, not alone, I recognized bitterly. The pages of history are filled with those who committed crimes against all human decency in the name of their beliefs. They saw no wrong, either. They pointed to Scripture, they had their reasoned, philosophic blocks, also, their ordered structures. Adam's words about giving oneself over, denying the self, they all fitted now, all part of the fabric of belief. It was fitting, so terribly fitting, I thought with both sorrow and anger. It was the final contradiction, the stuff of which inquisitions are made, witches and astronomers burned, unbelievers tortured, and the stuff of which a Joan of Arc, a St. Francis, a David, and a Martin Luther come into the world, the stuff of faith, hope, charity, of the one promise given us to carry into the dark.

Adam's voice rose, began a litany, the very tone of it carrying final things in it. I had no time left for inner wonderings. He had moved a step closer to the end. Philosophy was no shield now, no weapon, and yet, I paused, perhaps it was my only real weapon. Perhaps it would buy me time. I reached the tool bag at my waist, got my fingers around the end of the sharp chisel, and pulled it out as Adam turned his back on me for a moment, the chalice raised high. I managed to bring it up, using my fingers, position the edge against the wrist bonds. Slowly, carefully, I began to move it back and forth against one of the ropes. Adam turned, lowered the chalice. I had to reach him, to spear deeply enough. The belief that was his root, twisted as he had made it, was my only way.

"You're wrong, Adam," I said. "You're the one who doesn't understand."

I saw him pause, glance at me, and his smile was slow, tolerant. "You don't even understand why it ended the way it did," I pressed. "You don't understand the meaning of the crucifixion. You couldn't believe as you do if you understood."

I saw his eyes hold on me, intense, burning. "He gave his only begotten son for the redemption of man," Adam said.

"Why?" I flung out. "Why that sacrifice? Certainly, in his omnipotence, there could have been another way to redeem man. There could have been another sign. But the tragedy was left to play itself out. The sacrifice of his only begotton son was let go to its bitter end. Don't you see the real message in that, Adam?"

"To show man the enormity of his sins, to show man the terrible tragedy of rejection, disbelief, error."

"No, to show that man has the freedom, the God-given right to err. Man was let make the greatest mistake of all to show that he was free to be wrong, to find his own mistakes in his own ways. There was no divine interference. The sacrifice was made and it was a sign of man's freedom to choose."

"No," Adam thundered and came around the stone altar, his face darkened in anger. I felt the rope at my wrist starting to fray, but I needed more time. "No," Adam repeated. "It was a warning against rejection, against disbelief. It was a sign of men's irredeemable debt."

"It was a warning not to rule in His name, just as He refused to rule in His name then," I struck back.

"No," Adam shouted and came toward me. I stepped back, pressed hard with the chisel, my fingers cramped, aching now.

"Yes, yes, yes," I shouted back. "It was a sign of man's right to believe or not to believe, to see or not to see. To deny this in His name is the one absolute sin, for He gave his only begotten son to affirm that."

A strangled cry of fury burst from Adam's throat and he leaped forward at me. I ducked away, felt the wrist ropes part. His hands reached for me again. "Devil's child," he hissed. I shook the cord loose behind me, brought my arm around in a sharp arc, the end of the chisel still held in my cramped fingers. It caught him just above the right eye and I saw the redness leap from his face at once. He cried out in pain, stumbled backwards. I got a foot out and he fell over it, off balance. I felt my lips draw back in pain as his head slammed into the edge of the stone altar. He crumpled to the ground, tried to rise, fell back unconscious. I stood for a moment staring down at Adam Rood. He looked like a sleeping prophet. Only a day had passed since I had lain against his strong body, certain that I'd found a deeper kind of love than I'd ever known. Only a day, and now I had faced death at his hands. He groaned as I stared down at him and I shrank back, turned, and ran. He'd come around in another minute, and Randy, Joan, and Judy were due to return. I raced up the tunnel, into the dark section that led to the wall panel.

I had almost reached it when I heard the sound of it sliding open, the wedge of light snake into the passageway, flashlight beams. I heard voices, men's voices, and then a form entered, followed by another. The light fell on me and I could see nothing. Instinctively, I shrank back against the tunnel, foolish, automatic reactions of the trapped.

"Thank God," I heard a voice say, recognized the sound of it suddenly and then Lee Farrell was pulling me forward, out of the tunnel. I saw others, uniformed men, and I pointed into the passageway.

"Down there, at the very end," I murmured. The others rushed in and, abstractedly, I counted off five of them. Lee stood quietly alongside me. I heard the sound of more cars driving up to halt outside, saw more policemen come in, some in rain slickers still wet.

"Just him?" I heard Lee ask and I shook my head.

"Randy, Joan, and Judy," I said. I was aware suddenly that I was shaking, felt Lee's hand reach out, touch my arm, but the shaking wouldn't stop.

"Tell me the rest, the pieces I can't put together," I said. "Multy, under the tarpaulin beside your house."

"You were there?" Lee exclaimed. "God, I'm sorry."

"I was running from them," I said. "Tell me the rest."

"Later," he said. "Right now I'll get your things for you and take you out of here."

I nodded, turned, and walked beside him. I'd had enough of Cashelderg, of betrayal. Outside, the wind had died down and the rain was almost gentle. Dimly, I was aware of policemen hurrying past into the night, fanning out, of voices snapping out commands. Lee took me to the Land Rover and I sat in it as he went to my room, gathered my things. It had been no dream, yet it felt as though it had been that. I felt numb, an after-shock that was far more than physical. Lee would fill in the material details, I knew, but they would not be enough. Who would fill in the rest?

CHAPTER TEN

The cottage was a warm place, the fire reaching into my bones. I sat on the floor and sipped the whiskey Lee had given me while he perched on the edge of the couch, his wide-featured, disarrayed face quiet, gentle. He let me ask my questions first, answering each with patience. Surprise was no longer an emotion I could summon. It had been used up for now, at least. I could only listen and absorb.

"You're right, I'm not a free-lance writer," he said. "I was hired by a group of parents to try to make some contact with their children who had become part of Adam's Disciples of Light. Two girls, over a year ago, had left the community and had never returned home. They had just disappeared."

"As Beth just vanished," I murmured.

"There was no evidence of anything, and yet it was unusual. Adam had written each family, telling them the girls had left the community. He covered himself very well. But the two families contacted others and a group was formed. They all felt that their sons and daughters had been made into strangers, brainwashed, that they were a kind of prisoner."

"Yes, in a way they were. But they came to Adam wanting to be brainwashed, wanting their emptiness filled. He did that. He showed them something to look to."

"He made them give themselves to him, materially as well as spiritually," Lee countered. "That's a high-priced exchange."

"One that's made all the time, on less than spiritual levels. How often do men exchange free thought for comfort?" I thought of the time I'd spent during the affirmation session. The techniques and methods had been at least borderline brainwashing. But I had felt the power of the message, known how easy, soothing, and simple it would have been to give myself over. "It's not all that hard," I said. "To resign from problems, decisions, struggling, to put yourself in someone else's hands can be very attractive."

"For some," Lee snapped.

"Exactly, for some," I replied. "They who inwardly seek that. You could say it's another kind of dropping out."

"He used his personal charisma, his magnetism, and he used Scripture as a means to personal power," Lee said.

"That's been done before, too," I commented. Lee frowned at me, his eyes growing sharp.

"You sound as though you're defending him," he returned.

"No. I'm still bothered, though, by questions we can't answer here. Adam believed in the wrong ways, but that's all so common. History shows that it's almost a certainty. Why? Why is a force for love so often a force for hate? Why does believing lend itself so to abuse?"

Lee's eyes grew thoughtful. "I think that when belief becomes an absolute, it changes character, it turns from good to evil. I think man is not made for absolutes, not even absolute truths." He paused, as if suddenly embarrassed by having revealed a new level of thought. "Returning to realities, I learned quickly enough that Adam Rood had an absolute hold on his disciples. I concentrated first on the two girls who had disappeared. Their disappearance had been too complete. I couldn't find a soul who'd taken them to a bus or train, who'd seen them leave or arrive anywhere. It didn't smell right and I settled down to watch and wait."

"And then I came along, complicating things," I said.

"Not for me. In a way, you simplified them. Your arrival created the tensions that finally broke open," Lee said.

"Multy must have known something," I said. "That's why he left the old manuscript for me. It had to have been him."

"It was," Lee told me. "That night when he left it, Randy and the two girls saw him, took after him. He ran but they finally cornered him."

"Then when he was at my window he was looking for help," I said, shock flooding over me with the realization. "He'd come there expecting to find me there. When I called out for him to stop he thought it was Judy or Joan." I pressed my eyes closed, felt brushed by the spirit of betrayal. "It all went wrong," I murmured.

"You couldn't know," Lee said and I was grateful for his words. "They made a mistake then, their major mistake. They hurried the job of disposing of Multy. The weights they tied onto him when they rowed him out to sea came loose and they didn't go out far enough. He surfaced, more dead then alive, and he was washed up on shore. I found him and somehow he had enough life left in him to gasp out what I know now."

"The letter that brought me here, did he say anything about that?" I asked.

"He sent it," Lee answered.

"It was no fake. It was written three hundred years ago," I protested.

"He gasped out enough for me to put it together. The letter was real, all right. Lord Brian had written it to a prominent architectural expert of the day but had never sent it. It was among the old documents in the castle. Multy saw an article by you, by Pat Conway, in a magazine someplace and sent the letter to you."

"Then he knew something all along," I said.

"He had a gut feeling, apparently, and he believed in the curse of Cashelderg. But he knew his limitations, that if he searched too much himself it would alert Adam. He hoped that an expert going through Cashelderg room by room with a fine-tooth comb would unearth something."

"But he didn't want me there when I came."

"Shock. He thought Pat Conway would be a man, able to fend for himself. When you turned up, he wanted no more of it. He was afraid for you."

"When I insisted on staying, he decided to help as much as he could," I thought back. "He was probably afraid to reveal his role after a while, unsure of my involvement with Adam."

"That became my problem, too," Lee said. "I couldn't tell you anything for the same reasons. I didn't know how involved you'd become with Adam Rood, personally or spiritually."

The remark held a query in it and I didn't pick it up, stayed silent behind my own tumbling thoughts. Lee's quick mind would make its own conclusions, I knew. "When you came to my place tonight, I was with the police," he said. "I'd been with them most of the day, filling them in on Multy, and on everything I'd learned. They don't move hastily here. Papers and warrants have to be in order."

"Practical things, and pratical, rational answers," I commented. He caught the edge in my voice.

"You still say there's more," he remarked.

"There's more," I echoed. "The dreams, they were messages, warnings. Multy hadn't sent them to me, nor had he put up the round, oak chandeliers. They were shown me by something else, another force. Souls come back to habitations and familiar spots," I quoted.

"That's Yeats. The poetic mind," he remarked.

"Nothing more, is that it?" I said, leveled a stare at him, and saw that he waited for me to go on. "We speak of dreams, visions, prophecies, of premonitions, intuitions, insights. On a more common level, how often do we wake with a thought, an idea, a solution to a problem that has come apparently out of nowhere? Premonitions and intuitions come to us out of nowhere, too. But is there such a thing, a clear blue sky, a nowhere? I don't think so. The intuitions that come to us, the ideas and often the messages of our dreams, have an origin. They may be directed at us, or random, passing communications. Maybe some of us condition ourselves, subconsciously, to receiving such impulses. But they have an origin." I rose, went to where my bags lay, and took a small book from one, sat down on the floor again, an elbow on his knee.

"Let me read you something," I said. I opened the book, began to read from it notes I'd taken directly from the original.

Frankly, I do not accept the present theories about life and death. I believe that our bodies are made up of myriads of units of life. Our body itself is not *the* unit of life or *a* unit of life. It is the tiny entities which may be in the cells that are the units of life.

... To put it another way, I believe that these life units of which I have spoken, band themselves together in countless millions and billions in order to make a man ... further, that these life units themselves possess memory... that these life units are at work in the mineral and plant as well as in what we call the "animal" world. But are all these life units, or entities, possessed of the same memory, or are some, so to speak, the builder's laborers and are others the units which direct those laborers? In connection with the problem of life after death, the thing that matters is what happens to those that may be called the "master" entities.

... I am working on the theory that our personality exists after what we call life leaves our present material bodies. If our personality survives, then it is strictly logical and scientific to assume that it retains memory, intellect, and other faculties and knowledge that were acquired on this earth. These life units that make up our bodies live forever. When we "die," these swarms of units, like a swarm of bees, betake themselves elsewhere and go on functioning in some other form or environment.

... Numerous experiments have revealed that the memory is located in a certain section of the human brain called the fold of Broca. If the units of life which compose an individual's memory hold together after that individual's "death," is it not within the range of possibility that these memory swarms could retain the powers that they formerly possessed and thus retain what we call the individual personality after "dissolution" of the body?

... I am hopeful that by providing the right kind of instrument, to be operated by this personality (these life unit entities), we can receive intelligent messages from it in its changed habitation or environment.

I closed the book, met Lee's questioning eyes. "Who do you think wrote that?" I asked. "Some spiritualist? Some occult thinker? Or perhaps a poet toying with flights of fancy, someone concerned with abstract thought?"

"Possibly," he replied cautiously.

"Those words are notes from the diary of one Thomas Alva Edison," I said. "If ever, a man of practical, logical matters." I watched Lee's lips purse, then his slow smile.

"Point and counterpoint," he said.

"Like many of his projects, that instrument was not built before his death. But that's not the issue. He thought seriously of the presence of forces that communicate with us, of those extrasensory messages."

"Maybe there is more," Lee remarked thoughtfully. "Much more than we know." He put his hand out, against my face. "Messages are often hard enough to send right here. Communication between people is difficult."

"Not so hard if you keep sending them," I answered.

"I'll do that," he smiled, and I put my head down upon his knee. His quiet affableness held its own strength, one that would be nice to be around, I decided. I lifted my head, met his eyes.

"I could leave tomorrow," I said.

"Exactly what I was thinking," he said. His eyes watched me, caught the thought as it drifted across my mind.

"You're thinking about all the others, aren't you?" he asked.

I nodded. "What will happen to them?" I wondered.

"They'll find their way home, or to someplace else."

"That's the outside. What about the inside?"

"Those who were really reaching out to something will ride it out. Those who were hiding will be lost again," Lee said.

"It all comes down to how you believe, doesn't it?" I said.

"Or how you love," he answered. I met his eyes, shared the thought silently with him. He leaned down and his lips touched my forehead. No burning intensity, no charismatic, sweeping strength. Just tenderness, understanding. That was strength, too. That was a better beginning, I decided. The rest was there, just beneath that disarrayed, affable face, I knew.

I rested against his leg. He would be good to have near in the wracking, turmoil-filled nights. They would come, I knew. Terror is a cry that sears the soul. Love is a cry that heals. I had known them both, too close together. I would need time to hear only the one that healed.

www.ingramcontent.com/pod-product-compliance
Lightning Source LLC
Chambersburg PA
CBHW031229260626
47169CB00007B/2210